The Spectral Seduction at Mason's Hole

Devora Gray, Len M. Ruth

This book was not written by AI. Two humans armed with laptops, lattes, and question-able judgment hammered it out the old-fashioned way: with caffeine, chaos, and too much enthusiasm for paranormal smut.

Dedication

For my sister: giggle-box, math teacher, and all-around beautiful person. ~D

And for Tony, because ghost cock. ~L

ANOR

LIBRARY

SCHOOL

Y PEA
MPANY

CHAPTER ONE

JULIAN

Special Agent Julian Worthy sighed and rubbed his temples. He stared down at the file between his elbows, as though the secrets of his newest case might surface if he focused on the space between the lines. The wan light filtering through his office's minuscule window offered no help.

"Is that the Mason's Hole file?" a husky feminine voice asked from the door.

Julian turned to see Special Agent Nina Spearman leaning on the frame. Taking in her lean, athletic build, he suppressed a familiar wave of desire. "Yeah."

Spearman righted herself, tapping absently on the manila envelope in her hands. Her easy, casual manner clashed with the severe gray woolen skirt-suit and painfully tight bun of her dark hair. No one would guess she was ten years his senior. Until her full lips parted and the force of her authority scrambled his twenty-eight-year-old brain.

Those full lips were currently flat-lined in displeasure. "Your travel's been approved."

Julian reached across his desk for the envelope, but Spearman flicked her wrist, holding his plane ticket hostage.

"Don't take this case, Agent Worthy."

Julian stood to face his boss, a lock of his thick blond hair threatening to fall into his bright blue eyes. "Is that an *order*?"

Exasperation replaced Spearman's professional tone. "Come on, Jules. I'd rather not get into hierarchical games this morning."

He spread his hands in the air. "Then what gives?"

Spearman flicked the dusty horizontal blinds with something close to distaste. "Look at you in this tiny office..."

Julian knew what she meant. The department referred to his office as "The Closet." If Julian had to guess, the ten-by-ten-foot room had once been used as a coffee nook or maintenance storage. But in federal buildings sprinkled throughout the District of Columbia, any space was fair game for a desk and a phone. Could be worse. He'd heard of a guy in the basement working in a fire suppression room.

Julian waited as Spearman's eyes traveled his office. His mouth curved into an unwilling smirk. "You realize you haven't said anything, right?"

Her hazel gaze turned a smoky shade of irritated. "Ghost sightings involving kinky octogenarians won't get you out of the closet."

Julian raised an eyebrow. "Who says I *want* out of the closet? It's where all the good monsters live." Circling the desk, he reached behind Spearman and nudged the door closed. "Well, and under the bed."

The two agents stood toe-to-toe, their estranged lips inches apart. Julian's cock twitched like a pet who'd spotted a playmate. He leaned in and whispered, "The *closet* is where all the *taboo* things happen."

"Don't go there—" Spearman said, her voice strained, but didn't move away.

Her scent, dark and spicy, filled his nose. Since the first time he'd met her ten years ago, it never failed to grab him by the balls. "Why not? You did."

Spearman's eyelids lowered. "Are we still talking about Mason's Hole?"

Julian gave her a mischievous half-smile, pleased she couldn't seem to look away from his mouth. "What else would we be talking about?"

"I think *you're* talking about Slate Hill. That's in the past. *I'm* talking about Mason's Hole, which could end your career."

His grin widened. "Yeah, let's talk about the rituals of Slate Hill, where a whole town came under the influence of—" his fingers lifted in air quotes "—a secret government experiment."

Clearing her throat, Spearman gently pushed his shoulder until he moved back a step. "We spent an amazing time together, but—"

"In for a penny, in for a pound, Agent Spearman. You fucked a high school—"

"Graduate," Spearman interjected. "You were a high school *graduate.* As in, eighteen and legally an adult. Additionally, I was under the influence of an unknown phenomenon."

"That the government quickly covered up." Julian folded his arms. "But hey, it's water under the bridge. Unless you want to enlighten me on your side of the story. Which you never have."

After his erotic encounter with the gorgeous Agent Spearman, Julian had been put in quarantine. Watched. Tested. Interviewed relentlessly. He couldn't remember much about what happened, other than getting hot and horizontal with a woman who knew how to show him the ropes. During the quarantine, he hadn't seen Spearman, not once, and when the suits let him go, he wasn't just confused, he was furious at himself and at Spearman for not protecting each other.

He could have spiraled down a dark path. Booze. Meaningless sex. A half-ass job working at a half-ass company. But he'd gone off to college to study criminal justice. Only when Spearman popped up out of nowhere during his final year and actively pushed him to join the Secret Service had he felt invisible puppet masters pulling his career strings. Spearman's superiors, the ones that used him as a lab rat, probably used her as bait. But he wouldn't look a gift horse in the mouth.

His work at the Treasury Department landed him in Homeland Security, which quickly became a fast track to a unit no one wanted: lead investigator for the Supernatural, Extraterrestrial, and Xeno-Crimes Department. Laughingly referred to by everyone else in the department as "S.E.X.D."

Julian couldn't spare time for jokes from the over-sexed. He hadn't avoided regular dates to secure a happily-ever-after with Nina Spearman, but in those first years at the department, Julian had hoped the story would end that way.

It hadn't.

She was always professional, always slightly out of his reach. But she looked at him like she had all those years ago. As if he was the only one she wanted.

Damned if he'd let her downgrade their undeniable chemistry. "All you have to say is you didn't *want* to fuck me. Or that you did, and it didn't mean anything. Just tell me you believe the government dosed us with a top-secret love potion, and I'll never mention Slate Hill again."

Spearman's shoulders dropped. "You know I'm very fond of you. I encouraged you to join the Secret Service, so in a way, I feel responsible."

Julian rolled his eyes, smarting at the pity in her tone. She wasn't going to give an inch. "I do fine on my own."

Spearman wasn't having it. "And if you keep pursuing cases like Mason's Hole, you'll *remain* on your own. No one wants to work on paranormal phenomena unless they're attached to a cult or a serial killer. It's a hard road to travel solo, which is *why* I'm trying to wave you off."

"The S.E.X.D. unit is where *you* started."

"And look how quickly I moved on. This...woo-woo business...is for the tabloids."

Julian frowned at her out-of-hand dismissal of his work, then glanced at the file on his desk. "You have to admit, a haunted house with a woman claiming to be visited by spectral lovers has a lot of similarities to Slate Hill."

Spearman's chin came up. "That's exactly why I'm advising you to pass on it. Let sleeping dogs lie, Jules."

Heat flashed behind Julian's temples. He caught a fleeting image of a masked doctor in a green gown leaning over him before the memory sputtered and died. Every time he tried to remember the specifics of the night he shared with Spearman, he'd get a snippet, a taste of pleasure, then an opaque cloud smothered his recall. Asking Spearman for details was useless. She'd only change the subject, saying, "It doesn't matter. We live in the *now*." Julian wanted to live in the now, with her, but couldn't do that when a ten-year ghost stood between them.

Jaw clenched, he tried for an even tone. "They took something from me. From us. That doesn't bother you?"

Spearman looked away. "I don't know what you're talking about."

"Yes, you do."

Her hazel gaze sharpened, glowing like warm honey. "I won't always be your boss, Julian. And I want you around when that time comes."

Longing warred with frustration. He didn't need a babysitter or a secretive boss, damn it. He needed a partner. Someone to believe in him, watch his back, and let him watch hers. He couldn't wait until their career paths parted to find out if there was something other than great sex between them. If Spearman wouldn't take a chance on him here and now, she probably never would.

"I'm going to Mason's Hole."

She stepped back. "You're risking staying in The Closet forever."

Julian snatched the envelope from her and slid the top sheet out. "Looks like I'd better get packing."

He glowered at her, daring her to say something else to dissuade him.

Spearman shook her head, a sad little frown on her lips. "Safe travels, Agent Worthy."

Julian closed his eyes as the door shut behind her. The old wound of disappointment was like rereading a love letter from the one who got away. It hurt. And helped. He was an easy-going guy, but once he sank his teeth into a decision, he focused on it with the tenacity of a bloodhound.

He didn't need to pack. His 'go bag,' with a change of clothes, preferred toiletries, emergency tools and cold weather gear, sat in the corner. Snatching up his phone, he ordered an Uber ride to the airport. It was easier than having another agent take him. Spearman had hit the nail on the head when it came to inter-office politics. Julian knew he was respected from the deferential treatment he received when pulled onto large cases, but no one sought him out.

At the airport, it was both a blessing and a curse to pass through security, stow his bag, and settle into his assigned seat without the jabber of another agent telling him Homeland Security had bigger fish to fry. Why use department funds chasing one-night stands with mystical beasts when most of the cases led to dead ends?

Julian knew better. Slate Hill wasn't the only reported incident of strange activity infecting entire towns. The most recent case, Slaughter Beach, a supposedly sleepy town outside of Baton Rouge, had a file as thick as his wrist, but it was five years old. Beneath the tabloid headlines, there were *real* cases of criminal and paranormal activity thriving under the public's nose.

His gut told him the file in his hands held the answers he'd been seeking.

A month ago, Roland Hanford of Mason's Hole, North Carolina, called the police and reported a home invasion and assault of his eighty-year-old mother, Constance Hanford. When the authorities responded, there was no evidence of a break in. Further, Mrs. Hanford denied any knowledge of an assault. She claimed the noise her son heard came from an adult movie she was watching in her room.

Mr. Hanford made a similar call on a subsequent evening, claiming when he'd entered his mother's room, she hadn't been present. There, he'd been assaulted from behind and knocked unconscious. The responding officers found no evidence of physical injury to Roland Hanford, and his mother refused testing for evidence of sexual assault. Local law enforcement threatened to charge Roland with creating a public nuisance, and he'd backed off.

The file had come to S.E.X.D. because of a series of pings Julian set up in the National Sex Crimes Reporting Network. The report itself wasn't enough to get Julian on a plane to bum-fuck North Carolina. But when coupled with the weather reports on the dates listed, the climate patterns matched the anomalous reports of Slate Hill: heat lightning without the necessary atmospheric conditions.

On top of that, photos of the house looked like something from a horror flick. Overgrown weedy yard, peeling paint, shutters hanging askew. From the pictures, Julian had a hard time believing a caring son, a lawyer no less, would let his mother live in such a place.

The two cases shared other elements. Slate Hill and Mason's Hole had events of a sexual nature occurring at night. Both cases had unlikely, elderly individuals involved: Slate Hill, a middle-aged teacher and doctor of biology, Mason's Hole an eighty-year-old rocket scientist. Elderly educated women engaging in sex wasn't groundbreaking, but add the weather and the rural setting, the case stopped feeling coincidental.

One of the things he *did* remember from ten years ago, Spearman had insisted he get a criminal law degree so they could uncover illegal government conspiracies. He'd upheld his part of the bargain, but she hadn't. Something had changed. Whether it was fear of being fired or the desire to rise in the ranks, Julian didn't know.

Sighing, he tucked the file in his bag and tried to enjoy the flight. No sense rereading the same details for the tenth time. Nothing would come from endless speculation.

Outside the scratched plastic window, thunderclouds gathered and roiled. A flash of lightning illuminated the heavy gray vapor, making it glow from an electrical surge within.

Julian closed his eyes.

Ten years ago, he'd been shown into a private room at the Slate Hill Library. The sight of Agent Spearman's lean body in a tight gray suit had made his blood boil with lust, her scent filling his head with thoughts of hot sex in dark places. Pheromones floated in the air like free radicals, looking for, and finding, someone to land on.

Under Spearman's hand rested a copy of *The Lesser Key of Solomon* by Aleister Crowley and S. L. MacGregor Mathers, exactly the book he'd come to find.

The sexy older woman laid her hand on Julian's and got to the point. "What made you come to the library looking for this book?"

Lost in her hazel eyes, he hadn't been able to answer.

He was just an eighteen-year-old kid, and she was a world-wise federal agent. It wasn't fair. Part of him suspected she was using her feminine wiles to get him to talk about the town. But the chemistry, the visceral crackling energy in the air, made his penis stiffen in his pants. Was that tangy pungent scent her sex? Could he smell her arousal through her professional gray suit?

The agent's finger traced the vein on the back of his hand. "In a dream? Did you dream the name?"

"It wasn't a dream." Julian turned away. Just because he was a teenage boy didn't mean he wasn't a reliable witness. Whatever dream he'd experienced the previous night left him coated in viscous liquid that wasn't his own. He'd woken, stuck to the sheets with a sore cock. No wet dream had ever left him with the unsettling feeling that there was something... inside him.

Spearman grasped his chin and turned his head to face her.

Their eyes met.

She licked her lips.

Their faces grew close.

Lips touched.

Spearman lifted her other hand from the book and guided it where her pants stretched tight over her sex. Heat and moisture met Julian's fingers. She'd soaked right through the fabric. Julian's erection strained in his jeans, so hard he thought he might rip the denim.

She pulled her lips away. "Sir?"

Julian frowned. Why would she call him *sir*?

"Sir!"

Julian's eyes snapped open.

An attractive female flight attendant leaned into the empty seat next to him. The half-smile on her ruby lips told Julian she knew the nature of his dream.

"We're on approach. I need you to put your seat forward and tray table up."

Julian looked down. Thank god the tray table hid his bulge. "Of course."

The aftereffects of the dream stayed with him as the plane descended. He absently scratched at the scar on his stomach. The doctors said they removed a cyst. Well, not doctors. The news of the surgery had been delivered by a shadowy figure standing in an unlit corner of a mobile surgery unit. A man he'd seen around town. Haunting his steps. But Julian couldn't remember his name.

Why would sex magic give him a cyst? The nagging feeling there was more to Slate Hill than he remembered, persisted. It wasn't just about the horny town and a book of magic. Yet, when he tried to recall the details, it was like staring at the sun, then looking away, and having that yellow-green spot obscure every focal point. The answers were right there, just out of reach.

Goddamn it, why couldn't he remember?

Julian hustled out of Raleigh-Durham and into his rental car in record time. His federal law enforcement ID got him a decent sedan. Can't have Homeland Security agents driving around the North Carolina countryside in smart cars. The late-model black Chrysler 300 might be a bit conspicuous in truck country, but it provided a bit of gravitas. After all, Julian was a serious man on serious business, no matter how much he imagined Sheriff Billy-Bob laughing up his sleeve at an older woman watching porn.

There were plenty of bed-and-breakfasts, but no decent hotels within a half-hour drive of Mason's Hole. Not that his per diem would cover *decent* accommodations. Julian found a run-down, clean-ish place aptly named The Climax Motel, located in Climax, North Carolina, because, of course.

The faux-paneled room featured a queen bed with no apparent sag and a TV new enough not to have dials. Julian didn't care. When he wasn't reading or writing case reports, he liked a good, dark romance novel, his secret guilty pleasure.

After washing his face in the Pepto-Bismol pink sink, Julian headed for Mason's Hole. The huge swathes of grassland on either side of the road were trim and maintained. Instead of dilapidated homes and trailers at the end of rutted dirt tracks, there were perfectly manicured homes, driveways, and lawns. Julian doubted the upper-middle-class folks would allow a dilapidated, run-down house to hedge their property values.

So the tiny town wasn't a shithole as he'd assumed.

His conscience pinged. Making assumptions about the area based on the nature of a file was no way to start an objective investigation. And given the incorrectness of his assumptions, how far off was his assessment about the similarities between this case and Slate Hill? He'd have to check himself at every juncture. Getting personally involved on any level could spell disaster.

But Julian *did* take the past personally. And with good reason. He'd worked on cases where his experience—being brainwashed, drugged, and screwed for reasons outside his consent—made him the only advocate who could sympathize with the victim's confusion and distrust.

He hoped whatever was happening at Mason's Hole could give his work in S.E.X.D the credit it deserved. If he could just track down one concrete shred of evidence proving it wasn't all in his head, Julian could move on with his career...and his love life.

CHAPTER TWO

MADELINE

Madeline Da Vinci stifled the urge to rub her forehead as the couple sitting across from her took turns avoiding each other's gaze. Martin and Peggy Atwood had been married over thirty years. They'd weathered the highs and lows of commitment—but now, a withering sex life was pushing them toward divorce.

"How did last week's homework go?" Madeline asked, keeping her tone neutral.

The assignment had been to reinvent their first date in hopes an old spark would kindle a new flame.

Martin crossed his arms. "We didn't do it."

Glaring at her husband, Peggy pulled at the hem of her lavender cardigan. "Jackson came up for the weekend. We see so little of him, it didn't feel right to neglect family time."

Martin rolled his eyes. Jackson, their only son, was in his third year at Brown. He regularly dropped in for his mother to do laundry, meal prep, and edit his English essays. Martin loved his son, but insisted his wife cut the umbilical cord. The tough love stirred Peggy's maternal defenses, and a large chunk of their session time would be spent bickering over parenting styles.

It wasn't the first time Madeline witnessed couples using children, pets, or money as a way of avoiding deeper fears, but on this morning, the pressure behind Madeline's eyes continued to tighten as if she were made of wood and screws. She wanted to shake the couple, demand they remember they were staring into the barrel of old age. Hair loss, vaginal dryness, curving penises, the whole gamut waited for them. *Did they want to face the unknown alone?*

In her seven-year practice as a marriage and sexuality therapist, Madeline's client pool was made of unspoken desires leading to dangerous crossroads. Lack of physical contact wasn't the end of the world, but underneath the placid waters of day-to-day survival, an emotional clusterfuck waited to explode. Something in their relationship had to change, or it would break.

Not unlike Madeline's own personal life.

She glanced at the Georgia O'Keefe clock behind the couple. The minute hand cut a line in the dark purple flower's luscious folds, signaling they had fifteen minutes left. Madeline tried to stay engaged, but she couldn't help thinking about her boyfriend. Well, her ex-boyfriend.

Before she left for the office, Sebastian, a microbial biologist bent on having a by-line in *Science* magazine, had announced over a bowl of oatmeal he'd taken a position as lead scientist in a research facility deep in the heart of the Amazon rainforest.

Stunned, Madeline's only response had been, "What about our trip to Costa Rica?"

"You go," he encouraged, scooping beige lumps into his mouth. "Maybe you'll meet someone who is, you know, more into the stuff you like." His lanky arms dumped the bowl in the sink, not bothering to wash out the glue-like remnants. "Gotta pack. Plane leaves tonight."

Madeline had sat there, wishing she had the energy to tell Sebastian she hoped he got deep-throated by a snake, but she'd been numb.

Was he joking? Or was this a weird kind of test? She was a self-made woman with her own practice, a house, and no debt. Alexandria, Virginia, wasn't a hub of sex pots, but she knew she was a good-looking woman. Her red hair was maybe a shade too bright, but it framed a heart-shaped face and generous mouth. Perky breasts stretched the black knit of her sweater. A striped pencil skirt did great things for her rounded hips and thick thighs, the ensemble disguising the extra fifteen pounds she'd gathered listening to a full slate of clients.

And what had Sebastian meant, *the stuff you like*? True, not everyone enjoyed BDSM conventions or tantric crystal ceremonies, but the man fantasized about mummification, for god's sake. Owning her sex appeal was a delicate line, one she liked to walk, but today she wondered what was wrong with her.

Staring at the Atwoods, their faces blurred, her vision dimming. Madeline shook herself. She needed to get a handle on the session. "Peggy, have you been journaling every morning like we discussed?"

Peggy sniffed, plucked a crumpled tissue from her purse, and nodded without looking up.

"Do you want to share with Martin?"

To Madeline's surprise, the older woman lifted her chin and stared her husband in the face. "I've been dreaming about kissing Mr. Staffmore."

Madeline watched Martin's face congeal into harsh lines. Mr. Staffmore was Peggy's boss. Martin regularly complained his wife sung Staffmore's praises like he was the quarterback on a football team, and she the loyal cheerleader. The dream was proof his wife's feelings verged on inappropriate, and the intruder was getting the affection Martin deserved.

He straightened in his chair. "Has he tried to kiss you?"

Peggy frowned. "Of course not. You know he's married."

"I know he's a man."

Madeline fought back her wince. "Peggy, do you feel safe in this room?"

"Yes."

"Martin, do you feel safe?"

He shrugged.

"Let's focus on the dream. Peggy, how did it feel to kiss your boss?"

"I wasn't really me. I was—" she shot a glance at Martin "—another girl in the office."

This piqued Martin's interest. "Who?"

"Tania. His secretary."

"Go on," Madeline prompted. "Describe the scenario."

Peggy wrung her hands, but forged ahead. "Tania's a pretty girl. Young. She has her whole life ahead of her, but she flirts with Mr. Staffmore. To be honest, she's downright bold. Red lipstick. Wearing low-cut blouses. And she can be rude to anyone who wants his time, a regular gatekeeper."

The animation in her voice was like she was recounting a favorite scene in a rom-com.

"In the dream, I—well, Tania—closes Mr. Staffmore's door, but doesn't lock it," Peggy said. "Anyone could walk in, anyone could find them. She saunters over and sits on his desk. He tries not to give her any attention, but she opens her legs and her skirt rides up. He can't help but look. Then she leans over and covers his mouth like it's hers."

Madeline bit her tongue, trying to conceal her excitement. She'd been waiting for weeks for one of them to share something that could bridge their divide, and here it was, a tentative rope.

Martin turned away from his wife. "I don't think this is doing any good."

Madeline leaned forward, her voice gentle. "Why do you say that?"

"I'm nothing like Mr. Staffmore, and Tania sounds like a troublemaker." Anger turned his mouth into a sneer. "Am I supposed to share Peggy's fantasy if I'm not in it?"

A reasonable question, but it wasn't Madeline's job to pick sides. It was her job to illuminate what neither party was capable of seeing.

"Martin, that's a valid point. But Peggy isn't asking you to become her boss any more than she wants to become Tania. The dream is a representation of her feelings, her desires. She longs to be a sexual creature who has free agency to take what she wants. Mr. Staffmore is a safe conquest. He won't reject her. In fact, he's helpless against her allure. This makes her powerful." Madeline paused, wondering if she was getting through to them. "Your wife is saying she wants to explore her sexual power, to be swept up in lust and attraction and taboo. She's saying she wants to feel alive, and by sharing her fantasies, she wants the adventure to be with you."

Abruptly, Martin stood and faced Peggy. "Dragging me to therapy, making me listen to dream interpretations... It's selfish and vain." He shoved a thumb at his chest. "I don't need to change. There's nothing wrong with *me*. If you want something I'm not giving you, maybe you should go find it."

Peggy's face turned red. "Martin—"

Martin wasn't finished. "The real world is hard. It changes you, and after a certain point, you can't change back. Think about that when you feel sorry for the way your life has played out."

No one spoke as Martin quietly left the cushy beige office. Madeline got ready for more waterworks, but Peggy stared at the door with wide, dry eyes.

"Peggy," Madeline began.

"You know, maybe he's right."

The bottom dropped from Madeline's stomach. "Which part?"

"The real world *has* changed me. Do you think that's what couples mean when they say they've grown apart?"

"Growing apart doesn't mean you can't course correct and move toward your lover." Madeline glanced at the clock, then forgot about the rules. "If you need more time..."

"Martin will be waiting in the car," she said in a flat monotone. "We'll drive home and have dinner. We'll be polite, friendly even, because that's what you do after thirty years of marriage and you've said everything there is to say." She laughed without mirth and stood, collecting her purse and jacket. "I guess it's time I stopped talking, huh?"

"There are peaks and valleys to every relationship—"

"Madeline?" Peggy looked her over wistfully. "You're a fine therapist. You really know who you are. Your mother must be so proud."

Peggy left the office as quietly as her husband.

Madeline looked down at her hands, fighting the tightness in her chest, the twisting behind her eyes. What did the older woman see that Madeline couldn't?

No matter where she went, people talked to her, told her strange and wonderful details about their personal lives. Their sex lives. Madeline wondered if it was because she'd grown up in The Disciples of Creation sex cult, but no one knew that about her past. About how she'd run away with her sister Hatty. About how they'd had to stay in hiding while Madeline worked less-than-reputable jobs to stay off the radar. She seriously doubted her clients wanted to know she paid the rent cleaning a strip club, and later, became a sex phone operator to put herself through school.

All those years hearing secrets made her want to be a therapist, if only to give unspoken desires a place to live in the light. As for Madeline's mother, Jennie lived in Fort Lauderdale. When they spoke on the phone, she talked about Hatty and her watercolor paintings. Never the past. It was as if being too brainwashed to save her children happened to someone else.

With a sigh, Madeline stood. Pushed the memories away. She glanced at her calendar. No more clients for the next two weeks.

She'd cleared her schedule to go to Costa Rica, a trip she'd planned to jumpstart her and Sebastian's lackluster connection.

Sleeping in a rainforest, making love to the sound of howler monkeys, the vacation would have been a nod to her younger self, a symbolic, "See? I *can* trust a partner."

She snatched the framed picture of her and Sebastian hugging on Virginia Beach, muttering, "Fuck trust."

Sebastian was a lanky ginger, cute like an abstract painting of an octopus, and it didn't always annoy her when he sang *The Little Mermaid's* "Under the Sea" in a wonky Caribbean accent when they showered together. No one was perfect, least of all her, and it wasn't like she told him *everything*.

Some details were supposed to stay private, locked in the closet of fantasy, but maybe she should have confessed she masturbated to vampire erotica. Or imagined beating the shit out of Thoth, the leader of The Disciples of Creation. Or got a terrifying high from dreams of a stone demon sitting on her chest, threatening to pluck out her eyes.

Instead, she'd buried her darkness, thinking it was for the best.

So why hadn't she and Sebastian been happy?

Madeline's voicemail beeped. Reaching for her phone, she tried to calm her racing heart. If it was Sebastian, she'd convince him they could work out a long-distance arrangement. Maybe play around with an open relationship. There were worse things than living on two different continents. Like failing her clients.

But the voice recording wasn't from Sebastian.

"This message is for Dr. Madeline Da Vinci," said a nasal male voice. "My name is Roland Hanford. I'm a lawyer in Mason's Hole, North Carolina. You were referred to me by..." A long pause. "Look, that doesn't matter. Time is money and money is time. My mother needs professional help. She is eighty-two-years-old and believes—" he cleared his throat and continued in a rush "—she has a ghost lover."

Why Hanford was contacting a therapist in a different state, she couldn't fathom. But she did have a license to practice in North Carolina, and the case sounded fascinating. A smile twitched Madeline's lips but transformed into a scowl with Mr. Hanford's next words.

"My mother shouldn't be playing with imaginary friends. Her health isn't the best. She could fall out of bed, break a hip, er, damage her vocal cords. I'd like you to talk some sense into her, and if need be, prescribe her a medication that will keep her less...active. Call me back."

Hanford left his contact information, but Madeline barely heard it. The little prick. What did he know about how active his mother should be? Madeline considered deleting the message, but what if sonny boy jumped the gun? He could find an ass-backward doctor stuck in the Victorian Era with no clue about postmenopausal women. If mom refused treatment, Hanford could have her committed and use the "ghost lover" statement as evidence.

Thanks to her childhood, Madeline believed magic was for children, ghosts didn't exist, and paranormal events could be explained by science. Not that she discounted those who had preternatural experiences. Coping mechanisms for the lonely and neglected voices of the psyche came in all shapes and sizes. Had Madeline been raped or gaslit into being a sex slave for the morally bent, her worldview might have been different. Just the same, freedom meant she'd enjoyed her share of drugged interludes with questionable partners. Therapy and learning her attachment patterns let her face the fear of commitment, but she'd yet to disclose her past to a lover.

Grabbing the nearest implement on her desk, a rotund wooden fertility goddess, she paced the small office. She still had time to go home, catch Sebastian before he left, and ask what she'd done to push him away. But was it worth it? Arguing with him was like demanding answers from the ocean. The tide would come in and roll out, but it wouldn't change the fact he was leaving her.

That left a solo trip to Costa Rica. She could meditate and do yoga. Get plastered and cry if she felt like it. Find a stranger and fuck on the beach. Promising, but what would she do the next day? And the day after that?

A road trip might clear her head. A quick search on her phone revealed Mason's Hole was a five-hour drive from Alexandria. She could blast Radiohead's *In Rainbows* on repeat with no Sebastian to tell her, "Please, can we listen to something else?"

"Fuck something else," she muttered and looked at the goddess in her hand. The polished hardwood face didn't have distinct features, but she was a symbol of abundance and possibility. Madeline might not believe in woo-woo word salad, but she did believe in the power of symbolism, corporeal and otherwise.

"Fuck Sebastian and fuck Roland stick-up-his-ass. A lady should be free to explore her sexuality any way she sees fit. If Mama Hanford wants to suck ghost cock, she can suck as much as she wants."

If Madeline left now, she had forty-eight hours to find out if the octogenarian was in danger of hurting herself or someone else. If she wasn't, Madeline was going to sit Roland down and have a serious discussion on embracing sensuality through all stages of life.

"We should all be having great sex in our eighties," she said to the figurine and started shoving notebooks in her satchel. "We should all have a bevy of ghost cock."

CHAPTER THREE

JULIAN

When Julian pulled into the driveway of Mason's Manor, he thought he had the wrong address.

The handsome sky-blue, two-story colonial featured gingerbread molding, a friendly gable reaching for the heavens, and a wrap-around porch. A rainbow of flowers Julian couldn't name sprouted along the pathway leading to the front door.

According to his report, Constance Hanford lived in the ancestral home of Desmond Mason, the man responsible for founding Mason's Hole. More than a hundred years old, the property was supposed to be a relic of gothic neglect. A place teenagers dared their friends to trespass, scaring themselves silly listening for bumps in the night.

Where was the chipped paint? The rotting shutters? The sagging steps? Julian smothered his twinge of disappointment. Just because he had a thing for haunted houses didn't mean every low-country cottage in the rural South needed the inescapable aura of spilled blood.

Must be the wrong place. Had to be.

Scrambling for the reference photos in the backseat, he didn't see the man come up on his driver's side door until plump brown knuckles tapped against the window.

Julian turned to see a disgruntled, bespectacled black man in his fifties staring at him. He cracked the window, desperate to keep the cold air inside the compartment.

"What are you doing in my driveway?" the man said.

Julian reached into his blazer for his credentials and held the bifold ID to the window. "Special Agent Worthy, Homeland Security. Are you Roland Hanford?"

Roland straightened and crossed his arms. "Your ID says Treasury, not DHS."

"Treasury is a division of the Department of Homeland Security."

"What are you doing in my driveway, Special Agent Worthy of the Treasury Department?"

Julian rolled down the window. A wisp of dirty blond hair fell out of the part that crossed his forehead. He blew it aside. Every fucking time he tried to act with authority, that damn hair made him seem like a buffoon. "You recently placed two 911 calls, alleging that an intruder sexually assaulted your mother, correct?"

Roland took a step back and slashed the air with his hands. "Look, we got the whole thing cleared up. No more calls, okay? It's done. I can't believe the federal government sent someone all the way out here to laugh up their sleeve at me and my mother."

Julian held Roland's gaze to establish somber intent. "I'm not laughing."

Roland broke eye contact first. "So, what, you want to question my mother?"

For all his bluster, Roland Hanford wanted help from someone who believed. It was the kink in the armor Julian hoped for, but to get his foot in the door, he would have to tread lightly. "I wouldn't say question, exactly. More like have a conversation with her, and you as well."

Roland frowned and crossed his arms again.

"There's a long list of missing persons reported in this area, Mr. Hanford. Somewhere between your assault and your mother's assertions of pornography, the truth lies."

Roland's expression softened a notch. "About the porn... That's not like my mother. She's classy. Smart. Funny. But she never remarried after my father died. I think she's lonely, but she won't let me hire help, not that anyone would want the job."

"Is she ill?"

The older man's eyelids dropped. "Not exactly."

Julian could almost feel the waves of frustration rolling off the older man. "I'd like to help you," he said, "if you'll let me."

"I suppose a conversation couldn't make me any more of a laughingstock."

Julian glanced at the sky. "Any chance we could get out of the sun?"

As if the mention of the weather made it so, a bead of sweat trickled from the razor cut line of Roland's buzzed salt-and-pepper hair. He wiped his brow with the back of his arm. "Fine. Come up to the house."

Julian pulled the big sedan to the edge of a generous, tree-shaded parking area. An acorn crunched under his black rubber-soled dress shoes as he climbed out of the car. The overhanging trees shushed pleasantly in the wind as Julian took a few big gulps from a bottle of water, capped the remainder, and tossed it back into the car. The heat wasn't so bad in the shade. Good thing, too. If he removed his sport coat, his gun's shoulder holster would send the wrong message.

"I think Mom has some fresh lemonade. Care for a glass?"

"That'd be great," Julian said. "Will she be joining us?"

"She's napping," Roland said gruffly and gestured to a wicker basket of a chair. "Have a seat."

No way was Julian sitting with his back to the house. "It's been a long drive. I'll stretch my legs."

"Suit yourself."

The screen door screeched its need for lubricant.

In truth, Julian hoped for lemonade from powdered concentrate. At least with that, you knew what you were getting. If it was homemade, the whole time Julian sipped he'd be wondering if Mrs. Hanford had washed her hands before she'd made it, or the lemons, or the pitcher, or the glass. His stomach made a plaintive wobble. This was really the only part of the job Julian didn't like. But being receptive to courtesy built rapport. And that buy-in could make all the difference.

Julian tested the porch rail with a hard shove. No movement. Satisfied, he leaned against it, faced the picture window, and tried to make out the home's darkened interior through the reflections of sunlight dappled trees. He could have asked to sit inside out of the heat, but the screen door and whirring box fan in the second-floor window told him there was no escape from the sweltering temperatures.

The window fan masked any sounds coming from within. With no way to see inside, Julian turned his attention to the yard. Several flowerbeds dotted the well-tended lawn. He didn't know shit about flowers, but appreciated the red, yellow, and purple patterns interspersed with the vibrant green grass. Between the grounds, gardens, and the condition of the house, Julian surmised the Hanfords had money. So, not fools or bumpkins trying to get on a ghost-chaser reality show for a bit of prime-time attention.

Roland bumped the screen door open with the tray he carried.

To Julian's relief, there didn't appear to be any pulp in the pitcher, and the glasses seemed relatively free of filth or hard water residue.

"Here we are," Roland said, setting the wooden tray on the wicker table. He took one of the chairs and gestured for Julian to take the other.

Julian didn't want to sit. Why did people like creaky, poky, uncomfortable wicker? He didn't trust the chair, old and no doubt dry-rotted sitting on the porch for god knew how long. A strange tingling nipped at the edges of his nervous system. An ill-defined unease. As if something was amiss underneath the house's charming paint job or in the soil beneath the flower beds.

In situations like this, Julian would normally strike up an easy conversation with the person he was questioning. Find common ground. But Roland's off-putting personality, and the inexplicable tension the haunted rumors generated, set him on edge. He wanted data before he turned his back on the irrational, malevolent feeling the house represented.

"Mr. Hanford, could you describe the assailant that prompted you to call nine-one-one?"

Roland nearly spit a sip of lemonade back into his glass. When he'd recovered, he said, "You don't waste time, do you, Agent Worthy?"

What was he supposed to say to that? "I don't."

Roland sighed and set his glass back on the tray. He chewed his lip.

Julian waited, keeping his face carefully neutral.

Roland cast his eyes around the yard, as if the answer would materialize out of the shady pines like a familiar and unwanted guest.

Interesting. Roland *could* describe his assailant, but didn't want to.

Julian painted on a friendly smile and continued on a slightly different tack. "I understand this is difficult. Were you familiar with the assailant? Perhaps it was a friend of the family?"

A slight flare of Roland's nostrils, an increase in his blink rate, and the way the man's hands gripped the knees of his slacks was the answer Julian needed. Roland knew the attacker.

A surge of discontent threatened to derail his casual manner. If this was a simple case of domestic abuse, there wasn't a case. Except, who was the abuser? The eighty-year-old mother? Abuse had no age limit, but it didn't make sense. *Something* was here. The hairs on the back of Julian's neck agreed with his gut. His file said nothing about other people in the house. No other family.

"Mr. Hanford?" Julian prompted, realizing the silence stretched away from his question.

The sound of a car crunched up the driveway.

Roland stood. "Goddamn it, now what?"

A sparkling green Toyota RAV4 appeared through the trees and stopped next to Julian's rental in the driveway.

The car door swung open and a striking woman emerged from behind the wheel.

Julian froze, the glass of unwanted lemonade halfway to his lips. The woman's flaming red hair against the green car was like the sun rising over a verdant field. Or a fire burning it to the ground. Judging by the assertive way she moved, this woman could go either way. She had curves accentuated by a casual cream blouse and skinny black pants, as if she wasn't afraid to show her arsenal but held it back out of a sense of propriety. Taller than most, she wasn't fashion-model beautiful, but the everyday kind; solid, soft, and strong. The kind of beauty that lasts.

"Jesus, another ghost-hunting tourist," Roland muttered, then called out, "This is private property!"

The redhead squinted up at him. "Is this two-oh-one Farmington Road?"

"Yes, but—"

"Are you Roland Hanford?"

Roland hitched his pants over a bulge of belly. "If you're trying to serve me...."

"I'm Madeline Da Vinci. The therapist you called." She smiled. "I spoke to your secretary on the drive up. She gave me the go-ahead to meet you here."

Roland frowned. "I didn't order a therapist."

"For your mother?" Da Vinci put a hand on her hip. "I'm the *sex* therapist."

Julian came within a hair's breadth of spitting his drink all over the porch.

"Oh," Roland nodded. "Sorry. I've had a lot on my mind."

"What would you be getting served with?" Julian asked.

Roland turned. "Huh?"

"You thought she was a process server." Julian motioned with the glass of lemonade. He hoped it would slosh out, so he didn't have to drink it. "What would you be getting served with?"

Roland shook his head. "I'm not going to answer that."

Julian hated lawyers. "Why not?"

"One, I'm an attorney. We get sued. Two, you're here on my invitation, and I'm not obligated to answer your questions."

"This is an official investigation," Julian countered.

"Fine. Go get an *official* warrant."

"Whoa, whoa, whoa," Julian said. "We're just having a conversation."

"Hey! Hi!" Da Vinci waved an arm from the driveway. "Are you going to invite me up?"

Roland sneered at Julian. "Where are my manners? Would you like a glass of lemonade?"

"Love one," Da Vinci said.

She ducked back into her car. Julian watched her pants tighten, further accentuating the twin globes of her ass. The view stirred his lower chakras.

Roland cleared his throat. "I'll get another glass." The screen door clacked behind him.

Julian tossed his lemonade into the grass before anyone could notice. Sex therapist for the mother, huh? Da Vinci's arrival could help his investigation, or it could be a giant pain in the ass. As it was, she'd interrupted before he'd managed to get an answer from

Hanford about the identity of his assailant. Not that it mattered. Julian was a patient man.

When she emerged from the car with a small carry-on, Da Vinci's lips quirked when she caught him looking at her silhouette.

He decided he liked her on principle and motioned to her Virginia plates. "Long drive?"

She made a sardonic face and turned in a circle. "Do I look the worse for wear?"

Julian tugged at the collar of his suddenly too tight shirt and let his opinion on her curves slide. This was not the time or the place.

Da Vinci crested the steps. "You a cop?"

He stood and extended a hand. "Special Agent Worthy, Homeland Security."

"Treasury, actually," Roland said, returning with the glass.

Fire rose in Julian's cheeks.

Da Vinci fixed Julian with a speculative feline stare. "Which is it?"

"Treasury is part of the DHS." Julian wondered just how red his face was. As red as Da Vinci's hair, he'd bet.

She gave him a disarming smile. "Got it."

Roland handed her the lemonade.

Da Vinci took two big gulps.

Julian cringed.

"Delicious." She lifted her glass in salute. "Thank you."

"Would you like to sit?" Roland asked.

"Actually, I was hoping to speak with your mother."

Julian raised an eyebrow. "She's having her *nap*."

"I would be, too," Da Vinci said, but didn't elaborate.

"Well then," Roland sat. "Miss Da Vinci, this is awkward..."

Da Vinci gave him a professional smile. "Many people feel as you do, Mr. Hanford, but sex is a natural part of aging."

When Roland choked on his lemonade a second time, Julian imagined Da Vinci grasping the enormous stick up Hanford's ass and giving it a shove. For therapeutic purposes, of course. He turned

28

his head so only Da Vinci could see his face and shared an approving grin. She kept her face neutral, but those feline eyes sparkled with mischief.

Julian returned to nudging Roland. "I'd like to discuss exactly what occurred on the occasions you called nine-one-one."

The flustered lawyer looked from Da Vinci to Julian. He coughed again and took a sip of lemonade. "I'm sorry." Roland pointed to his throat. "A bit of pulp. What was the question?"

Lawyer trick. Roland was delaying so he could think of a polished response. Julian paid extra attention to Roland's face, because clearly, the man's words would be, at best, a carefully curated version of events. At worst, they'd be total bullshit. Julian wished the mother would wake up. "I asked why you called for help. Twice."

"Very well. I was staying the night—"

"You don't live here?" Julian asked.

"Agent Worthy," Roland frowned, as if the lemonade had suddenly gone sour. "I have a successful law practice in a major city. I don't live *with my mother* out in the sticks."

Da Vinci grinned like a lioness who'd spotted a gazelle. She snapped her fingers. "That's why you look so familiar. I saw your billboard as I passed through Durham." She straightened and held up a finger, her expression dead serious. "Injured at work? You need Hanford. The lawyer you can afford!"

A vein on Roland's temple throbbed. His mouth drew into a thin line. "Are you mocking me, Miss Da Vinci?"

"Just quoting your billboard."

Julian hid his amusement. "Can we get back to the issue at hand? You alleged someone assaulted you and your mother on two separate occasions. But she denied your claim."

"And I dropped the issue when it was evident no one took me seriously. Whoever called your office didn't run it by me." Roland turned to Madeline. "I don't buy the sit-around-and-talk-about-our-feelings stuff, and my mother has never listened to me, anyway. If you can get her to see reason, I won't have to force my hand."

As if called from the shadows, a melodious Southern voice floated from inside the house. "Who's out there coughing and causing a ruckus on my porch — Oh!"

The screen door opened, and Constance looked from Julian to Da Vinci doubtfully, then ducked back inside. "Ronnie, why didn't you tell me we had company 'stead of lettin' me walk out in a housedress with my hair a mess?"

Roland's head vein started pulsing again. "Mother, I—"

"Invite these folks inside and offer them something to eat while I fix myself."

Julian's hair chose that moment to succumb to gravity. A dirty-blond wisp fell in front of his right eye. He blew it out of the way with a puff of his quirked lips. Da Vinci cocked her head, brow furrowed. For the five-hundredth time that day, heat rose in Julian's cheeks. What was it about this situation that turned him into a twelve-year-old boy?

Da Vinci tested the rail, just as Julian had, then rested her hourglass bottom on the white-painted wood. Her sensible heels clacked on the floorboards as she crossed her ankles.

Julian's eyes sought the sound, then against his will, traveled upward, surreptitiously tracing the curve of her thighs and the swell of her breasts.

Their eyes met.

Da Vinci tilted her head, letting Julian know his appraisal wasn't at all secret. She then looked *him* up and down.

Things were definitely heating up on the porch.

Roland rolled his eyes. "I don't think it'll be any cooler inside."

The screen door screeched. Constance stepped out, looking put together as if she'd spent hours primping, instead of mere seconds. A tasteful touch of lipstick framed the warm, wide smile on her surprisingly vibrant brown face. Large white curls bounced as she moved toward Julian.

Julian offered her a hand. "Special Agent Worthy, Department of Homeland Security."

"Actually, he's—" Roland began.

"Hush now, Ronnie." Constance waved at her son. She put a cool hand in Julian's. "Constance Hanford. Pleased to make your acquaintance."

Julian gave a slight bow. "The pleasure's mine."

Constance turned to Da Vinci, who smiled with gentle candor. "Madeline Da Vinci, Certified Marriage and Sex Therapist."

"How nice to meet you, Miss Da Vinci."

A look Julian couldn't identify passed between the two women as they shook hands. Some kind of secret female code.

"Call me Madeline, please."

"And you call me Constance, but not Connie. Sounds like dried-up corn." She turned her gaze to her son. He stared back.

"Do you think another chair is going to drop out of the sky?" Constance asked.

Roland grumbled but fetched another chair from the far side of the porch.

Constance took the empty chair, frowned at the pitcher and glasses on the little table, then cast a reproachful glance at her son.

"I'll grab you a glass, Mother."

After the screen door bounced shut behind Roland, Constance sighed. "He's a good boy, but we're at odds more than not, especially when he decides to poke his nose into my affairs."

Da Vinci nodded, her mouth a thin line.

"On the nights he called the police—" Julian started.

Constance cut him off. "My nightly adventures are none of his concern. And if you'll pardon my bluntness, none of yours."

"Of course," Julian said. He'd have to switch tactics if he wanted to talk to her about paranormal visitors. "Strange weather you've been having down this way. Lightning with no clouds?"

Constance kept her smile, but gave her head a little shake. "I see you, Special Agent Worthy. You didn't come all the way from..."

"Washington," Julian supplied.

"Right," Constance continued. "You didn't come all the way from Washington to talk about the weather." She turned to Da Vinci. "And Madeline, I don't know what made my son call you, but I assure you, I don't need counseling."

This didn't faze the therapist a bit. Da Vinci let out a soft chuckle. "I believe that. From what Roland told me on the phone, I could take some pointers from *you*."

Constance let out a hearty bark of laughter. "I know that's right."

Da Vinci's smile softened. "But I wonder how long it's been since you had another female to talk to?"

"Since you put it like that, it *has* been a while." She studied the ceiling for a moment. "I think I'd like a little girl talk."

Roland returned to the porch and filled his mother's glass.

She took a sip and smacked her lips. "You can go home, Ronnie."

"But, Mother," Roland protested.

"I'll be fine talking to these nice folks a while."

"You shouldn't talk to *him*," Roland pointed a finger at Julian's chest, "without a lawyer present."

Constance waved a hand. "I know my rights."

"I'm not leaving you with these strangers—"

"Strangers you called." She sighed, a menagerie of tired frustration passing over her face. "I appreciate your concern, but I don't need it. Run along back to Durham so you don't hit traffic. I'll call you later."

"I...." Roland looked like he wanted to say more, but her stern stare deflated him. "All right, Mother."

She held out an arm.

32

Roland leaned down and gave her a half-hug. "Are you sure—?"

Constance patted his back. "I'll see you for Sunday dinner."

Roland gave Julian and Da Vinci each a curt handshake, mumbling their names as he left.

Constance contemplated Roland's Mercedes as it rolled down the driveway. "Don't know what's gotten into that boy. He's always been a bit sensitive, but the last couple weeks he's down-right skittish." She threw up her hands in a what-can-you-do gesture and turned to Julian. "Agent Worthy?"

Julian raised his eyes. "Ma'am?"

"Why don't you give me and Madeline some privacy?"

He opened his mouth to protest much like Roland had.

"I don't mean to be ungracious," Constance said, "but I would like to talk to my therapist alone. Come back for dinner and we can jaw about the weather."

This wasn't going at all the way Julian planned, but he knew when he'd been beaten. Perhaps an afternoon session with Madeline Da Vinci would loosen Mrs. Hanford's tongue about the goings on in her home. He forced a smile. "I'd be delighted to join you for dinner."

Before Julian left, he pulled a card from his coat pocket and pressed it into the warm, soft skin of Da Vinci's hand. His fingertips lingered a moment too long on hers. "In case you need anything or there's...trouble."

Da Vinci accepted the prolonged contact as if she were comfortable with trouble. "Pleasure to meet you, Agent Worthy."

Julian replayed the scene as he drove back to the motel. With no sign of a proper haunted house and no indication Constance was in jeopardy, this might be a goose chase. Perhaps Spearman had been right. The department would get a laugh, and his reputation would take another hit, but he'd had to check it out.

Still, there was something strange about Mason's Hole, no doubt about it. Roland Hanford wasn't on the up-and-up. To call a sex therapist for your eighty-year-old mother.... The hair on the back of Julian's neck stood to attention, sitting on that porch. And his gut had told him there was a long history of unspoken secrets between Roland and his mother, not to mention a battle of wills.

The Hanfords weren't the only people on that porch eager to spar. A less professional thought came forward: the way Julian's name sounded coming from Madeline's lips was its own invocation.

Agent Worthy....

His cock twitched in his pants. For sure, when he returned for dinner, he'd have his go-bag in the car. Just in case. One never knew what strange specters waited in Constance Hanford's house.

CHAPTER FOUR

MADELINE

Madeline's eyes lingered on Agent Worthy as he walked to his car and drove away. He had a nice, round ass, and the thing he did with his hair, swiping the golden bangs out of his eyes, was adorable. She bet he knew how to touch a woman.

"That one's got a solid head on his shoulders," Constance murmured, her voice slow as a southern rain. "Nice backside, too."

Madeline jerked her eyes away from the road, heat flaring in her cheeks. What was she thinking? Hooking up wasn't why she was in Mason's Hole.

She gave Constance her full attention.

Thick white hair swirled at her crown, giving Constance an aura of royalty, and the knowing smile created a fine network of wrinkles and crevices that reminded Madeline of a handmade quilt's soft folds. Her yellow housecoat was clean and covered in tiny white flowers. Underneath, Constance wore what looked to be expensive cotton loungewear. If the older woman was suffering from neglect, it wasn't obvious. What a relief.

Now that they were alone, they could talk about real things. Rather, ghost things.

"Mrs. Hanford—sorry—Constance, I won't beat around the bush. When your son called, he implied your current relationship might not be safe. I believe he's concerned about your wellbeing." Madeline shifted on the porch railing but kept her body open, her tone steady. "You don't know me, and I'm not here to judge, but I'd like to hear your side of the story."

"That boy..." Constance gave a long-suffering sigh and settled back into her chair. "He was always one to jump at every shadow. Can't say I blame him. Thomas, his father, wasn't an easy man. Always had his mind on business, money, and well, propriety. My husband cared too much about how the world saw him, even though he drank like a fish and sometimes got too handsy. I'm afraid Roland adopted his father's mindset."

"Is he still in Roland's life?"

"Lord, no. Died shortly after we moved into this house. That must have been when Ronnie was ten or so."

Madeline paused, imagining the struggles of a mother without the comfort and stability of a partner. "I'm so sorry."

"Water under the Lake Lure Bridge."

"You never remarried?"

Constance huffed in disgust. "Thomas and I married late, had Ronnie when I was thirty-two. When my husband died, I didn't see the point of giving up control again." She shot Madeline a look. "I bet my boy didn't mention I worked at NASA or that I have a Master's in aerospace engineering."

A pleasant jolt clanged against the dislike Madeline felt for Roland. "He did not."

"I'm not one to put on airs, but look around." She waved at the colorful bounty of her yard. "A little old lady set off in the country, a black woman at that, with no man and no job. Folks take on certain assumptions. I must be deep in the voodoo or communing with demons to live in a haunted house."

Madeline frowned. "Haunted house?"

"This here is Mason's Manor. The founder of the town, Desmond Mason, built it for his wife and son. After Desmond passed, the property sat empty. Folks tried to live here, but they saw things—felt things—they couldn't understand. When you go into town, you'll hear all kinds of tales."

Madeline had forty hours before her flight to Costa Rica and doubted she'd stick around long enough to talk to the townsfolk. She didn't see the point. For all intents, Constance knew her own mind and had yet to show any signs of trauma, cognitive or otherwise, that would bring on hallucinations. Then again, shifts in attitude could only be observed over time. Then there was the aspect of medication. Constance could be stable in the morning, but slip into confusion or depression by nightfall, a pattern commonly known as sundowner syndrome. And she was out here all alone. Keeping an invisible friend was a plausible coping mechanism for isolated elders.

Might as well get to the point.

"Constance, have you seen anything or felt anything strange while living in this house?"

The older woman's eyes twinkled with mischief. "Ah, you want to talk about my sex life."

Madeline chose her words carefully. "I want to know if you're lonely living in a place that might not meet your needs."

"That's a fancy way of asking if I like it when things bump me in the night." She gave a hearty chuckle. "I believe the term you'd use is spectrophilia, correct? Have I passed on human patty cake to take up with ghosts and spirits?"

Madeline nearly slipped off the porch rail. "Umm..."

Constance gave her a sly grin. "I may be old, but I can Google."

Madeline couldn't help but smile back. "Touché."

"When I first came to town, the people were polite but suspicious. I thought, we're in for a fixer-upper, and I'm not talking about floorboards and a new coat of paint. I tried to make friends, what with Ronnie being school-age, but when I'd invite folks over, not one came callin'. I thought we were being snubbed. Turns out there were too many accidents on the property in previous years, it made those mamas scared to let their kids roam our hills. Then Thomas died and got the rumor mill cranking on all cylinders." She lifted an elegant shoulder. "It took time, but eventually I figured out, people are always going to see what they want to see."

Madeline tried to repress a wave of sadness. No one should ever be left alone, particularly not a vibrant woman such as Constance. "You don't have a support system besides your son?"

"I wouldn't say that." The older woman suddenly reached out and wrapped Madeline's hand in a grip surprisingly strong for its parchment-like appearance. "I'm quite selective in my confidants, Madeline, and pleased as punch you're finally here."

What did Constance mean by *finally here*? "Thank you, Ma'am."

"Not that Desmond isn't excellent company, mind you, but when he told me about you, I didn't know what to think."

Madeline kept her face neutral. "Desmond? As in the original owner of the house?"

Constance held her gaze with a level stare. "Yes, dear. He's my lover."

"Your...lover. Right."

"The look on your face." Constance giggled. "The cogs are turnin'. Is the old gal batty or just delusional? Desmond doesn't mind the label of 'ghost' and neither do I. It's romantic." Her lips twitched. "Not that he needs help in the romance department. That creature is hung like a stallion, and he's as generous as the day is long. That's rare, don't you think? Most large men can't fuck worth a buffalo nickel."

38

Madeline gave a choking cough and carefully put her lemonade down. Honesty was important, but she couldn't tell Constance she didn't believe in ghosts. Not when they'd yet to develop real trust. "Is there any chance I could talk to Desmond?" She glanced around the porch. "Is he here with us now?"

"He's not here. Not yet." The octogenarian's face showed amusement, but her tone held a hint of warning. "When you meet him, I don't want you to be alarmed. You're going to hear some things and feel some things that might strike you as unusual, but I promise, no harm shall come to you. Desmond is a gentleman, through and through."

Dread leveled Madeline's optimism. Constance's calm assurance could mean many things, namely she *did* have a lover, but he wasn't a ghost and he wasn't a gentleman. Financial and emotional abuse of the elderly was a common problem and made Madeline see daggers. If Constance was being taken advantage of, fuck Costa Rica. She'd find the bastard and nail his ass to the wall.

As if reading her mind, Constance patted Madeline's knee. "Thomas was an abusive man when he was deep in his cups. For a good ten years, I was like a dog he beat just to see how often I'd crawl back. Mind you, when Ronnie came along I'd had enough, but I couldn't run off in the night. Desmond convinced me I didn't have to live that way."

A scene began to play in Madeline's mind. If Constance was scared of her husband and trying to do right by her boy, the extreme trauma could have triggered the creation of a fantasy man to save her from despair.

Softly, she said, "How long have you and Desmond been together?"

"Coming up on forty years." Constance squinted in reflection. "Do you know I never experienced an orgasm until he came to me? I owe him more than I can say."

Madeline tried to do the math. "Has your son known about Desmond all this time?"

"My son hasn't the sense God gave a turnip, bless his heart. He wants to sell the house and the land. I gather he's been approached by developers." Constance's easy smile settled into a grim line. "I can't let that happen."

"You were in the house the nights Roland was attacked?"

"Oh, definitely."

Madeline was wading into a sinking tide, but she had to ask. "Did Desmond assault him?"

"Desmond feels sorry for my son. He wouldn't intentionally hurt him. It's not his style."

Which wasn't an outright rejection of assault. "Constance, it sounds like there's reason for Roland to be concerned. You're out here in the country. If you fell or if someone broke in again—"

"Desmond would protect me," she said with absolute certainty.

Madeline couldn't sit still. She turned and faced the yard. The blush of evening traced the sky, and the forest swelled with shadows. Irrationally, she wanted Agent Worthy to return. Now.

Constance sighed. "Oh, I've worried you. That wasn't my objective. Would it be better if I lied, said ghosts don't exist, and if they did, they can't harm you?"

Madeline spun around. "I don't think you've lied to me once. Please don't start."

Constance's intelligent brown eyes deepened, gleaming like whiskey in the fading light. "The truth is, a ghost is a label we invented for something we can't understand. Much like angels and demons, there are forces in the world that make us feel protected or threatened. At the end of the day, what we're dealing with is our own expectations. Do we believe in love or fear?"

Madeline opened her mouth to say belief wasn't as easy as picking a side. Love was tricky. Fear equally devious. But facing off against Constance, a swell of vulnerability sucked the words from her throat. This woman knew things. Things Madeline wanted to know. So *what* if she'd made up a relationship with a ghost? There were worse fantasies.

Constance nodded, her eyes deep as a cavern and just as mysterious. "I'll answer your questions to the best of my ability, and I won't lie to you. Not ever. My life has been a wild ride, but I'm tired. It'll be good to lay my secrets down, once and for all."

Alarm skittered down Madeline's spine. "Are you sick? Or being threatened in any way? We can leave tonight, if that's the case. Just say the word."

Constance stood, the wicker creaking in concert. "I'm not sick, sweetheart. I'm just old and ready for what's next." She swung the screen door open. "Don't think too much about it now. We'll have supper. You and Agent Worthy will stay the night. In the morning, you'll know what you need to know."

Madeline followed her but paused on the threshold, blinking rapidly. It was a trick of the fading light, but for a second, she thought she saw a dusty, abandoned room with peeling paint and rotting furniture. Then the image faded like a dream.

When she spoke again, her voice was barely above a whisper. "Constance, what's next?"

"You, dear. You're what's next." Constance gave her a wink. "Now how 'bout you come help me fix supper before that cute federal boy gets back? We all need to keep up our strength for what's comin'."

Two hours later, Madeline shut the door to the guest room and let out a long breath. Her back hurt from the car ride, and her head was a jumble of contradictions. At least the guest room was comforting. Trimmed in crown molding and smothered in a cabbage rose print, fringe lamp shades cast the room in a rosy glow. The four-poster bed looked old, the mattress lumpy, but in the luxurious way of down feathers. Constance liked pillows with ruffles. No complaint there.

Downstairs, Agent Worthy camped out on the couch. Somehow, this made her feel better. He'd returned right as she and Constance set the table and made no argument when Constance informed him he'd stay the night.

Over a simple vegetable soup and homemade biscuits, Constance was true to her word. Every question Agent Worthy had about strange weather patterns, she'd answered. When he switched to questions about the town's crime rating, the older woman said she didn't keep up with the local news but whatever gossip he craved could be found in the Mason's Hole Town Hall.

Rubbing the back of her neck, Madeline checked her cell phone. A single bar of service said if there was an emergency, help might take a while to get to the house. This would have bothered her had Roland stayed. Caring for an elderly parent was no walk in the park, but she'd seen her share of middle-aged men who became a jumble of nerves and thumbs when the matriarch took ill. That wasn't why she didn't trust Roland. He loved his mother, anyone could see that, but he was hiding something.

Out of habit, Madeline wondered what Roland fantasized about, a thought she abruptly cut short. Did she really want to know if a slimy lawyer with mommy issues liked to be spanked with a wooden brush? Not really.

Then there was Agent Julian Worthy. He was...different. Handsome. Definitely quirky. None of her spidey senses said he was physically dangerous, but he was withholding information. By default, that made him a threat.

And Madeline could have a field day guessing his sexual kinks.

Her body gave a delicious tightening. That thick hair, those broad shoulders. He acted like a Golden Retriever, but he wasn't a pushover. There was muscle and heat and confidence beneath his derpy office suit.

She shook herself. No. She wasn't going to go there. The sooner she could determine if Constance was mentally stable, the sooner she could focus on Costa Rica. If nothing else, this jaunt down a country lane confirmed her need for a vacation.

Madeline flipped open her carry-on and rummaged until she found her collapsible baton. One pound of titanium that could expand into an eighteen-inch nightstick made for a decent weapon. She'd keep it close, just in case Agent Worthy wasn't who he said he was, or the house got another nighttime visitor.

Placing the baton on a rose-printed armchair, Madeline wearily undressed and slipped into a silky peach nightgown. She thought about washing her face, but couldn't be bothered.

The night air coming through the open window was cool and sensuous. Tree frogs and crickets sang in the lawn, and it was dark, so dark beyond the thin pane of glass. Madeline knew she should keep her guard up, but as soon as her head hit the pillow, the tension drained from her body.

The mattress and its feminine dressings cradled her. Floating, her thoughts turned to supernatural exploits. Ghosts. The Treasury Department. Spanking. Agent Wonderbread had rolled his sleeves up at dinner. He had nice forearms. The kind that could hold a woman up...or hold her down.

She wanted to be held down. She wanted to feel a male body pressing into her, warm and hard, as he whispered hot commands into her neck, urging her to give him what he needed. Sebastian had never been strong enough to pin her, and she'd been so long without the overwhelming tremors of a body flooded with sensation. Julian was just downstairs. She could tiptoe her way to his side, wake him up with a caress. The look he'd given her when she arrived implied the gesture wouldn't be rejected.

No, dammit. Bad thought. Bad therapist.

Huffing, Madeline beat at her pillow and turned over.

Her main concern was Constance. There were clues to her personality in what she'd shared. Intelligence. Wisdom. A bawdy sense of humor. Her relationship with Roland was stretched to the breaking point. Madeline sensed this bothered Constance more than she let on, but she couldn't possibly say, "I know how you feel." Being a mother was...something you could never take away. And how had she managed to be a single parent in a small town?

Probably the same way Madeline managed to run away from a cult with Hatty. Grit and resilience opened a lot of doors. Madeline still had fond memories for the band of exotic dancers who had sheltered them, given them a home, and taught Madeline how to hide in plain sight. Those women had interesting stories, interesting sex lives.

According to Constance, she'd had help, too. Desmond wasn't a ghost, so maybe he was an outlaw of sorts. Or married and living a double life. That would explain the subterfuge, but forty years was a long time to spend with one person.

What would it be like to have deeply satisfying sex into your 80s?

At the rate she was going, Madeline would never know. Sex with Sebastian had been sporadic. He was open to tantric breathing and delayed orgasms, but on some level, his mind was hunched over a microscope, yearning to climb into a tropical canopy and play with monkeys.

Drifting into a fitful sleep, she couldn't help but ask herself why he didn't want her anymore. What had she done wrong...

A deep male voice slipped into her dreams. *Shh. Don't think of him anymore. You're free to have every experience you want. No boundaries. No limitations. You're free.*

Large, strong hands slid down her shoulders and arms. Madeline moaned into the pillow, melting with languor. Able fingers found her nipples. Stroked them, light as a whisper. The ache of arousal intensified between her legs. She stretched under the covers, her back arching, and was rewarded with a wet mouth at her breast.

Did it matter she didn't know who this fantasy represented or what he looked like? Nope. There was a master seducer playing her body to perfection. She needed to come to North Carolina more often if she could have sex dreams this good.

The man's fingers slipped into the plump folds blooming between her thighs. Gliding along the bud slick with dew, they gently scissored her clitoris, pressing and releasing, using a technique she'd have to remember when she woke up.

Yes, lovely one, the dream man said. *Open for me. I want to use my mouth.*

Did ghosts do cunnilingus? Wait. She didn't believe in ghosts. She was dreaming, and she wanted him to use his mouth. His tongue. His cock. Hell, if he was this adept at manipulating her lady parts, he could use whatever implement he wanted. Cucumber, drumstick, ice cube...

The tongue fondling her clit sent electric pulses down her thighs. Definitely not a ghost if he felt so much like firm flesh.

Madeline's body crested a wave of pleasure that defied gravity. She was weightless and hungry, surging and empty. Sex had never been this otherworldly. She wanted to give back what she was being given, to touch and stroke and kiss, but if she moved, if she reached for his shoulders to pull his weight on top of her, she might wake up. What a tragedy.

The dark voice chuckled, and the vibration made her nipples tingle.

You don't have to do anything but take your pleasure. You can feel how much I love giving it to you, can't you?

Madeline *did* feel him. A man with powerful arms and shoulders was between her legs and giving her the best head of her life. Her eyes were definitely closed, but she could see his face in her mind's eye. Warm brown skin. Kind eyes. High cheekbones. Full lips. God, those lips. Beautiful. She must be having a lucid dream, a place her imagination could unravel the confusing information of the day. That was the only reasonable explanation.

The spectral being cupped her bottom, lifting her higher into spirals of pleasure. She could feel his strength, the length of his erection pressing against her legs as he moved up her body. A sob grew in her chest. She couldn't wait for him to drive himself into her and end the tension.

But the dream lover wasn't interested in rushing. He eased over her, letting her accept his weight and get accustomed to the heavy girth of his loins rubbing into her swollen folds. Madeline blinked sluggishly. He smiled at her, revealing straight white teeth. Were those dimples winking at her? God, he was too beautiful to be real.

I think you're beautiful, too. Luscious. And this flower between your legs is so wet. I want to give it what it wants.

Yes, please. Her hands slid down his broad, muscular back, lingering on the lean taper of his waist. The head of his shaft was nudging at her, teasing. Normally, she liked foreplay, but he was right. She was wet and ready.

When I come inside you, it will be a celebration. A homecoming. We will be joined, and you'll never know another moment of disappointment, another day of loneliness or doubt.

Geez, what a promise! It sounded heavenly, and nothing like the waking world. Who needed the angst, the constant compromise of dating, mating, and marrying? Not her. Not if she could have a dream lover who was gently, patiently grinding the base of his wonderfully large cock against her clitoris. But what was he waiting for? Did he want her to beg?

No. Nothing like that. He wanted her to want him so much she demanded he enter her.

What a gentleman.

She stretched again, opening her legs wide to wrap them around the dream man's waist. She'd tell him to take her now, knowing she wouldn't wake up until he fucked them both into oblivion.

"Madeline. Madeline!"

Another pair of large, strong hands took hold of her shoulders, shaking her.

The dream man and his sex disappeared.

Thrust forcibly into the waking world, Madeline's eyes snapped open. Julian's concerned face hovered over her in the shadowy dark.

"Agent Wonderbread?" she mumbled.

"It's Julian," he muttered and yanked the coverlet off her body.

Madeline squeaked a protest and sat up. Scrambling off the bed, she snatched her self-defense baton from the chair.

"Agent Worthy," she hissed. "What are you doing in my room?"

He dropped to his knees to look under the bed. "Where did he go?"

Madeline would have been scared, but he sounded more excited than aggressive, and his enthusiasm wasn't directed at her. Plus, he was wearing striped pajamas. What a nerd.

To be on the safe side, with a flick of her wrist, the baton extended.

Julian stood and held up his hands. "Hey, now. You were moaning so loud I could hear you downstairs. I came to help."

"I was dreaming! Don't you think I would know if someone was in my room?"

"There was someone under the covers with you." He shook his head as if he couldn't believe what he'd seen or heard. "But when I said your name, he disappeared without a trace."

CHAPTER FIVE

JULIAN

J ulian eyed Da Vinci's self-defense baton, thinking it resembled a large and impressive vibrator. Which would explain the moaning, if not the disappearing lover. "I'm telling you, someone was *here*."

"Your imagination has gotten the best of you, Agent Wonderbread," Da Vinci bit out. "The only man in my room is you."

"Agent Worthy," Julian put in.

"Whatever. I was having a very pleasant dream," she said. "One I'd like to get back to."

"I don't think that's a good idea," Julian said, his stomach quaking with excess adrenaline.

Da Vinci tapped her nightstick against her leg. "Why would that be?"

Julian's gaze rested on the shapely curve of her thigh, drawn instinctively to the meaty sound of metal on skin. He shook himself, raising his eyes to meet hers. "If the entities in this house see you as a threat, they may find a way to attack you while you're sleeping."

"I wasn't being attacked!"

Julian held up a hand and ticked off the points on his fingers. "One, an unknown assailant attacked Roland in this house. Two, Mrs. Hanford has an unknown lover, but there is no physical evidence of another person in the home. Three, when I entered the room, there was someone under the covers with you, someone who disappeared into thin air. Four, whatever is happening, happens at night. *Ergo*, you shouldn't go back to sleep."

She waved the baton around the room. "Then where are they?"

"We need to search the house," Julian said, making a B-line for the closet.

"Now wait a minute, Agent Wond—"

"Worthy," Julian repeated, irritated. He opened the closet door.

Da Vinci crossed the room and closed it, standing between Julian and the door. "I'm staying in this room. And I have a right to privacy. So does Mrs. Hanford. You can't just go rifling through her things."

The faint smell of perfume and arousal penetrated Julian's lizard brain. Being in close proximity to this beautiful woman sent unwelcome hormones coursing through his system. He opened his mouth. Closed it. She had him feeling like an addled schoolboy.

Da Vinci crossed her arms, unwittingly plumping her cleavage. "Well?"

Julian pinched the bridge of his nose as if he could squeeze the chemical reactions in his traitorous body out of his bloodstream. He took a breath, let it out, and tried again, pointedly not looking at the outline of her curves under her peach nightgown. "I know you're concerned about Mrs. Hanford's safety. That's our common ground. I need you to believe I have investigated cases of..." the words 'ghost sex' died on his tongue "...this kind of phenomenon."

"A dream is now considered phenomenon?" she scoffed.

Julian's hair chose that moment to fall across his eyes again. He blew it out of the way absently. "You were not alone in that bed."

"Look, you come into my room, invade my privacy, and invalidate my experience. You're either a fraud, under-sexed, or in desperate need of attention."

Julian held up his hands. "I surrender. But if you want to psychoanalyze me, just know that the coolest thing about my job is my title. Secret Service agents don't get paid that much. I can't afford your services. Also, my sex life is just fine, thank you."

They stared at each other.

Julian's eyes fell to the outline of her magnificent breasts, drawn by the powerful pheromones coursing through the air between them. The contour of her nipples stood in sharp relief against the satiny fabric of her nightgown.

Da Vinci followed his gaze, snorted, and stared directly at the bulge of his semi-erection tenting his striped PJs. "So, what do you propose we do for the rest of the night?"

Was she flirting with him or manipulating him? His pants said it didn't matter. Discretion, rather misdirection, being the better part of valor, Julian tried a different tactic. "I'm sure you're excellent at your job. I need you to accept that I'm good at mine, too. When it comes to paranormal events, I know what I'm talking about."

"Convince me," Da Vinci said.

"Can we sit and talk?" Julian waved toward the easy chairs by the window.

She cast a longing glance at the disheveled bed. "Okay, but not here. If we're going to play Scooby-Doo, I'm going to put on my Thelma clothes."

Julian smiled. "Daphne."

Da Vinci tore her eyes from the bed. "Huh?"

"Daphne. The hair. The...." Don't say curves. "Everything. You're Daphne."

Her smile turned feral, showing perfect white teeth. "And you'd be...?"

"Fred, I hope. Because if you say Shaggy, I'm going to have sharp words with my tailor."

"On *your* salary?" she taunted.

Julian bit his tongue. "I'll put some coffee on."

As he rummaged through the kitchen for the java makings, Julian tried to order his thoughts. Energy crackled through the house. Was it his hormones? Or a repeat of the tingling power of supernatural magic like Slate Hill?

As if in answer, silent blue-white lightning lit the kitchen. Julian turned to the window over the sink but saw only darkness outside.

The second thing, then.

Once the coffee started perking and bubbling, Julian took his go-bag to the bathroom and changed out of his pajamas. He wished he had jeans and a T-shirt. But no. He packed only for work. And work meant suits. The best he could do was an undershirt and slacks. He placed his compact flashlight and backup pistol, snug in its ankle holster, on the closed lid of the toilet. Casual or not, he wouldn't be without a weapon.

As he changed, all he could think about was seeking vindication from his boss. Spearman told him not to take this case. But this *was* like Slate Hill. He was right. She was wrong. Without thinking, he hit call and put her on speaker.

"Julian?" Spearman's groggy voice echoed loud in the bathroom.

Beyond the door, a floorboard creaked.

He grabbed the phone and took her off speaker. "I was right," he whispered. "It's like Slate Hill."

"Do you know what time it is?"

Julian glanced at his phone. "One seventeen."

"You couldn't have called me in the morning?"

"I...."

"Jules," Spearman's voice softened. "I never said you were wrong. I only encouraged you not to take the case. You need to be careful."

Her words provoked a strangely angry reaction. Never said he was wrong? His mentor wanted him to *knowingly* wave off finding the truth. Maybe she wasn't the person, the Special Agent, he thought she was. "I won't be seducing any high school students, if that's what you mean."

She hung up.

Yup. He'd totally fucked that up.

He finished changing, feeling like an idiot.

Da Vinci sat on the couch. She had changed into sleek leggings and a slouchy cardigan. She sipped her coffee, curling her legs under her. "No red scarf?"

"We're going to stop with the Scooby-Doo thing soon, right?" It came out harsher than he meant. He was still flustered from the call with Spearman. Deep breath. Coffee. Julian went to the kitchen and poured himself a cup, trying to decide how much to tell Da Vinci about himself, the file on Mason's Manor, and Slate Hill. Enough to make her stay without revealing the far-fetched and racy parts of the story. If he were honest, most of the story was pretty racy.

Tricky.

"So, your past cases with the paranormal...?" Da Vinci asked, as Julian settled into an armchair.

"Right." He sipped his coffee, stalling.

The grandfather clock across the room ticked out a sonorous rhythm. She waited. Damn therapists. He knew this game. The one who talks first, loses. But he did owe her an explanation. Barging into her room was a serious offense.

"In 2015, a small town about an hour from here—"

"Slate Hill?"

"Yes. Anyway. There was a spate of inappropriate sexual activity."

"What qualifies as inappropriate? Shaming and labeling—"

Julian cut her off. "Can you give me five minutes without the therapist hat?"

Da Vinci shook her head. "Doesn't work like that."

He rolled his eyes. "Fine. Inappropriate, as in, the townspeople experienced a total loss of inhibitions, self-control, and propriety."

She sipped her coffee. "That's pretty vague."

Julian sighed. She wasn't going to settle for the sanitized version. "Basically, the whole town went sex crazy. Teachers and students. Librarians and soccer moms. They reported encounters with...."

Don't say ghosts.

"With?"

"Supernatural elements."

She raised an eyebrow.

"The case had a *lot* of supernatural elements."

Da Vinci choked on her coffee, coughing and laughing.

Heat rose in Julian's cheeks. "What?"

"Like, a bevy of ghost cock?" she managed.

"Huh?"

She waved a hand. "Private joke. Keep going."

"When I investigated the scenes, there were arcane symbols found surrounding the town—"

"Oh, come *on.*"

"I'm serious. You can't tell me you haven't noticed the weird energy in this house."

"If you're trying to convince me this house was built on native burial grounds or used by pagans in fertility rituals, I've had my fill of history lessons." Da Vinci shook her head. "It's gibberish, or to use my pretty therapist words, confirmation bias."

"I'm acting on personal experience," Julian countered.

She waved a hand at him. "Do tell."

There was no way he was going to share the deeper secrets prompting his career choice. "I've felt this before. This..." *don't say sexual* "...energy. The lightning. All of it. There's something in this house with us."

"Maybe so," Da Vinci conceded. "But whatever it is, there is a rational explanation."

Julian fought the urge to stomp his foot. Fucking shrinks. After Slate Hill, he'd spent years in a therapist's office, twice a week, while a stogy old bastard tried to convince him his memories were creations of his mind masking some deeper psychological issue. Gaslighting, that's what it was. Institutional gaslighting by myopic doctors who couldn't open their minds to the truth. Julian knew he'd been abducted. Slate Hill was real. And it was happening again, more or less the same, in this house. He was *goddamned* if Mrs. Hanford or Da Vinci would suffer the same fate. No hospitals. No surgery. No shrinks laughing up their sleeves.

Just like Slate Hill, there had to be a summoning circle. A portal to another dimension. Something. If only he could find it.

"Hey."

Julian realized he'd been staring out the window into the darkness. "We need to search the house."

"I told you I'm not going to rummage in the middle of the night," Da Vinci said firmly. "We'll ask Constance in the morning."

Lightning flashed. Julian felt his body swell with sexual awareness and heard Da Vinci's sharply indrawn breath.

"That," Julian pointed out the window, his voice a husky rasp, "is exactly what I'm talking about. To get lightning, you need a column of warm wet air and cool air colliding. There are no clouds. You can see the moon."

Da Vinci stared at his mouth. She looked sleepy, her eyes heavy-lidded, despite the coffee. Sex magic, he reminded himself. It worked fast, and she probably wasn't aware of what was happening to her.

She put down her coffee cup, still looking at his lips, and gave a feline stretch. "What about heat lightning?"

Her V-neck revealed a distracting amount of cleavage, and the gentle light hugged the soft curve of her shapely legs. Julian's resistance caught fire and threatened to go up in flames.

"Jules?"

She'd called him Jules. Not Agent Wonderbread or Worthy. Did that mean something? Well, she must have heard the beginning of his call to Spearman. Had she been eavesdropping, or the speaker volume was turned up? Either way, he'd stick to formal addresses. He was a professional. "Miss Da Vinci—"

"Madeline," she corrected and gave him a smile that nearly stopped his heart.

"Uh...." This wasn't fair at all. How was he supposed to work if she kept distracting him with smiles, cleavage, leggings, and.... "Right. Madeline."

She let out a tiny giggle, looked away, and rubbed her hands slowly over the sweater.

Julian straightened in his chair, squared his shoulders, and started over. "Heat lightning is a misnomer. It's just energy from a distant thunderstorm. Flashes can be seen on the horizon when clouds can't. The storm is so far off, the sound doesn't travel." He rose and walked to the window. "But this isn't that."

He smelled her at his side before he saw her: vanilla and cinnamon and something else. Did he still smell her arousal from earlier, or was it caught in his nose?

"There are so many stars on these dark country nights," she whispered. Her soft sweater brushed the sparse hair on his triceps.

"They're there all the time," Julian said absently, pulling out his phone. He wanted to stop the blood pulsing to his lower chakras by checking the weather radar. Sure enough, it showed clear on his app.

Julian held the phone out. "See?"

Madeline leaned in to get a better view, not quite resting her head on his shoulder. "Huh. No storms nearby. I'll be damned."

"Hopefully not," Julian said, feeling more at ease now that science had vindicated him.

She leaned back in mock surprise. "Why, Special Agent Worthy, are you concerned for my soul?"

Their eyes locked.

Her half-lowered eyelids barely concealed the glittering emeralds in the dim room. The crackling energy flowing between them wasn't in his head.

Time slowed.

Her inviting scent enveloped him.

Had he moved closer to her, or the other way around? They drew together, pulled trance-like toward a destiny that seemed suddenly certain, natural, and unavoidable.

Her lips parted.

So close now. Julian closed his eyes and bent his head toward hers, his mouth seeking....

A heavy *thump* across the room sent them jerking apart.

Julian spun around. In the second it took him to turn, a different image of the room flashed through his vision.

The sedate floral wallpaper hung in yellowed strips. Broken, dusty furniture littered the room. Black mold crept across the ceiling. The impression lasted only an instant and disappeared so fast, Julian questioned whether he'd seen it at all.

Everything was as it should be, almost. The only thing out of place: a photo album on the floor close to the couch, its loosened pictures splashing across the carpet.

Julian reached down and drew the backup pistol from his ankle holster.

"Really?" Madeline asked. "It's just an old house. Probably settled or...something." But there was no belief behind her words.

Julian stepped carefully toward the photos on the floor, inspecting the room for what caused the album to jump from the shelf. Or signs of the decay he swore he'd seen. Or a ghost, cuz' why not?

Madeline passed him and stood staring down at the mess. Her hand flew to her chest. "No way."

Satisfied there was no one else in the room, Julian drew up beside her. "What?"

She reached down and grasped a weathered black-and-white picture. "Oh, my god...."

"Seriously, what?"

She held up the picture for Julian to examine. "This is the man from my dream."

CHAPTER SIX

MADELINE

The next morning, Madeline sat at the kitchen table across from Julian, but didn't make eye contact.

The sunflower yellow cupboards and white Formica counters were like stepping into the 1950s. Happy energy pulsed from dappled sunlight streaming through the lace curtains, but Madeline's head swam with lethargy. Agent Wonderbread—err, Julian's—info dump demanded attention. Weird weather patterns and sex-crazed townspeople sounded like a conspiracy theory podcast, not reality. If she hadn't found her dream lover's face in an old photo album, she would have said Julian lived in a land of wishful thinking.

Then there was that moment of shared intimacy. They'd almost kissed. Maybe sneaking around in the middle of the night hadn't been the best idea, but she'd been captivated by the luster of Julian's lips moving, smiling, forming words while blue lightning flooded the cozy living room. Here was a real man, an available man, at arm's reach. It seemed completely reasonable to ditch her reservations, lean forward, and taste him.

They'd been interrupted, but that didn't prevent twangs of lust from clawing at her with devilish, ghostly fingers. She should have taken five minutes and masturbated before coming downstairs. It wouldn't have been satisfying, but hunger doesn't argue with the menu.

Constance hummed at the stove. Bacon sizzled and pancakes bubbled on the griddle, sending waves of deliciousness through the bright kitchen. The matron in her quilted housecoat was going all-out on breakfast and refused help from her visitors. Setting a bowl of cubed melon, strawberries, and blueberries on the table, the older woman shot Madeline a twinkling smirk.

"Did you two have fun last night?"

Madeline swallowed a lump of guilt. "I don't know what you mean. I slept like a baby."

"I slept like crap," Julian announced, eyeing the fruit with trepidation.

"Both of y'all are terrible liars." Constance sat between them at the table, hands steepled in old lady wisdom. "I heard you roaming around the living room like mice in a rice sack."

Madeline winced and hid behind her coffee cup. Julian had no such compulsion.

"Constance, can I ask you about Desmond's photo album?"

"That's a wonderful idea."

Without the preamble of ignorance, Julian sprang from the table, went into the living room, and returned with the ancient leather binder. Madeline willed herself not to send him a disgruntled look. He was sure to lean into Constance's delusion of a ghost lover, and that would *not* help Madeline's cause.

If she could convince Constance that Desmond was a healthy figment of her imagination—not a paranormal specter—Roland would stop insisting she needed medication, or worse, to be moved into an assisted facility. At some point, that might be necessary, but

Madeline couldn't advocate for intervention when Constance was obviously vibrant.

That meant offering Constance contradictory information until she could decide for herself it was normal to have an imaginary friend when you were sad, depressed, or lonely.

Unless, that is, Constance wanted them to believe Desmond's spirit inhabited the house for another purpose. Maybe one more nefarious than attention-seeking.

The older woman had said you could touch a ghost, feel a ghost. But ghosts were supposed to blow cold air on your neck, make the lights flicker, and scratch you when you asked stupid, and frankly invasive, questions about their personal lives. With the help of her secret, living lover, they could have put a speaker in Madeline's room, or rigged the photo album to fall from the shelf.

If this was a hoax, it was an elaborate one.

Constance smoothed her wiry hand over the leather and opened the cover. She pointed to a print of a painting. He was a handsome man with smooth, dark skin, wearing a smart suit and cravat. His slight, knowing smile had Madeline's nipples tingling in recognition.

Julian shifted in his chair.

She shot him a look. When their eyes met, a shower of sensual possibility shimmered between them. From his flared nostrils and dilated pupils, he felt it, too. What the hell was going on?

Constance seemed oblivious to the currents of chemistry. "This is the first picture I could find of Desmond, painted right after Louisiana gained statehood in 1803. The original is hanging in the library. He was a member of the free people of color before the racial divide cleaved our baby country in half." She traced a finger along his strong jaw and turned the page. A sepia-toned photo of a stately black man and his pretty wife stared up at them. The woman held a plump toddler on her lap. "Desmond moved to the DC area with his wife Lula in 1859 to support the abolishment of slavery."

Madeline frowned and leaned over the album. Fifty years had passed, and Desmond hadn't aged a day. "How old was he when he married his wife?"

"The records say thirty-one," Constance shrugged. "Lula was twenty-two. She was a spirited girl. Look at those daring eyes. The boy was hers from another man, but Desmond raised him as his own." Another turn of the page, Desmond, an older, rounder Lula, and a young man in military garb posed in front of what was now Constance's house. "The boy died in his twenties, bless his heart. Lula made it to fifty-three, a decent age back in those times."

More pages turned. Lula's face bore the lines of gravity and sorrow, the clothing aged, but her husband remained unmarked by time.

"May I?" Julian reached for the photo album.

Constance handed it over and returned to the stove. "I collected photos of Desmond over the years. I hadn't met him, not officially, until after we moved into the house."

Madeline's mind spun. Photos could be altered, easy to do with today's technology, but what if they weren't? Desmond could have had other offspring with different women. If his descendants looked like him, they could dress the part, show up on Constance's doorstep, and claim to be the long-dead Desmond.

Madeline opened her mouth to ask about Desmond's family tree, but out of the corner of her eye, she saw Julian pull a folded piece of parchment from the album, frown, and put it in his pocket. When he caught her looking, he just gave a subtle shake of his head.

Constance placed a plate of pancakes on the table. "Roland was ten when we moved in. Thomas lasted two years before the heart attack took him."

Julian broke his concentration to offer a sincere, "Constance, I'm so sorry."

She waved this aside. "I wasn't sad to see him go. He had old-fashioned ideas about what a wife should and shouldn't do. Never took to me being a NASA mathematician."

Julian looked up sharply, a dog catching the scent. "You were a NASA computer?"

"Indeed. Got my bachelor's from Hampton Institute of Mathematics and Physical Science just like Mary Jackson, then went on to work at the Langley Memorial Aeronautical Lab in Virginia."

Madeline dumped maple syrup over her pancakes and bacon, wondering what kind of husband could let himself sink into his insecurities to the point he'd turn against his brilliant wife.

Constance sat down, smiling fondly. "They were difficult but good times. I don't know how you kids do it today. Everyone is trying to tell you go-with-the-flow, make it easy. Nothing worth doing is ever easy."

Sound advice, Madeline thought with a ping of conscience. It was entirely possible she hadn't fought for Sebastian because their relationship wasn't worth the effort. They liked doing things together, but as soon as he moved in, he'd acted more like a roommate than her partner. The last time they'd had a real conversation, she'd sat across from Sebastian, listening numbly to his trite breakup script. "I don't want this to turn into a big deal, but I can't live like this, Maddie. It's not you. You're a great gal, but I feel like I'm suffocating."

In Madeline's professional opinion, "It's not you" meant the one leaving didn't want to explain why it *was* you. Sebastian knew she wasn't going to change. Neither was he. Why hash it out? Then again, she'd picked Sebastian for his laser focus on his career. She'd never had to entertain him, never had to give up her individuality. Then there was the issue of money. Madeline's private practice made three times that of a non-tenured research biologist.

Queasy, Madeline put down her fork. "Constance, tell me to mind my own business, but how are you for money?"

"I'm not ashamed to say my late husband made terrible business decisions, and that I, knowing what I was getting into, hid money I later invested. Desmond has always given me pointers on stocks, but overall, he is very proud of the way I've handled money."

"Desmond knows about the stock market?" Julian asked, frowning.

"Oh yes, but not from a greedy perspective. He told me I'd need to shore up enough capital to resist corporate land acquisition. Considering I've been approached three times by smart fellas in business suits thinking they can write me a half a million dollar check for my property, I'd say he was right."

Madeline realized her mouth was hanging open and sealed her lips. What possible argument could she make? *Constance, a ghost isn't supposed to know the difference between a Bull or Bear market.*

"What about your son?" Julian asked. "Does Roland plan to keep the land?"

"My son followed in the footsteps of his father. Poor business acumen." She nibbled on a strip of bacon. "He knows he'll be taken care of when I leave this earth, but the majority of my wealth will go to the township."

Julian and Madeline shared a look of uncomfortable realization. If Roland knew his mother wasn't leaving him all her assets, he might want her to move into assisted care as a bargaining chip to get more money.

"If y'all are finished with breakfast, there's something I want to show you." Constance stood and gave a limber stretch. "Get your boots on. We're going on a field trip."

Ten minutes later, Madeline and Julian waited on the front porch. She felt like elbowing him in the side, but resisted the urge–the need–to make contact. "You didn't touch breakfast. On a diet?"

"I'm a picky eater," he hedged.

She patted her hips. "I don't have that problem."

His gaze settled on her lower half with appreciation. Madeline swallowed, once again aware of her runaway hormones.

Constance appeared in sensible cotton pants and a bright green linen blouse. Walking stick in hand, she led the way down the short porch steps, around the flower beds, and into the surrounding forest. They passed dogwoods, old-growth pine trees, and healthy white hickory. Julian peppered Constance with questions about her time at NASA, most of which Madeline ignored.

Walking behind the science-loving pair, she watched Julian's hair glint gold, then platinum, then umber in the stippled light of the tree canopy. What would the silky strands feel like between her fingers? Rebound sex was generally hot, but Julian was her colleague for the time being. And his motives were still in question.

Constance didn't seem to be suffering from confusion, memory loss, or Sundowner's Syndrome. By her ease in the kitchen, she could probably outwork them, a fact Madeline marked with more than a little pride at the woman's resiliency. The more Constance told them about her life, the deeper Madeline genuinely cared about what the woman thought and felt. Rapport with a client was a must, so was trust. Being drawn into a fantasy world, not so much.

Madeline took a deep breath, luxuriating in the scent of moss, wildflowers, and morning dew. God, it was nice here. What would it be like to linger in the solitude and stillness of the forest? To know you were surrounded by protection? By love?

She collided with Julian's back, the impact sending a wave of excitement down her front. And her back. And her feet? Julian reached back to steady her, but she stepped away, not wanting to make the tension worse. He didn't seem perturbed, and she craned her neck to see what had captured his attention.

They had entered a small clearing filled with soft green grass and purple-blue flowers with dainty yellow centers.

"Welcome to the family cemetery," Constance said, her voice rippling with joy.

Ancient stone markers, some pre-Civil War, the epitaphs worn away by weather and time, jutted from the earth in lopsided crosses and statues. Constance began absently plucking random weeds obscuring the stones. Madeline pitched in, as did Julian.

Constance said, "The newer stones are some of my family members. Two of my aunties. My nanny on my mother's side. Here's Lula and her son's marker."

Both stones were made of thick yellow marble a foot square and detailed with a bas-relief flower. The same species of purplish flowers dotted the clearing. The flat oval face of the flower held an almond-shaped hood and, peering closer, looked a lot like a woman's vulva. Madeline smiled, thinking of her Georgia O'Keeffe clock, but something else nagged her. Post-Civil War times in the South weren't known for a boom in commerce. Most people were lucky to get a marker, much less a marble headstone with an embellishment.

"Constance, what did Desmond do for a living?" Madeline asked.

Constance gave her a level stare. "He owned a mining company." She pointed to the grave's flower. "That's the masthead for the Butterfly Pea Quarry."

Julian perked up. "Did Desmond tell you why he picked that flower?"

Madeline glared at him. The next opportunity she got, she would warn him about feeding into Constance's fantasy.

Constance stood, plunking her hands on her hips. "I didn't ask. Why do you want to know?"

"Just curious. It looks like...well..." He cleared his throat, an attractive blush marking his cheeks. "A vagina."

"That's right," she chuckled. "The butterfly pea is in the Clitoria ternatea family."

Julian changed subjects. "This is Desmond's grave?"

Madeline hurried to Julian's side to look at the would-be ghost's last resting place. Desmond Mason. Loving husband and father. B 1792- D. 1888. The butterfly pea relief adorned the plaque, but it was joined with a geometric shape of intertwining circles that looked cosmic in origin. Nothing that would have been in vogue in the 1800s.

Julian stared at the marker. "How did he die?"

Constance gave him a thoughtful look. "Poison."

The bottom dropped from Madeline's stomach in a clench of sympathy. Before she could stop herself, she asked, "By whom?"

"Self-administered." The older woman rubbed at the dirt on her hands. "After Lula and the boy died, he tried to put up a good show. Ran the company. Traveled. But you know, a handsome black man with money in that day, no one ever left him alone. There was always some yokel trying to steal from him or accuse him of theft, the usual. He killed his physical body, but something kept him here, in a less corporeal form." She smiled to herself. "I'd like to think I was the reason, though we wouldn't meet for decades to come. His family wasn't thrilled he'd decided to stay."

Julian's was voice sharp. "His family?"

"The others like him." She nodded, lost in memories. "Took me by surprise, too."

"How were they like him?" Julian asked.

"Non-human," Constance said calmly. "I won't say alien. Bad connotation."

Madeline could barely keep up. Julian pushed ahead. "Forgive me, but how did you say your husband died?"

"Julian," Madeline hissed.

"The coroner's report said heart attack." Constance shrugged. "That was over fifty years ago. Not much on toxicology reports back then, aye?"

"Did Desmond have a hand in your late husband's death?"

Madeline whirled on Julian, her patience at an end. "This is how rumors get started. Bad rumors. What if Roland believes his mother is being visited by a copycat murderer of his father?"

He gave her a considering look. "That's a stretch, but a plausible one."

Madeline's fists clenched. "Even if it's the furthest thing from the truth, he could use the story to convince the state Constance is incompetent. They might commit her!"

Her angry voice faded into the wooded border. Just for a second, in the time it took for a cool breeze to ruffle the flowers in the clearing, Madeline saw the shadows of the surrounding forest swell and contract. She had the unsettling feeling the land was not only listening, but responding to her urgency to keep Constance safe.

Was she losing her grasp on reality, or did everything about Mason's Manor hint at a darker, more menacing agenda?

Then the older woman was beside her, taking her hand. A rush of calm eased Madeline's shoulders.

"Sweet girl, don't worry about me. There are a million ways to break a heart and an infinite number to put that heart back together." She waved at the pristine beauty of the forest. "This place is special. You can feel it. *It* can feel you. If you wanted, you could stay. Both of you could. You'd be happy, like I was."

With a final squeeze of Madeline's hand, Constance left them alone in the graveyard, her voice like the scent of flowers faithfully trailing after her. "We're getting to the end now, and whether you believe it or not, it's no accident y'all are here. Best decide what you want the future to look like before someone—or something—decides for you."

CHAPTER SEVEN

JULIAN

"What do you think you're doing, Julian?" Madeline asked as Constance disappeared down the forest trail.

He held his palms up in defense, but he was pleased. She'd called him Julian. "What did I do?"

She parked her hands on her generous hips. "You're feeding into Constance's delusions. If you reinforce all this paranormal hanky-panky, they're going to lock her up. Is that what you want?"

Julian's shoulders tensed. "Look, my questions aren't going to suddenly convince her she hasn't been fucking the ghost of the guy who used to live in her house. She believes what she believes, and I'm not going to tell her she's wrong. Gaslighting people is the province of shrinks like you."

He didn't mean to say that, but the bitterness of his memories left him raw and boiling mad.

Madeline's mouth hung open, and her eyes grew cold. "There is so much wrong with what you just said I don't know where to start unpacking it."

Julian crossed his arms. "If you don't believe her, or me, why are you still here?"

Madeline looked at the weathered stone grave marker, a muscle twitching in her clenched jaw. "You don't think protecting her from people who think she's too old to enjoy an active sex life is a good enough reason?"

He raised an eyebrow. "Even if you think it's all in her imagination?"

"*Especially* if it's all in her imagination We all fantasize about something."

"Is that how you rationalize your dream about Desmond? The photo album falling from the bookcase? The lightning?"

She remained mute.

"Madeline, you know I'm not a threat to Constance. Hell, I'm more on her side than you are. So, I'll ask you again, why are you here?"

She turned her big green eyes on him, stormy with a chance of showers. "You want me to go?"

"Of course not!" Julian's abrupt confession stunned both of them, but he refused to backtrack. Something about her confidence spoke to his heart. He wanted her next to him. "I might not agree with your views, but I value your input."

"Doesn't feel like it."

Julian took a deep breath and let his shoulders drop. "I'm sorry about the gaslighting crack."

Madeline nodded, but didn't meet his eyes.

His stomach took the opportunity to complain, loudly. "I haven't eaten for twenty-four hours. I'm getting hangry. Will you come to town with me? After I eat, we'll poke around, see what we can find out about the house, Desmond, all of it."

She hesitated. "I'm supposed to be on a plane to Costa Rica in thirty-six hours."

"Did you rob a bank? Are you on the lamb?" Julian asked, trying to lighten the mood.

Her face darkened. "Doesn't matter."

He wanted to ask what was bothering her, but it might stretch their tentative truce. A slow-motion movie of their almost kiss the night before played in his mind. Did he want her to stay because of the case or...? "Give it one more night. Help me solve this case."

"I'll go to town with you. We'll see from there."

"Cool." God, he sounded like a horny teenage boy. He puffed that damned lock of hair out of his eyes again.

Madeline spun on her heel and found the trail back to the house. He followed, mesmerized by the twin globes of her retreating bottom.

"What was the deal with breakfast?" she asked over her shoulder.

Sunlight filtered through the trees, setting her red hair on fire and alternately quenching it in shadow.

"I'm not big on eating at other people's houses."

"Interesting," Madeline said. "When did that start?"

"I can't afford your rates," Julian said. "Remember?"

The sound of her grudging laughter broke the tension and faded through the trees. Julian spent the rest of the walk thinking of ways Madeline could see what was really happening at Mason's Manor. When they reached his car, he asked, "You've had a private conversation with Constance. What is your professional opinion of her condition?"

Madeline gave him a tight smile and slid into the passenger seat. "My professional opinion is that I don't discuss the details of my client's cases. It's not legal or ethical." She sighed. "But because we're supposedly on the same side, I see no signs of prescription abuse, obvious addictions, or chronic ailments that could be wearing her down. She doesn't even complain about her joints!"

Julian put the car in drive and crunched down the long dirt driveway, nodding thoughtfully.

Madeline continued, "What really bugs me is her son. There's something off about Roland. Do you get that impression?"

"Yeah. But sometimes it's hard to tell if a guy like that is just an asshole or if he's complicit. I'm starting to see why local law enforcement blew him off."

The car bumped off the gravel lane onto sturdy asphalt. "Where are we going, exactly?" Madeline asked.

Julian fingered the folded yellowed paper in his pocket. "Any chance I can get away with telling you it's a surprise?"

"*Julian....*"

He couldn't hold back the grin. It was nice, working with someone. If he could just get her to believe he wasn't a kook, she'd truly be a partner.

She stared at him expectantly. "You realize you haven't said anything yet?"

Julian pulled the map from his pocket. "I found this in the photo album hidden beneath Desmond's picture."

"Yeah, I noticed." Madeline unfolded a map of the Butterfly Pea Mines tunnel structure. "We're going to a mine?"

Julian couldn't help showing off a little. He wanted her to know that he wasn't just a conspiracy theorist with a badge. "We're going to the town clerk's office to get records of Mason's Hole."

"Why?"

"Because Desmond was responsible for digging the tunnels. I'm willing to bet it goes under the house." And that there was an interdimensional portal hidden under the town. "Constance hinted we'd get some good gossip there."

Madeline surrendered with a shrug. "After you, fearless leader."

They drove Julian's rental car in silence for several minutes. It felt good to be back on firmer ground. The sex life of an octogenarian might be more in Madeline's wheelhouse, but digging through obscure details no one thought important was Julian's specialty.

The summer sun turned the sweeping rural lawns sapphire green. Trees hung over the blacktop, creating a kaleidoscope of light and shadow. Hard to believe a so-called haunted house could exist in this well-to-do suburban utopia of perfectly kept homes.

He parked in one of three spots in the converted colonial house that served as the Mason's Hole town hall.

"Well, this is cute," Madeline said and shot him an ironic look. "Another picturesque house that doesn't look remotely haunted."

He tapped his fingers on the steering wheel, momentarily distracted by the memory of Constance's house in the shambles of ghostly disrepair. "You noticed that, too? I have half a dozen reports talking about paranormal events in the area. Most of them mention Mason's Manor being prime real estate for a horror movie."

Madeline shrugged. "It could be a guise to drum up tourism."

Large oaks and maples along the sidewalks provided ample shade for a drugstore, coffee shop, post office, library, and an antique emporium. The only thing that stood out was a garish advertisement for Roland Hanford's law firm plastered on a sidewalk bench.

They got out of the car. Julian paused, giving the quiet, clean streets of downtown a thorough glance. "If they want to attract the ghost-hunting crowd, they'd advertise, right? Maybe offer a tour?"

Madeline squinted. "I'm going to check out the library. You know, divide and conquer?"

The euphemism gave Julian a jolt. He'd love to divide and conquer a number of secret places with her. "Keep an eye open for flyers and pamphlets."

"Will do," Madeline said and headed down the street.

The sun blazed hot on Julian's dark suit as he advanced up the walk. Inside, the town hall had shed all traces of its former life as a genteel sitting room. Straight-back wooden chairs lined a wall facing a tapioca-colored counter, behind which a rotund woman of about sixty clacked away at a computer. Beyond her desk crouched a phalanx of filing cabinets and a door marked 'Mayor's Office.'

"Good morning!" The woman at the computer rose, eyes growing wide at the sight of him. Her ample chest quivered with an indrawn breath. "And who might you be?"

"Mr. Worthy, but please call me Julian." He didn't pull his badge. Sometimes small-town folks clammed up when 'the feds' came poking around. But from her reaction, Julian guessed she might respond to a little male attention. He gave the clerk his warmest smile. "That's a magnificent blouse, Miss...?"

In truth, the garment was a cacophony of swirling colors that hurt his eyes. One more button than was appropriate perched undone over three inches of exposed cleavage.

She blushed and returned his smile. "I'm the town clerk, Sarah Dubois."

He leaned in and rested his chin in his hand, keeping eye contact. "Dubois, is that French?"

"Why, yes," the clerk's blush deepened. "My people settled here after the revolution."

"Then you're exactly the person I need. I'm interested in some local real estate. Could you show me the records for an address?"

"I'll have to ask you to fill out an information request form." She pulled a sheet of paper from a pile behind the counter and slid it toward him without taking her appraising eyes from his broad shoulders.

Julian's grin deepened. "I bet you know a lot about this town."

Dubois touched a hand to her chest. "I *am* the clerk."

"Yes," he pressed, "and I bet you know *secret* things."

"Well...." She waved away the flattery, clearly enjoying the attention.

"You could tell me things about the town I can't find in the records."

Dubois's eyes flashed with mischief. "Like what?"

"What would a person moving to Mason's Hole want to know that they can't find in a brochure?"

"Let's see." She clamped the end of a pen between her lips and blinked coyly. "They might want to know that the government has been buying up land around town. No one knows why."

"Oh," Julian hid a frown. "Maybe they're planning a new facility. That could bring more jobs."

She held a hand to her cheek in a stage whisper. "Between us, we don't want that. They are trying to buy up all the property on Farmington Road."

"They?"

Her chin lifted. "Some fancy-pants corporation out of DC. They probably want to put up a city block of warehouses, the god-awful eyesores. If the government's behind it, you know what that means."

"No, tell me," Julian purred.

"Keeping secrets is what they *do*." She gave a shrug that enhanced her cleavage. "I guess they have reason. This town has been a hotspot for alien abductee stories and strange goings-on in the forest since before I was born."

"You mean thirty years ago? That's not *that* long."

Dubois preened.

Julian cast a conspiratorial glance around the office. "Miss Sarah, I hope I'm not being too forward, but have you ever experienced a spectral visitation?"

She giggled and shook her head. "Goodness, no! But I will tell you, the locals are...open-minded. We enjoy country living, sharing with our neighbors, that sort of thing." Lowering her lashes, she let her eyes rest on his mouth. "If you bought a house here, you'd be a local, too."

"I just so happen to be looking at a house on Farmington Road," Julian put in.

"Oh, which one?"

"Two-one-one."

Dubois straightened, and the shiver rolling down her shoulders had nothing to do with being open-minded. "The haunted house? Sorry. I meant Mason's Manor?"

"Um, yes," Julian said.

"I don't think you'll be able to buy it. Jamie Saunders, she's the realtor in town, told me the corporation offered twice the market value, but the Widow Hanford won't sell. And that awful boy, Roland Hanford, is trying to get...." She covered her mouth with her hand. "I shouldn't. Really. How unprofessional."

"That's all right, Sarah." Julian touched the back of her hand. "You've been so helpful I wouldn't dare betray your confidence. Do you think I could take a quick look at those records?"

"Of course." She turned to a table behind her and began shuffling through papers. "You might have more competition than you think. Someone else was looking at them this morning. Another stranger, this one as dark and brooding as you are a streak of sunshine."

Julian's radar went up. A dark and brooding stranger in the flesh? Maybe Roland hadn't made up a mystery intruder.

Dubois returned with a file. "Here you go. I'll have to ask you not to remove any of these materials from the counter."

"Of course." Julian smiled, opened the beige folder, and began taking pictures of the documents without breaking the conversation. "You said Mason's Manor, the house I'm thinking of buying, is haunted?"

"Silly rumors, really. There was that business with Roland calling the police." She gave an eye roll. "Judy Marsh said that Alma Snelling, the deputy's wife, said that Roland got beaten up by a poltergeist."

"How about that?" Julian didn't know what else to say. "Anything else you can tell me about your beautiful little town?"

"I really shouldn't."

Julian leaned in again. "Now you *have to*. This sounds good!"

Dubois moistened her lips and used the counter to pillow her bosom. "Jane Willis over at the pharmacy thinks they might be putting something in the water. Over the last three days, they've sold out of every type of birth control in the *whole store*. Also..." she blushed, "all the um, *adult* items...."

He thought of touching her hand again, but Dubois was all but signaling she'd like to drag him into the Mayor's office. "I could get to like this town."

Dubois took the initiative and laid her hand on top of his. "I know you could. I bet you could get to like me, too."

"Miss Sarah, you're going to make me blush," Julian said, straightening. "And you've given me plenty to think about. It's been a pleasure."

"Not yet, Julian. But it could be." She waved her fingers. "Too-dle-loo."

Humidity had Julian sweating as soon as he stepped out of the air conditioning. Should he meet Madeline in the library? His stomach growled again. Food was more important.

He eyed the quaint café next door, but he didn't want to take the time to look up the health code rating. Nothing less than 'A' would suffice. Why risk it? A few doors down, a sign lettered 'Ye Olde Convenience Store' hung from another converted residence. A few protein bars and a piece of fruit would do for now.

A bell affixed to the door rang overhead as Julian entered. The sound drew a thin, handsome man with frosted hair and tan skin from behind a curtain.

"Hel-lo," the man said, fanning himself with his hand. "How can I help *you*?"

"I'm looking for a good piece of fruit," Julian said.

"There are so many ways I could respond that my mind is paralyzed by a plethora of possibilities." He gave Julian a wicked, serpentine smile and picked something out of a basket on the counter. "Apple?" he said, holding it out.

"Perhaps," Julian replied, eyeing an escape route down the aisle. "I'm going to grab a few protein bars first."

The man made a gesture like a game-show model, drawing Julian's eye to the hot dog roller further down the counter. "The wieners are fresh. I could slide one into your...um, a bun for you."

Julian bit the inside of his cheek. Like Sarah Dubois, the clerk was throwing more than his share of 'open-for-business' signals. It wasn't completely unpleasant. "I'll stick to the protein bars, thanks."

"Aisle three, just down from the empty condom section. I've got a few of those left behind the counter, if...uh, you need one."

Julian's face burned. Just the mention of the word 'condom' had him thinking of Madeline's swaying hips as she walked ahead of him on the trail. He must be the color of a sunburned tourist right now.

Selecting a handful of bars, he put them on the counter next to the apple.

"Are you sure I can't interest you in my... I mean, *a* wiener?" the man asked.

"No, thank you," Julian said. "But I will take that apple."

"Excellent!" the man said, scanning the barcodes.

Julian caught his name tag, which read '*Even*.' "Even, huh? Cool name."

"It's Irish." He looked down at his screen. "Ten ninety-seven. I haven't seen you in town before. Just passing through?"

"I'm what you call a dark tourist. No monuments or theme parks in my itinerary, just the macabre," Julian said. "I heard there might be some cool paranormal stuff to check out around here. Any suggestions?"

"Lots." Even stopped tapping the keys on the register and fixed Julian with a smoky gaze. "Sack?"

It took Julian a moment to realize the man wanted to know if Julian needed a bag. "No thanks." He scooped up the protein bars and pocketed them.

"Don't forget your apple, Adam," Even said, holding the fruit in his palm.

"Haha. And in this scenario, you'd be...the serpent?"

"No, silly." Even held a finger over the N on his nametag. "I'd be Eve, of course."

Julian reached into his pocket and handed Even a twenty.

Even made change and handed it back. "The apple is on me."

Julian felt the tug of sex magic on his lower chakras and decided to lean into it. Guys weren't normally on his radar, but the right person with the right energy made all the difference in the world. He made eye contact with the clerk, rubbed the apple on the inside of his sport coat, and took a big bite.

Even touched a hand to his chest. "Oh!"

Julian slowly chewed and swallowed. "I suppose this means we'll have to wear clothes from now on."

Even fanned himself with his hand again. "Only if you want to, handsome."

"You said you had some ghostly suggestions?" Julian took another bite of the apple, savoring the sweet, juicy fruit on his tongue.

"Well, there's Mason's Manor," Even said. "It's an old haunted house out on Farmington Road."

Julian covered his half-full mouth with the back of his hand. "I just drove by there. Didn't *look* haunted."

Even leaned on the counter, resting his chin in his palm. His eyes traveled down Julian's body. "You can't always tell what's underneath someone's pants." He shot bolt upright. "Roof! I meant roof!"

Julian ignored the slip. "What's under the roof?"

"Some people say the ghost of the town's founder lurks in the basement, angry they closed his mine." Even smile ruefully. "Of course, some people think there's a nest of lizard people under there, too, so, you know...." He perched a hip against the counter. "There's been talk of some kind of sex ritual, what with the whole town acting like a bunch of horny teenagers, but that's nothing new. If you look at Mason's records, we've had spikes in weird events going back a hundred years. You'd think we'd learn and stock up on condoms." He paused. "Are you sure you don't need one? I have some behind the counter. You never know...."

Julian's mind connected condoms with Madeline again. As much as he desired her, staying platonic held the least risk. "My partner and I don't need them."

Even's eyes lit up.

Julian realized too late, the word *partner* had a totally different connotation.

"If you're looking for a third—"

No need to get the clerk riled up any further. "Maybe next time. Thanks for the apple!"

Julian left the shop. The exchange with Even, and Miss Dubois before that, sent his mind tumbling back to the sex magic of Slate Hill. Mason's Hole was turning out to be the same thing all over again. The lightning. The ghost sex. The town full of inexplicably aroused townspeople. He was certain somewhere in Mason's Manor, or in the mine, he'd find a summoning circle, or a portal, or an altar similar to what he and Spearman found in the woods.

Or had they? Every time Julian tried to recall the exact details of the case, they slid away like butter on hot toast. He'd always wondered how much the mental block was due to trauma and how much could be blamed on chemical intervention. This town gave him the feeling, no matter how deep you buried a secret, it would find its way to the surface.

Lost in thought, Julian devoured his forbidden fruit, but the sight in front of him brought him up short.

An enormous statue of Desmond Mason stood in a grassy square. In front of it, Madeline stood transfixed, the sun sending halos of fire through her crimson hair.

Julian stopped mid-chew.

Behind her, a mysterious figure in a dark suit approached like a predator who had selected his next victim.

CHAPTER EIGHT

MADELINE

Madeline made her way down Main Street, eagerly soaking up the Mayberry-like essence of the sleepy hub. There was pep in her step and a sense of purpose that had evaded her over the last two years. Her liveliness was emotionally connected to meeting Constance, but spending time with Julian ignited her body. He was interesting, no doubt about it, and not just in a rebound way.

She passed a country boutique, and the charming arrangement of dresses and hats, old-fashioned jams, and assorted knickknacks threatened to distract Madeline. Most of the merchandise had the Butterfly Pea Mining insignia. The town certainly embraced nature's nod to floral vaginas. How fun was that?

If she were lucky, she'd chance upon a curio selling the alien abduction theme, what Julian called "sex magic," but the thought made her gut clench. How would it help Constance to go along with the town's— and Julian's—mass hysteria? Madeline believed in chakras and energy, power exchange and connection, but anything smelling of cults sparked a force field of cynicism.

Not that she wanted to think about the past, or god forbid, share her memories. Not even Sebastian knew the extent of the terror she'd endured waking her nine-year-old sister to escape the power-obsessed leader. Those who stole innocence were worse than human, lower than scavengers. Becoming a therapist had been Madeline's act of rebellion, but helping couples hadn't dampened the torch of white-hot anger she carried in her chest. At least Hatty was in a Portland, Oregon, art school, and had two successful art exhibits, thankfully not large enough to put her on the national radar.

The time for running and hiding had ended, but Madeline didn't put anything past Thoth, who wouldn't know a true partnership if it bit him on the ass.

With a pang, Madeline wondered how the Atwoods were doing. She'd all but ditched them in their time of need, and if you didn't feel your partner had your back, who could you trust?

Blinking, Madeline found herself in front of the library, almost as if she'd been led there while her mind wandered.

An impressive colonial structure with stone pillars, the large teak double-doors had butterfly pea flowers carved into it. A plaque on the wall said this was the first building Desmond Mason had dedicated to the town. His love of books had made him a successful man, and he wanted to continue the legacy. The added quote "Knowledge is the nectar of the gods. Drink of it often and gain access to the stars" was a nice touch. Desmond must have been a bit of a philosopher.

Inside the library, Madeline's shoulders dropped, unchecked tension sliding from her like rainwater. Libraries were a special place. Surrounded by voices of the past, one could always find a confidant.

Soft, golden light illuminated the circular information desk from palatial skylights. At either side, tables displayed the librarian's book recommendations for paranormal events and, no shocker, sexuality. The curation had everything from ghost-sighting tour books to the latest #booktok steamy romances. The town might have been quaint, but it leaned into its reputation like a champ.

There was no one at the desk, but a murmur of voices deep within the stacks let Madeline know she wasn't alone. Circling a shelf, she glanced down the aisle and saw two females enshrouded in a bubble of intimacy, their playful hands skimming the other's curves. Madeline hadn't made a sound, but they both looked at her, sheepish but not apologetic.

"Sorry," Madeline said. "I'm looking for the librarian."

"That's me, Effy," said a small Irish woman with dense flaxen curls. She wore an emerald green cardigan over a t-shirt of a black cat holding a giant cup of coffee and scratching off a to-do list. "Coffee. Read. Nap." Pointing to her girlfriend, Effy said, "This is Rosamund, the town's baker."

The other woman had light brown skin, a head taller than Effy with thick dark hair, broad shoulders and sculpted eyebrows. She tucked her hands into a baker's apron and gazed at the librarian wistfully.

"Madeline. Nice to meet you both. I like your selection," she nodded toward the sex table, "but was hoping you could recommend historical books on the town. Anything with pictures."

If Madeline could research the town's founder, the lore might help her relate to why Constance had the hots for Desmond. She might also find reference to relatives Desmond might have left behind.

"Happy to help." Effy made a bee-line for a shelf near the information desk, her sweetheart following behind. She plucked several leather-bound volumes and placed them on the counter. "This one is my favorite." She tapped a title, *The Birth of Mason's Legacy: How One Man Created a Free State in the Heart of the South.*

Madeline opened the book and took in the photographs of Mason's Hole, pre-township. "I've heard of free states in the South," she murmured. "Entire communities refused to partake in the slave trade."

"Oh yes, few people know about them, but we're up there with Fort Moses and Winston, Alabama." The librarian leaned an elbow against the desk. "Desmond Mason accepted all types, free or escaped. There are family accounts of bounty hunters showing up and demanding slaves return with them." She shared a smirk with Rosamund. "Desmond paid for their freedom, but anyone that didn't want to make a deal disappeared."

Madeline's eyebrow shot up. "There weren't repercussions?"

"The tunnels are said to go on for miles. Some have dead-ends, some drop into caverns that were never explored." Effy shrugged. "Back in those days, it was pretty easy to have an accident or get lost."

Rosamund lifted her chin proudly. "Don't forget about the miners. Those are my people, and they were as committed to Desmond as he was to them. You tussle with tough folk, they're gonna tussle back."

Madeline felt a jolt of excitement. Ruffling through her pocket, she unfolded the yellowed map and spread it on the desk.

The librarian cooed as if someone had shown her a collector's edition of *The Invisible Man*. "Where did you get this?"

"I'm staying with Constance Hanford."

No one moved, but Madeline felt the shadows of the library pulse as if a cloud had passed over the sun. Both women stared at her with wide eyes.

The baker was the first to speak. "You got balls, girl."

"She's a lovely woman," Madeline said, irked in Constance's defense. "Very hospitable."

"We know." Rosamund's eyes softened, turning the color of warm molasses. "She gave me seed money to start the bakery and refused to let me pay her back when we started to turn a profit. But that house…"

Madeline frowned. "What about it?"

"It's spooky," Effy said, stepping close to Rosamund. "The plot of land surrounding it, that's where most folks disappear. Everyone knows to stay away, lest they go the way of the bounty hunters."

Rosamund encircled Effy with a strong arm. "The forest is—I don't know—alive with spirits. If you don't belong there, you'll hear things, see things, feel things. Things you won't like."

Madeline thought back to Constance's cemetery. How the trees swayed together, and the flowers seemed to whisper to one another. A chill tickled her back.

The librarian added, "We've tried to get Constance to move to town, but she refuses."

Madeline bit her lip. "We share a common goal. I want to make sure Constance is safe, but can I ask you both something? Have either of you experienced, err," she refused to say *sex magic*, "spectral phenomena?"

The baker nudged her girlfriend with an elbow and elicited a giggle. "You mean ghost sex?"

Effy's cheeks flushed pink, but she held Madeline's gaze. "I can't speak to being haunted, but I'm a lover of all things mystical. If there are nasty ghosts who don't like people with bad intentions, there are friendly ghosts who make it clear they mean us no harm."

"The opposite of harm, in fact," Rosamund said, a twinkle in her eye.

Madeline couldn't be sure they weren't pulling her leg, and resisted the urge to ask for more details. She turned back to the library book, flipped a page, and caught her breath. A photo of Desmond, not unlike Constance's original, jumped from the page.

He was a big man, built like Adonis, but it was the lazy confidence emanating from his expression Madeline remembered from her dream. A shiver of arousal—and dread—made her step back.

Rosamund's smile widened to a grin. "Looks like you've had your own ghost sighting."

It was Madeline's turn to blush.

Effy studied the map and tapped a spot that looked remarkably like a scroll. "This is the library. From the looks of it, all the main buildings in Mason's Hole connect to the tunnel system."

Madeline thought the lines connecting the structures were roads, not tunnels. "There's a mine entrance under the library?"

The librarian's curls jiggled a negative, but her eyes told another tale. "All I can tell you, there are places in this town that feel different. More intense. Outsiders say they're haunted. Locals say they're blessed. Want to study for a test and remember everything? Go to the old schoolyard. Run into business problems? Go to the bank. You don't have to do anything, just show up."

"She's right." The baker cupped her girlfriend's shoulder. "I had a wedding cake collapse this morning. Rotten luck. But as soon as I stepped through the library doors, I felt great. Then my client called and asked if it was too late to change the flavor. Problem solved."

Madeline refrained from pointing out canoodling probably helped with the attitude adjustment, but what did she know about this town, these people? "Okay, say I'm worried about a friend, and don't know how to protect them. Where do I go?"

"That's easy." Effy pointed to a tiny picture of three conjoined circles in the center of town. "Go visit Desmond. He's the town's personal guardian."

Visit Desmond? This was getting weirder by the second. "Awesome. I'll do that." Madeline folded the map and stashed it. "Thank you both. You've been very helpful."

Effy smiled. "Anytime. A friend of Constance's is a friend of ours."

Madeline stepped back into the afternoon sunlight, humidity wrapping her in a damp hug. She didn't need to consult the map. Her feet took her down Main Street and across a circular drive. Every step filled her with gathering excitement. Her skin flushed, ultra-sensitive to the caress of the breeze; her mouth watered, longing for the taste of another; her legs felt strong, as if she could wrap them around a sturdy waist and cling till the miners came home.

Then she saw him.

In the center of the roundabout, a large and in charge statue of Desmond rose in orange-patina steel. Butterfly peas planted at the statue's base ruffled in the breeze, their lovely purplish faces tilting up to gaze at a benevolent champion.

"Hello there," she murmured, acutely aware her breasts were swelling by looking at his huge hands and chiseled jaw. "You've got everybody acting like sex-crazed teenagers. Congrats. Now, how the hell does that help me protect Constance?"

Faster than she had time to process, a wave of menace stirred the surrounding air, transforming her arousal to fear. She stepped back, confused.

The danger wasn't coming from Desmond's statue. In fact, it seemed like he was willing her to look over her shoulder.

Spinning around, Madeline swallowed hard.

Julian was running straight at her.

CHAPTER NINE

JULIAN

A shadowy stranger stared at Madeline, intent as a piranha catching the scent of blood. Julian felt deep in his bones he'd seen the man before. A gut clench told him his body was keeping the score of a game his mind couldn't quite remember.

Without questioning the impulse, Julian's legs pumped into action. The slap of his shoes on hot pavement echoed off the buildings. He wanted to call out. Warn her. But he didn't dare, for fear that the ominous stranger could grab her before he got there.

The squeal of brakes and a blaring horn made him stumble and almost lose his feet. The bumper of an old Cadillac gleamed inches from his legs. He couldn't spare the breath or the time for a 'sorry.' And when he turned his eyes back to the scene at the foot of Desmond's statue, Madeline stood gaping at him. A quick turn of his head, and the stranger was nowhere in sight.

"Fool!" the senior woman in the Caddy shouted.

Julian ran up to Madeline. His chest heaved as he reached for his gun, scanning for threats around the circle.

"Julian, what—?"

"Did you see where he went?" Julian managed between ragged breaths.

"This again? I didn't see anyone."

He pointed. "The guy in black under that oak tree?"

She cast her gaze up at the giant bronze effigy of Desmond. "I was looking the other way."

Julian couldn't stop the frustration boiling under his skin. This was the second time he'd seen or, almost seen, a strange man preying upon Madeline, and she'd been none the wiser.

"But I felt him," Madeline supplied awkwardly.

That brought Julian up short. He raised a sweaty eyebrow. "You...."

Her face flushed, but she gave a brief nod. "Right before you ran up, it was a vibe. A shift in energy. I don't know. It's stupid."

"It's not stupid," Julian insisted. "You can trust me. I won't make fun of you, swear it." He pulled a handkerchief from his pocket and dabbed the sweat from his face. "What did you feel?"

Madeline squinted against the hot sun. "Right before you showed up, I felt a wave of.... Menace is the best way I can describe it. Then I turned around and saw you running toward me. The feeling disappeared."

"Shadow Man," Julian muttered and cast furtive glances all around them.

She looked around too. "Who? What was he doing?"

He didn't want to alarm her, but felt he owed her the truth. "Hunting you."

Madeline put on a brave face but couldn't keep the fear from her voice. "Well, that's creepy."

"Can I ask what you were thinking about?"

She gazed at the statue, sucking in her lower lip.

Julian got the impression she was holding back, sanitizing the accounting of her thoughts. "The librarian thinks Mason's Manor and the surrounding forest is haunted, but those that belong to the town have nothing to fear. She told me I should visit Desmond. As I looked up at him, the hair stood up on the back of my neck. I had this churning, sinking feeling in my stomach. But that feeling wasn't because of the statue." She sighed. "Maybe it was something I ate."

"That's why I don't eat at other people's houses," Jules smiled, trying to lighten the mood.

Madeline gave him a weak grin. "We *will* be digging into that at some point in the future."

Julian let her premonition go for now. But he filed it away. One more inexplicable event in the Mason's Hole file.

She stared up at the statue, whispering to herself. "I came here to ask Desmond to protect Constance, but it was as if he wanted to protect *me*."

Julian could barely make out her words over the shifting of the tree leaves and sounds of the street around them. "Come again?"

"Nothing," Madeline said. "Just being silly."

He didn't press the issue, but felt secretly gratified Madeline might be starting to believe there was more to this case than just Constance having an imaginary lover.

"I think we should get out of the sun," Julian said. "I'd like to discuss this someplace with air conditioning."

Madeline followed his eyes and drew in a breath. "Yeah. Air conditioning would be good. There's a little café—"

"I don't want to hang around downtown. Everyone I've met this morning has propositioned me. It's distracting. And—" Only an iron force of will kept Julian's eyes from dropping to Madeline's breasts again. "—I'm already distracted."

Madeline stared back. Magnetism crackled between them. "Yeah. Sexual energy is contagious."

They stopped at the café, but only long enough to get two giant cups of ice water. Julian set the rental car's air conditioning as close to 'arctic tundra' as he could get it. The cold blasted the sweat from his face while he sipped. He'd shed his jacket before getting in the car. It lay rumpled on the seat between them. Still not enough, Julian rolled up his shirtsleeves and pointed the vent at his chest. Sweet relief.

"What did you learn at the clerk's office?" Madeline asked.

Julian wasn't ready to reveal that the dark stranger snooping around was familiar. And what would he say, anyway? Shadow Man was a creepy guy that he half-remembered from a case he could barely recall? No. But with that dark presence lurking and leering at Madeline, Julian vowed not to let her out of his sight while they were in town. "You first. I'm still cooling down."

She shrugged, wrapped her lips around the plastic straw, and sucked.

Julian shifted. Damn it! How was he supposed to work under these conditions?

Madeline reached into her pocket and held out the map. "The librarian told me The Butterfly Pea Mining Company constructed tunnels before the town was a town. The symbols on this map are landmarks of the major buildings, the implication being, each building hides an entrance to the tunnel."

"I'm impressed, Miss Da Vinci. You're a real Renaissance woman. Therapist, amateur sleuth, what other tricks do you have up your sleeve?"

"Who are you calling an amateur?" Her tone softened. "I accept the renaissance thing, though. Your turn, Agent Worthy. What did the *professional* sleuth learn this morning?"

Julian's lips lifted in a grin. "*Special* Agent Worthy. Mostly, I learned that everyone in this town is DTF!"

She frowned. "Details to follow?"

"Err, no. Down to fuck," he amended, contrite. "Both the town clerk and the convenience store attendant were trying to get in my pants."

Madeline rolled her eyes. "Anything relevant to the *case*?"

"Oh." Julian puffed an errant lock of hair from his forehead. He filled her in on an unknown stranger poking around the records of Mason's Manor, the alleged government corporation trying to buy the entire street, and the store clerk's assertions that the town was haunted.

"The plot thickens," Madeline said with forced joviality. "What do you think this shadow person's motives are?"

Whoever he was, it seemed like he was trying to get control of the supernatural energy surrounding the town. And his interest in Mason's Manor confirmed Julian's suspicions that the phenomenon centered around Constance's property. But if land rights were all of it, why was he watching Madeline? The encounter at Desmond's statue implied she was mixed up in the big picture, but how?

A memory materialized. He'd seen Shadow Man in Slate Hill the day he went to the library, which was also the first time he saw Spearman. Why hadn't he remembered that before?

"Other than wanting the house, I don't know why a strange guy would be stalking you."

That wasn't entirely true. Julian had a list of reasons why a man would follow Madeline around, but again, the impulse to protect her invaded his forebrain.

She gave him a quizzical look and took another sip of her drink. "I think you're withholding."

"Yup. Still not a therapy session."

She slapped a hand on the seat in exasperation. "I'm not trying to therapize you. I'm trying to solve this thing with you."

Heat rose in Julian's cheeks, despite the air conditioning. "Sorry. I'm just..." He sighed, trying to decide how much to say. "I'm worried. A creepy guy shows up and wants information on Constance's house. Then I find him breathing down your neck. I don't like it. Until we figure it out, I think we should stick together."

"You think it might be the same person who assaulted Roland?" Madeline's hands curled into fists. "What about Constance? Is she safe from him?"

"Everything happens at night," Julian said. "We'll make sure to be back at the house by sundown."

"You think she's in danger." It wasn't a question.

Fucking right, he did. But whoever was scooping up land wouldn't come to Constance's house in broad daylight and drag her away. No. Whatever was going on, it all came back to the mines. To Desmond. To ghost cocks. Julian didn't know how to say all that without sounding bonkers.

Madeline turned to face him. "Julian, this isn't easy for me to say. I mean, we just met. But I feel safe with you. And I hope you feel safe enough with me to tell me what you're really thinking."

Their eyes met. Those liquid green pools could melt the stoniest heart.

"Sure," Julian said, but decided voicing his thoughts wasn't the best play. Not yet. He needed backup. "I'd like to make a call first."

"Okay, but can we drive? I feel a little conspicuous sitting in this parking lot." She clicked her seatbelt into place. "Besides, if we wait much longer, someone is bound to proposition you again."

Smoky green eyes traveled his body. Julian coughed on a sip of his water. Watched her chest swell under her shirt as she absently rubbed her palm on her thigh.

If she came on to him right now, he doubted his ability to resist.

No. Goddamnit. She might not know she was under the sex spell of this town, but he did. And if anything was going to happen between them, Julian wanted it to be authentic.

Sighing, he put the car in drive.

Madeline cleared her throat. "Who do you want to call?"

"Doctor Otto Vaughn, defrocked MIT professor of astrophysics and consultant to a dozen UFO watchdog organizations. Sometimes he helps me. Sometimes the other way around."

"MIT kicked him out?"

"Yeah." Julian couldn't help feeling defensive. He knew the UFO thing made Otto sound ridiculous. Truth be told, Otto was a little bit of a nut, but a very smart, useful nut.

"Do you have a lot of guys like Otto on speed dial?"

"Maybe." He shot her a look. "Bet you have a decent Rolodex of spiritual practitioners, eh? Folks into astral projection, standing on their heads, playing with reiki?"

"Mostly experts in tantra." Madeline huffed out a pent-up breath. "I concede there's something really weird going on in this town. Maybe a pharmaceutical company is putting testosterone in the water or something. Or there's a toxic buildup of microplastics." She tapped her fingers on her knee. "I'm down to think outside the box, but there's a rational explanation."

Julian took a breath and let it out. She wasn't attacking him. She was struggling to believe things that clashed with the world she knew. "The thing is, there isn't an elevated crime rate. Outside of Roland's attack, there have been no reported incidents of rape, theft, or aggravated assault in the last five years. Mason's Hole has a small population and a stellar birth rate, but no crime? That's unheard of. None of that is consistent with an overabundance of testosterone."

She held out her hands. "Okay, okay, just trying to get a feel for this."

"Anyway, Otto and I have consulted on a few other cases. Some had, as you say, rational explanations. Some didn't. I trust his data. Admittedly, I take his opinions with a grain of salt. But his facts are always spot on."

Julian hit a button on the car's screen. The words 'calling Autobahn' appeared.

"Autobahn?" Madeline asked.

Julian held a finger to his lips. Then he made circles with his fingers next to his ear, and whispered, "Paranoid."

"Well, well, well," a high reedy voice crackled through the car's speakers. "Special Agent Brian Julian Worthy, I have four minutes and three seconds to chat."

"Speeding right to the point, Autobahn," Julian replied.

"Peddle to the metal. Spit it out."

"I've got something, and I don't know what it is."

"Hit me."

Julian described the ghost reports in Constance's house, the atmospheric lightning, and the DTF attitude of the town.

There was a long pause. "To be blunt, sounds like you need to get laid. How long has it been?"

Julian cast a glance at Madeline, who raised a questioning eyebrow.

"Let's leave my manhood out of it," he said while Madeline snickered.

Keys clacked in the background on Otto's end. "The lightning is interesting. And you've called at a busy time. Lots of UAPs this week. Check this out. We've got the same planetary alignment of Earth, Venus, the moon, and the sun, as during the Slate Hill incident on August twelfth through the fifteenth, 2015. And again, there's alignment during the Slaughter Beach event on January second through the ninth, 2022."

"Huh," Julian said.

"*Huh* might be the understatement of the year, BJ."

"Don't call me that," Julian warned.

Madeline silently mouthed, "BJ?"

Fuck.

Otto plowed ahead. "One incident is okay. Two similar cases with this kind of alignment might be coincidence. But three? Nope. This is some next level shit."

And those were the cases they knew about. How many more could have slid under their collective radar? "Next question, Otto.

Do you think there's a chance they're putting something in the water? Testosterone maybe?"

"Come on, BJ, you're not turning into one of those conspiracy guys on me, are you?"

"Nope."

Madeline frowned and folded her arms over her chest.

"If it were testosterone, there'd be a spike in violent crimes. This is consensual sex, right?"

"Right," Julian agreed and gave Madeline a told-you-so look. "Will you look through the archives to see if any other weird cases line up that we haven't looked at?"

"Will do," Otto replied. "Watch your ass out there, BJ. It's getting weird right now."

"I told you to st—" Julian started.

Otto hung up.

Madeline shifted in her seat. "I didn't really believe the testosterone thing. I was just looking for answers."

"I wouldn't have mentioned it to Otto if the idea didn't have merit," Julian said. "And if we hadn't brought it up, Otto would have. That's just how he is."

A smile twitched the corner of her lips. "Like calling you BJ?"

He rubbed his face with one hand. "Please, can we not?"

"Your name is BJ Worthy?"

"Ugh!" Julian grunted.

Madeline raised her hands in mock surrender. "How long *has* it been since you got laid?"

Julian thought about telling Madeline to take the wheel so he could jump out of the car. "Two years," he growled. "You?"

"Not fair!" Madeline protested. "I'm asking the questions here. Why so long?"

A surge of familiar energy crackled between them.

"I travel a lot, and I'm sort of married to my job."

"That doesn't mean you can't—"

"Casual sex is not my style," Julian said. He thought of Spearman in her pencil skirt, one hand letting down her hair from its severe bun, and felt a pang. He wanted to share a life with someone. Sharing a bed would follow. "Come on. What about you?"

Did she just move closer to him? He could feel the heat rolling off her in waves, matching his own suddenly heightened senses.

"I'm just coming off a long-term relationship."

"How recent?"

Madeline shrugged. "What time is it?"

"That recent, huh," Julian said.

His mind drifted to the motion under the sheets as he'd stormed into her room last night. The shape of her erect nipples under the satin nightgown. The scent of her arousal. Except, maybe he didn't have to imagine that. He stole a peek from the corner of his eye and found hers on the crotch of his tented slacks.

She *was* leaning closer.

"Two years," she mused. "Is that true?"

"Yes," he grunted and abruptly pulled the car onto the shoulder. They had unfinished business from the night before. The kiss thwarted by the ghost of Desmond, or, whatever. And now, with pheromones filling the car, he meant to have it out with her.

"Why are we stopping?"

Julian swallowed hard. "That's what I wondered last night. A photo album jumped out of the shelf, and we stopped."

"Yeah," she said, as if in a trance, her voice low.

Their eyes locked.

"Two years is a long time," she repeated, then licked her lower lip.

"It is," he agreed, staring into the twin emerald windows to her soul.

She placed a hand on his thigh, just like Spearman had done all those years ago, on a road like this one. Under circumstances like these.

Fuck.

Julian pulled back. "We can't."

Madeline removed her hand and crossed her arms, staring at the lush forest looming close to the road.

He hated the words but had to say them. "What we're feeling...It isn't real."

"What are you talking about?"

"This huge need for sex? This internal, insatiable desire? Have you ever felt it before?"

"It's called chemistry," Madeline protested. Then frowned. "And maybe rebound sex."

He appreciated her calling a spade a spade, but had to make his point. "It's not, though. It's the mine, the lightning...." He stopped. If he included planetary alignments, Desmond's ghost, or an inter-dimensional portal, he might lose what little ground he had gained. "Don't you feel how *off* the energy is?"

Madeline considered this. "I suppose you could call it that."

"Full disclosure: There's nothing I'd rather do than spend the night with you. But I've been hurt by this kind of phenomenon before." Spearman. Always Spearman.

Madeline nodded. "You're right. We shouldn't. Thank you for pumping the brakes."

He'd rather be pumping her. But, yeah.

"Still got the map? Let's look exactly where we are in relation to the mine and Mason's Manor."

Madeline unfolded the paper and leaned in so he could see, their heads almost touching. It was maddening. She had to orient the map to the compass rose and check with the navigation display on the car's console, but as soon as she turned the paper counter-clockwise, she sat back and started to giggle like they'd been caught in a practical joke.

"Holy shit. You've got to be kidding me!"

CHAPTER TEN

MADELINE

M adeline hunched over in the passenger seat of Julian's car and tried to control her laughter. Once she'd turned the map around, the outline of the tunnels struck her as familiar. It wasn't obvious until she knew what she was looking at, but she'd seen diagrams of a female's parts in the gynecologist's office often enough.

"What?" Julian demanded.

"I can't believe I didn't see it before. All this talk of sex magic must be screwing with my mind." She pointed to the roads making up a rounded triangle and two smaller ovals. "Tell me the shape of these tunnels doesn't look like a woman's reproductive system?"

He coughed discreetly. "It's been awhile since Sex Ed, but now that you point it out, I see the uterus, ovaries, and vagina. It's unmistakable."

Madeline raised her eyes to meet his. "Is this town just a giant tourist trap? I mean, this map could be fake. Desmond could be fake. The locals could be hamming it up for spectacle—"

"That doesn't explain why someone is trying to buy up all the property."

She couldn't help it; she had to ask. "Why do you want to believe in the paranormal so much?"

Julian pulled back and blew his bangs into place. "Why do you find it so hard to believe there are forces we can't explain?"

She gave him a level look. "Because I study human nature, and humans tend to want three things: money, sex, and status."

"Constance already has those things. What's her excuse?"

Damn, he had a point. Constance's life story, Desmond's grave, the unsettling low-frequency vibrations keeping the town sex-drunk—it was a lot to take in. Was staying one more night the answer? Maybe, maybe not. Either way, she needed to make a choice. Bail or play ghost hunter.

"Fine. I'll suspend my disbelief...for now."

Julian gave her an encouraging smile and pulled the car back onto the road. "Then I suggest first thing tomorrow we try and find a tunnel entrance on Constance's property."

Madeline tried to sulk, but his excitement was adorable. And it wasn't just about his case. He seemed genuinely interested in her help, and being appreciated always gave her the warm fuzzies.

The car bumped down the gravel road toward the picturesque homestead. Madeline rolled down the window and took a deep breath of greenery. God, it was pretty. The porch, the flowers, even the air was softer on this path of rolling forest, as if fairies had blessed this specific plot of land.

The image of woodland nymphs sprinkling glitter through the air made Madeline think of her sister. It was time for their monthly check-in. Hatty was busy with school and her art, but she was also living in an artist's community. Raising chickens and goats while selling diorama pumpkins and gourds for the autumn Halloween crowd wasn't a lucrative business, but her sister seemed happy. Madeline needed to touch base on a regular basis just to remind herself Hatty was a grown woman, not the child who clung to her legs when a raised male voice startled them in the night.

She started a text, "What's up, buttercup?" but before she could hit send, Roland's number popped up on her cell phone. A jolt of energy raised the hair on her arms. This was an opportunity to clarify Roland's intentions about his mother's care.

Madeline was out of the car and answering the call before Julian could come to a complete stop in front of Mason's Manor. "Mr. Hanford, it's good to hear from you. Are you on your way to your mother's house?"

"No. Should I be? Has there been another attack?"

"It's been as quiet as a graveyard." Madeline turned her back on the house and caught Julian's eye as he came around to her side of the car. "Speaking of attacks, would you mind if I asked you some questions about your encounters?"

Julian's eyebrows rose, but he quietly bent to listen to their conversation.

"What do they have to do with my mother's mental state?" Roland sputtered.

"You are her only son. Anything that threatens you is a cause for motherly concern and might be causing her anxiety."

"I suppose that's true."

"When I asked your mother who she thought attacked you, Mrs. Hanford mentioned a company was looking to purchase the house and the grounds. She turned them down, not once, but three times. A half a million dollars for a handful of acres in the middle of nowhere is generous, don't you think?"

"Miss Da Vinci, are you implying someone is trying to scare my mother off her land?"

Madeline thought she caught a hint of eagerness in Roland's voice. The faithful son was taking the bait. "Your mother is no spring chicken. In a house far from town, all by herself, I'm sure you worry about her nonstop. I mean, you could always install surveillance cameras, maybe get her a German Shepard, but if a grown man was attacked, what's stopping them from going after an elderly woman? It's simply not safe."

"That's what I've been trying to tell her," came Roland's nasal whine.

Julian shot her a confused frown, but Madeline shook her head. "Has the same company approached you?"

"When Mother didn't accept their offer, yes."

"Did they tell you why they wanted the land?"

"Something to do with a historical anomaly," he said vaguely.

"Did they mention The Butterfly Pea Mining Company?"

"It might have come up, but the mines were abandoned before my parents bought the house." Roland cleared his throat. "Look, we both agree my mother can't stay out there. Their offer will provide a comfortable assisted living facility. All we have to do is convince her it's in her best interests."

"Agreed," Madeline said smoothly. "But there's only one problem. Your mother is of sound mind and body. In fact, she's got better mental recall than people half her age, and she's limber as a jackrabbit."

"But what about the ghost stories? You can't tell me that's normal."

"It's not in my purview to determine what is normal or abnormal for my clients, but it's natural to have fantasies about someone she feels emotionally connected to, even if that person has passed on. Constance has an active imagination and a healthy sex drive. It's been known to happen, even for women her age."

"Can't you—I don't know—make something up?" Roland caught himself and backtracked. "Not that I'm implying you'd bend the rules, but I'd be willing to compensate you handsomely for your expert assessment."

There it was, the complicity Madeline was waiting for, but hoped wouldn't find. She and Julian exchanged a knowing look.

"Mr. Hanford, if I willfully and wrongly diagnosed a patient, I could lose my license."

"I'm trying to protect my mother. She could fall, break a hip, get so caught up in her escapades, she...she..."

"Could live another twenty years?" Julian interjected.

"Is that—Agent Worthy?" Roland bit out. "Am I on speaker phone?"

"Did I not mention that?" Madeline said. "My apologies, Roland. Must have slipped my mind. But no bother. We're all on the same side. All trying to protect Mrs. Hanford. Your mother."

Before she could feel guilty, Madeline ended the call and caught Julian staring at her intently. "What? Too much?"

"You don't pull your punches. I like it."

She smiled sheepishly.

They turned toward the house and jumped to see Constance standing stoically on the porch. If she was upset over the conversation, nothing in her demeanor showed displeasure. Her face was radiant, and an aura of peace floated around her like a beacon. Seasoned hands shooed them forward. Madeline and Julian didn't hesitate. They came into the house like two loved children who'd been called in for dinner.

Constance's strange assurance didn't falter the rest of the evening. She served a marvelous repast of pot roast and carrot puree. When she set a warm apple pie on the table, Madeline's hips grew another inch.

The older woman savored every bite but barely ate. She let them help clean the kitchen, adding a gentle, "I want you to make yourselves at home."

Madeline watched her, concern growing in her stomach along with the food in her belly. They collected in the living room. Constance took a seat in a green velvet armchair and settled a knitted blanket over her knees. Madeline and Julian took their places on the settee, careful not to touch each other.

Madeline nibbled on her bottom lip and shot him a look. His bright blue eyes were dark, as if he too were concerned with Constance's tranquil vibe.

She took it as a cue to jump into the deep end of her concerns.

"Constance, we need to talk about what's going to happen in the coming months. You don't seem to be suffering from an ailment that requires intervention, and I don't think displacing you is a way to mitigate future problems. However..." Madeline leaned forward, her hands massaging her thighs. "I am concerned with the depth of your involvement with Desmond. I think it's something Roland will use against you."

Constance's serene smile didn't waver. "Do you know what time it is?"

The couch couple shook their heads.

"The gloaming. Isn't that a beautiful word for twilight? The lingering children of light make their final plays." She sighed, a whoosh of sound like a woman who was tired but satisfied. "Roland cares too much about what other people think of him, but he's a grown man. There's nothing more I can do but let him find his own way." She tilted her head. "You know, when Roland's father died, I wasn't afraid because I wasn't alone. I had Desmond, and I had my son. But I never thought of it from Roland's perspective. He had every reason to be jealous of a ghost."

Madeline looked at her lap. She was getting nowhere. Constance was going to stay put, as was her right, and there was nothing Madeline could do, save move into the guestroom.

Constance's eyes sparkled as she stood from the chair and gently folded the caftan. "Look at you both. So young and full of energy. And doubt. I don't envy you the road ahead, but something tells me as long as you have the right partner by your side, you'll make the right decisions."

"Thank you for welcoming us into your house," Madeline said out of the blue, just to keep the woman talking.

She patted Madeline on the shoulder and made for the stairs. "They say hindsight is twenty-twenty, but sometimes looking back isn't necessary. You carry the past with you, always. Why not use it to build a better tomorrow?"

Madeline sprang to her feet. "Constance?"

The older woman paused, but Madeline didn't know what to say.

"Good night, sweet dears. It's been quite the ride," Constance chuckled softly. "Yes, an amazing ride."

Madeline watched until she heard the soft click of Constance's door closing. Apprehension seeped into her muscles. She imagined the older woman getting ready for bed. Brushing her teeth. Slipping a light cotton nightgown over her head.

Constance had a lovely home and an imaginary man's love. So what if the townspeople thought her house was haunted? What made that a bad thing? She'd suffered loss, betrayal, hate, all manner of abject cruelty that should have beaten her down. But adversity had made her happier, more resilient. Madeline wished she knew her secret.

Other than stellar ghost sex.

She turned to Julian. He looked as glum as she felt.

He rubbed a hand over his face. "Something that Otto said about the stars aligning has me worried. I thought...Constance isn't tormented by the past. If anything, she accepts it. Like it was always supposed to be this way. That's not the mindset I would expect. There's more going on here than an imaginary lover."

Madeline flopped back on the loveseat. "Julian, mysterious things are happening, I can't deny it, but how can you say it's supernatural?"

He shrugged, a slight smile making him look young and slightly reckless. "There are worse things than trying to track down supernatural encounters."

Madeline thought of her mother, her sister, Sebastian, even the Atwoods. Unlike Constance, they were constantly reaching toward something beyond them, never satisfied to be in the *now*. If Madeline was honest, she could admit she hadn't felt satisfied in a long time, either.

As if on cue, a streak of blue lightning flashed from outside. She jumped and found herself clutching Julian's hand. Their agreement in the car demanded she release him, lest weakened inhibitions run amok, but the warmth and vitality thrumming under his skin sparked a chain reaction in her palm. It traveled up her arm and caressed the tips of her breasts.

Damn it, not again.

"Let's change the subject," Julian said. "Like Constance said, we only have so much time."

"You want to talk about the weather again?"

"I want to talk about the mines Desmond created." He pulled the old map from his back pocket and smoothed it out in the small square of cushion between them. "Does anything look familiar to you? Other than the vagina?"

Madeline squinted. Now that he'd mentioned it, the quarry was on the outskirts of a town Desmond's business acumen had funded. But the map annotated other sites sprinkled over the countryside.

She pointed to a square outline. "That's the County Hall. And the girls from the library said there were other entrances to the tunnel system."

"Not exactly X marks the spot, but close." Julian pointed to another symbol, this one shaped like a bull's eye. "Here's the high school."

Madeline snickered. "No wonder birth control is heavily promoted."

Julian looked up sharply. "You're right. The town's infrastructure is related to the reports of heightened activity. But where is...?"

Both of their fingers found where Constance's house was located on the map. Its symbol was a butterfly pea insignia.

Julian muttered, "All roads lead to Mason's Manor."

Another flash of blue light briefly illuminated the room and showed the sharp beauty of Julian's profile. Immediately, Madeline's womb clenched with a primal heartbeat.

"This place is better than Viagra." she tried to joke, but Julian was staring intently at her breasts. They swelled under his appreciation. "Julian—"

A moan swept through the house like a gusty breeze. It sounded...different. Not completely human.

Julian jumped to his feet, putting space between them.

The energy in the room, in the house, changed. The small hairs on Madeline's arms and neck tingled. Sweet languor invaded her nerves, making her feel lighter, almost weightless.

Focus on Constance, she told herself. *Keep Constance safe.*

Julian's voice was thick, slightly hoarse. "How many of the nice town folk are getting it on in Mason's Hole, you think?"

"What does that have to do with anything?" Madeline whispered.

A full-throated female groan reverberated from upstairs. Definitely Constance.

Julian discreetly adjusted his pants. "You said yourself sexual energy is contagious."

Had she? Yes, in town. To try and explain the feral musk exuding from the sidewalk cracks.

Abruptly, Julian headed for the staircase.

"Wait," she hissed and sprang off the couch. "What are you doing?"

"This may be our last chance to get a look at Desmond."

Madeline had to hurry up the stairs to meet him at Constance's bedroom door. She grabbed his belt from behind, ignoring the wave of pleasure that radiated from the contact. "You can't barge in on Constance!"

"I'm not—" Julian swept his hair back, gathered his composure, and knocked on the door. "Constance? Are you okay in there?"

They were answered by a cry that could have been misconstrued as pain had they not been around the "let's fuck like bunnies" block.

"Geez," Madeline breathed. "I mean, it's supposed to get better with age but…"

Another moan, rising in intensity, shook the house.

Madeline shuddered and closed her eyes. Her hand tightened on Julian's belt. This was some *Phantom of the Opera* shit. There was a liquid river running down her spine, pooling between her legs. If Julian turned to her now, she wouldn't be able to stop him. Wouldn't want to. He could push her against the wall, slide his hand into her pants, and she'd melt over his fingers like warm honey.

The echo of the moan was answered by a primal growl saturated with raw encouragement.

A man was in Constance's room.

Julian took charge and pushed the door open.

Madeline was prepared to see just about anything. Constance watching back-country booty porn and going to town with a giant back massager. Anything, even a ghost, except what they found.

Constance's bed was empty, the covers thrown back as if she'd been asleep but something important had called her from slumber. Madeline rushed forward, praying the older woman wasn't lying collapsed on the bedroom floor. "Check the bathroom."

Julian was already moving.

"She's not in here," he said from the doorway. "And there's no television. If she was watching porn, where are the sounds coming from?"

A tangle of voices rose in sumptuous enjoyment. Madeline turned toward the fireplace.

"What the hell?" She dipped her head under the mantel. The bricks were blackened but clean, and the open flue broadcast the voices like a megaphone.

"Madeline," Julian said. "Come here."

He stood in the closet next to the fireplace. As she watched, he stepped into a cavity of hanging clothes and disappeared. She inhaled sharply and rushed forward, but Julian hadn't fallen into a parallel universe. He stood on a stone landing, a spiral staircase at his feet.

Julian was almost giddy. "It's a secret passageway."

"Wait," she gasped. "Let me get my phone or find a candle."

"No need." He produced a small flashlight from his pocket and started down the stairs.

Julian moved like a lynx, fast and graceful. Madeline had to follow his bobbing light down the narrow steps or be left behind. Their intimate panting breaths echoed in the small space, and the tang of moisture and moss filled her nose.

Beyond the meager beam, greenish light radiated from the floor below. Where it was coming from, Madeline couldn't pinpoint.

Constance's cries grew louder and faster.

Now that they were closer, Madeline heard a masculine voice accompanying Constance's ecstatic moans. She couldn't make out the words, but the tone dripped with praise.

Madeline bit her lip until she tasted blood. The excitement and electricity wafting up the stairwell was so thick, the air almost wavered in front of her face. If she didn't stay focused, she'd grab Julian's shoulder, push him down on the stairs, and mount him.

They continued down, their footsteps muffled by slapping sounds mingling with moans. The green light grew, almost pulsing with its own intensity. What could be solid enough to make the raw slapping of skin on skin, if not a human?

Madeline tripped and tumbled against Julian's back. He twisted to catch them, pressing his chest into her soft breasts until they were pinned against the wall.

"Sorry, sorry, sorry," she whispered, but couldn't help savoring the male heat soaking into her hands where they clutched his shoulders. A sizable bulge pressed into her hips, and it wasn't his gun. She briefly wished he'd slide his thigh between hers.

A fine tremor ran beneath Julian's skin. He opened his mouth, but the masculine voice coming from the archway cut off whatever words he meant to say.

"Come now, my darling, my love," the male voice said, sultry as velvet. "Come for me one last time."

Constance obliged, her peeking pleasure a soprano's exclamation of release. The wave of sound hit Madeline and Julian, freezing them in place. It slowed time, highlighting the tender droplets of sweat clinging to Julian's temple, and the flutter of Madeline's heartbeat pulsing at the cleft of her collarbone.

A hallowed silence descended as the last echo of Constance's orgasm faded. Madeline couldn't look away from Julian's intense gaze. All she had to do was lean forward and press her lips to his. He could ease the ache, end the madness.

But a new sound stiffened her spine. Someone was crying. The sound of soft, immeasurable sorrow broke Madeline's heart.

Julian heard it, too. Easing back, he took Madeline's hand and pulled them down the remaining stairs and through an arched doorway.

They stepped into a cavernous room filled with eerie green light. In the center of the chamber, an immense stone slab rose from the floor as if it had been fashioned from the earth's crust.

Atop the granite artifact, Constance's body lay motionless, her nightgown perfectly in place. The sweet smile of a lovely dream spread across her face. There was no ghost crouched over her body, weeping. She was alone.

Madeline covered her mouth to keep the scream of denial trapped. Yelling wouldn't do any good. She knew without having to touch her friend, Constance was dead.

Chapter Eleven

JULIAN

J ulian swung the beam of his light to Constance's chest, watching for signs of respiration. Then he checked for a pulse. Nothing. Without conscious input, he cast aside his flashlight, folded his palms over her heart, and began compressions.

Madeline reached across him, placing heavy hands on his arms. "Julian," she whispered, shaking her head.

He ignored her gesture. "Do you know how to check her airway?"

"*Julian,*" she said again, forcefully clamping down on his wrists. "I know this is your training kicking in, but take a breath. Remember how she said goodnight? *It's been quite a ride.*"

Julian let the fight drain from his arms. Constance's smile was eerie, and wholly unconcerned. "She knew."

Madeline gave him a faint, sad nod. Then she released his arms. "So did whoever was in here. It was a man's voice. He said, *Come for me one last time.* Where is he?"

She cast a wild glance around the great, stony chamber. A battery lantern sat on the floor beside the altar. With the strange green light gone, it was the room's only light source apart from Julian's flashlight.

Despite his conviction that Constance's partner was Desmond's ghost, or some kind of being pretending to be a ghost, he couldn't afford to make assumptions. He grabbed his abandoned flashlight and drew his gun. Then he scooped up the lantern and handed it to Madeline.

Their lights barely reached the far recesses of the almond-shaped stone chamber. He whispered, "No obvious exits."

"There could be a secret door. Like the closet," Madeline whispered back. "What's that protrusion at the far end?"

Her voice echoed strangely in the cavernous space as she pointed at a domed structure where the chamber's two walls curved to an apex.

Julian warred with himself. He should insist she stay back, but who knew what threats could come from behind them? Had they missed other doors or clues in their sex-trance state? She'd been so close to him when they came down the stairs. Having her near proved distracting, to say the least, but having her far away where he couldn't protect her seemed the worse evil.

"Let's have a look," he said.

Something about the room demanded quiet reverence. The dust and grit of decades crunched under their feet. The only tracks, their own. They skirted the curved walls toward the knobby structure at the end of the room.

"This part of the wall looks hand-shaped, but it doesn't seem to have a purpose," Julian said. "Who would carve this much stone for no reason? I feel like there should be a door here or something."

The structure protruded into the room about six feet and was so tall Julian could barely touch the top with his fingertips. The smooth stone featured an outer arch housing a bulbus knob inside, like a blank face in a hooded sweatshirt. Had the knob structure not been there, Julian would swear the whole thing was some kind of arched doorway. He pushed on it, hard, with no result. The sound of Madeline's muffled chuckle made him turn. "What?"

She gave him a crooked grin. Strange, under the circumstances. "Really? No purpose?"

"Huh?"

"Come here," Madeline beckoned.

"I don't—"

She waved a hand, cutting him off. "Just come here."

He walked over to where she stood, meeting her eyes.

She put her hands on his arms and spun him around.

He stared at the stone mound. "I still don't—"

"This room is shaped like a vagina, right?" she said, exasperated. "Julian, meet the room's clitoris. Clitoris, this is Julian."

Her gallows humor surprised him, but he wouldn't be deterred. "Okay," Julian admitted. "I see that now. I still think it's a door." He walked back and shoved against it.

"Oh, my *god*."

Julian turned back to her. "What now?"

"Just like a man, banging away like you're swinging a hammer."

"Okay, smarty pants, what's it for?"

Madeline grinned at him. "For pleasure."

"Ugh!" But he smiled back, wondering if joking about anatomy helped her process Constance's sudden passing. It was definitely helping him.

"Okay, okay, besides a love button statue, I don't know what this structure is supposed to represent," she said. "But I *do* know that if you want to get where you're going, you don't thump at it like a wrecking ball. You rub and tease it from different angles." She walked to the side of the rocky clitoral hood, her hands sliding along the smooth stone, caressing it. "I feel something—Ah!"

She leaned into the stone. The 'clit' retracted, leaving an open doorway.

"Yup." Madeline gave him a satisfied nod. "Do you think this goes into the mines?"

Julian nodded, hiding his annoyance that she'd found the secret button instead of him.

Madeline took the lantern and started for the opening. Tiny streaks of blue lightning arced from the entrance, zapping her head, shoulders, and legs. "OW! Fuck. What was that?"

"No idea," Julian said. "You okay?"

"Yeah. Just shocked."

Julian stepped forward to get a better look. Nothing obvious. When he pushed a hand through the tunnel's entrance, nothing happened.

Madeline reached out, putting her palm into the opening next to his. Again, blue fire arced from the stone. "Damn it!" she said, shaking the offended appendage.

"Weird that you're getting shocked and not me," Julian said.

"If I was a superstitious person, I'd say something didn't want me to know what was on the other side."

"Or didn't want you to leave," Julian said, casting his eyes back at the altar.

Madeline followed his gaze. "Maybe we take the hint. I don't want to leave Constance like that. Plus, with no tracks in the dust, I doubt whoever was in the room came this way."

"Agreed," Julian said. "Do you think you can close it again? I'm not thrilled about leaving open doors to secret tunnels at my back."

"Worth a try." She moved to the side of the hood.

Julian followed, wanting to see what she'd done to activate the door. He pointed his flashlight at a fist-sized square protruding from the wall. "Look. It has the Butterfly Pea logo etched into the surface."

She pushed the square rock again. The almost imperceptible grate of stone followed.

"Our designer liked it rubbed on the right," Madeline smiled.

He could still feel the room's tickling energy and blurted, "What about you?"

Madeline turned away from the door. Even in the dim light, her emerald eyes glinted with feral intent. "Is this how you want to find out?"

"You," he swallowed, "want me to find out another way?"

She gave him a faint smile, then looked toward the altar. "Maybe another time."

Of course, she was right.

Madeline sighed. "I'd like to take care of Constance somehow."

"We're trying to find the truth. I can't think of a better way to honor her. Let's look over the rest of the room." He turned away from the clit, examining the wall opposite the one they'd skirted on their way to the tunnel's secret door. More symbols caught the gleam from his flashlight. Something about the etchings carved into the living rock tickled at his brain, seeking neurons leading to recognition.

Madeline stepped past him, holding the lantern up to better examine the glyphs. Several steps ahead, she stopped and put a hand to her lips. "Oh my god...."

Julian drew up beside her.

Madeline's voice trembled as she spoke. "I know this symbol."

He waited for her to elaborate. "Madeline?"

"Sorry. I just.... I never expected to see it again." She reached out, her hesitant fingers stopping just short of the stone, as if she expected another shock. "It's the symbol of the Disciples of Creation."

"The sex cult?"

"You know it?" she whispered without taking her eyes from the carving.

"It's my job. The question is, how do *you* know about it?"

When her words came, they had a wooden quality, as if part of her mind was elsewhere. "I'm a sex therapist. It's my job, too."

He strongly suspected there was more to it than that, but decided it might be best to leave it for now.

"I need to call my sister," she whispered.

Julian wasn't entirely sure he was meant to hear the comment and tucked the information away for later speculation.

They followed the wall with its strange carvings back to the altar. "Madeline," he said, staring down at Constance. Her face was still and serene, but the flush starting to fade from her cheeks. "There's no evidence of anyone else."

"Desmond poisoned himself. What if she took something, Julian? To be with him?" Madeline's voice retained the soft, far-off quality it had as she looked at the sex cult symbol. "Constance was so happy. There were signs in her words last night, but I didn't think... I should have put it together. All that stuff about choice, about our future, about it being quite a ride...."

"You can't do that to yourself," Julian said. "You know damn well this isn't a suicide."

"I don't know," she said. "I feel like we should call the police, but I don't want a bunch of middle-aged cops in here smirking at her, making jokes about the crazy lady in the haunted house."

Julian didn't want the local cops there for reasons of his own. They'd do the things Madeline said, plus fuck up his investigation. Admittedly, Constance's death was a pretty big nail in the coffin of this case. With her gone, would Desmond hang around? Would the paranormal activity continue? Julian had his doubts.

Maybe Spearman could help. Besides trying to wave him off the case, she was the one person who had cause to believe what he told her. For the bureau's own purposes, she might help keep local law in the dark for a while. He turned to Madeline. "I'll call my boss. If my people handle this, there'll be no jokes."

"How can you be sure?"

Julian gave her a half-hearted smile. "Most agents have their sense of humor chemically removed at Quantico." He sighed and closed his eyes, gearing himself for the inevitable. "But I'm going to do a preliminary exam of Constance before we call anyone. Is that cool with you?"

Madeline caught a tear at the corner of her eye and sniffed once. "I'd like to stay, if that's all right. There's nothing I can do, but I feel protective of her."

Julian nodded. He did, too. But he also didn't think watching him do the exam would do her any good. "If you wanted to get a shower curtain or a blanket to cover her, that would help."

"You're trying to get rid of me."

"I'll be quick, respectful, and professional."

"Okay."

When he heard her steps on the spiral stairs, Julian held his flashlight in his mouth while he checked Constance's airway— clear. He didn't want to remove the nightgown, so he did a tactile exam, running his hands down the length of her arms and legs, checking for the liquidity of blood and the crunch of broken bones. Nothing.

To be thorough, he needed to check for foreign objects in her vagina and anus, but not here, and not like this. He'd have to wait for the medical examiner's report on that one. Instead, he photographed the body, altar, and surrounding area with his phone.

Madeline came back with Constance's caftan.

"Find anything?" she asked as they draped the knit fabric over Constance.

"No signs of anything other than what we expected. She went out with a bang." Julian blanched, worried he'd gone too far with the joke.

Madeline guffawed. "Yeah, she did." Her smile fell. "Julian, dealing with the deceased might be business as usual in your line of work, but in mine, it means I've failed."

This intelligence hit Julian like a gut punch. He straightened. "You didn't fail anyone."

"Intellectually, I know that. I barely knew her. I just...."

Julian checked his phone to give his eyes some place to be. No service. "We should go back to the house. I need to make the call."

"Yeah," Madeline said. "I'm pretty keyed up. I wonder if she's got any valerian tea?"

"I'll take some of that action. Or Scotch." He followed Madeline back up the spiral stairs, and noted the sober mood couldn't stop him from appreciating her hourglass silhouetted in the lantern's light. Damn, sex energy.

In the kitchen, she said, "I'll put the kettle on."

Julian retreated to the corner of the table and turned his back. Spearman was not happy to hear from him.

"Agent Worthy?" she grunted, but sounded awake.

"There's been a fatality in Mason's Hole."

"It's the middle of the night. Let local law enfor—"

"I don't think we want that. It's like Slate Hill. Like the Arborist."

When Spearman spoke next, her voice was cold and calculated. "I'll have mobile ops there by morning."

"Can we get them sooner?"

"Is the body or the scene in danger of being disturbed?"

Julian gave one fleeting thought to the Shadow Man he'd seen staring at Madeline in town, but just as quickly, the thought dissipated from his memory like a nail popping a bubble. "No," he admitted.

"The team will be there in the morning. I'll see you then." She hung up.

"Shit," Julian said, pocketing his phone.

"What?" Madeline asked, turning from the stove.

"My boss is coming."

She frowned. "Isn't that what we want?"

He blew at his bangs with an agitated huff. "It's complicated."

"When does he get here?"

"She. Morning."

She pulled a chair out from the kitchen table. "Then you have plenty of time to uncomplicate it for me. And explain about the Arborist in Slate Hill."

He should have made the call out of earshot. Except he wasn't sloppy or unprofessional. Subconsciously, he'd wanted Madeline to hear. To ask questions. To continue acting as an unofficial partner in this investigation.

She waited patiently, hands folded on the rose-printed tablecloth.

Julian wouldn't let her therapist's mojo rush him into revealing more than he wanted. He let the silence stretch while he arranged his thoughts, deciding which details to obfuscate or omit altogether.

Lightning flashed in the starry sky.

Julian looked out the window. So, it wasn't over. Not yet.

The kettle whistled.

He found his tongue a little looser when she got up to make the tea. "The Slate Hill case started a lot like this one. A town with unusually high rates of sexual activity, as evidenced by reports from physicians, birth control prescriptions skyrocketing, and the empty condom aisles in the local drugstores."

"How did DHS get involved?" Madeline poured the tea into a couple of earthenware mugs.

"They put a flag on instances of multiple sex crime complaints."

"Crimes?" Madeline paused, holding the kettle awkwardly in front of her.

"Not assaults. Statutory stuff. High school kids getting busted in their parents' station wagon. Stuff like that."

Madeline offered him a tea bag. "No valerian. But I found some chamomile."

Julian plopped the herbal satchel into his mug. "It wouldn't have been a case had it not been for the lightning and atmospheric disparity. And the whole town was affected."

"Including you?"

"Yes. There was a visitation. I was..." He could do this. "I was taken."

"Like, abducted?"

Blood burned in Julian's cheeks. "Close enough."

Madeline jerked the string trailing from her cup up and down, then dropped it, and gave him her full attention. "Tell me as much as you feel comfortable sharing."

He pressed on. "At first, I thought it was a dream. A man and a woman came to me. They were...like Desmond. Spectral. I kept thinking, wow, it's just a sexy, sexy dream. But the sensations were too real. The feel of their.... It wasn't a dream."

Madeline fiddled with her tea again.

"Folks all over town were having this experience. Anyway, there was a hiking trail that ringed the town, famously haunted, of course. We were out there to investigate. Anyway—"

Madeline raised an eyebrow. "We?"

"Special Agent Spearman, my boss." Julian left out Spearman hadn't been boss at the time, and hoped Madeline didn't do the math. He also left out graduating high school wasn't nearly as exciting as helping Spearman, a gorgeous, confident agent who'd captured his thoughts since the moment they met in the town's library.

"Anyway," Julian continued, "there were these weird trees out there. Bent into impossible, unnatural shapes with strange symbols carved into their trunks. They weren't new etchings, which was really strange."

He felt himself relaxing, and he hadn't touched the tea. It felt good to talk to someone about this. He hadn't since he'd quit meeting the psychiatrist before college.

"The trees formed a ritual ring, and in the center, the limbs bent and twisted together, forming an altar, kind of like the one downstairs." Julian stared into his cup. "Madeline, the entities were...."

Words vanished. One moment they were there, cued up in his mind, ready to speak. And now, Julian did not know what he'd been about to say.

"Julian?"

He shook his head. A head he knew the government shrinks had fucked with. He couldn't tell her *that*. It was too bad she wasn't a federal agent. Wasn't trained at Quantico. She was under his protection. And she needed protecting from this, too.

"Julian!"

The present and the past collided.

His name. Uttered in Mason's Hole and Slate Hill. Mouthed by the beautiful Madeline Da Vinci in the present, and the sexy Special Agent Spearman in the past.

In the present, Madeline sat across the table from him, her gaze urgent. In the past, Spearman gripped his arms in front of an altar made of twisted trees. They were naked. Sunbeams created a halo over the dark brown hair pulled loose from Spearman's ponytail during their exertions. Her lips moved. He couldn't hear her words, but he could read her lips. He knew what she was saying. "The entities put something inside us!"

He must have said that aloud, because Madeline's alarmed face had an aura of tenderness. Gently, she asked, "Do you mean they used occultist paraphernalia?"

"No." Why was this so hard? Why couldn't he remember when he tried to focus on the details? It was like looking at the world through glasses painted black. He could only see things he wasn't trying to look at. "No probes or toys. It was organic."

The scar on his belly tingled at the half-hid memory. He wasn't sure how he kept the tremor from his voice. "Something that had to be surgically removed."

"Oh," she said, sitting back in her chair. "That's...."

"Bizarre? I know." Julian said. And just for a moment, he wanted to joke about the whole episode, tell her he'd been fucked up over

123

Spearman's attention. Instead, he pivoted to take the focus from his spotty memory. "What's the truth about your connection to The Disciples of Creation? Your reaction to the symbol wasn't academic, it was personal."

Madeline flinched.

He instantly regretted his words. "Sorry. You don't have to answer that."

She held a hand up, her jaw set. "It's okay. You shared. It's my turn. My mother joined The Disciples of Creation when I was eight, and my sister Hatty was born on the compound. We ran away when I was fifteen."

Julian sat back in his chair. "Whoa."

"Tell me about it." Madeline sipped her tea, her eyes haunted. "The cult was loosely based on the Egyptian goddess of beauty and fertility, Hathorista, but they could never stick to a deity. They believed if they danced long enough, kissed until their lips were raw, and sang until their voices became whispers, redemption in the form of alien rescue would arrive on their love-drunk shores."

Julian wanted to reach across the distance separating them and hold her hand, but it wasn't the time.

"When the aliens failed to show up year after year, they'd screw some more, usually with the help of alcohol and whatever hardcore drugs they could find." Madeline gave a shrug, and Julian could see the effort it cost her. "Outside of being forced to watch the rituals, they didn't rape us. Not that Walter would have let that happen. He was...is...an older gentleman who'd lost his wife and daughter in a flood and helped build the commune. It wasn't that bad, as far as organized bullshit goes, but over time, the leader..."

Her hands relinquished the mug and curled into fists.

"He renamed himself Thoth, after the Egyptian god of wisdom and magic, can you believe that? One minute he told us we should believe whatever our hearts felt was true. The next, if we disobeyed him, we'd be cast out of paradise. The man has a serious Dr. Jekyll, Mr. Hyde complex."

Julian chose his words carefully. "Why did you run away?"

She looked at him briefly, her feline eyes hard as flint. "Hatty started menstruating. Somehow, Thoth got it in his mind since she was able to bear a child, the aliens needed a sign—a sacrifice—to prove the commune was ready to ascend."

Julian flinched. No wonder Madeline hated talk of paranormal events. And he'd been pushing her to open her mind.

Well, didn't *he* feel like a jerk?

"Madeline—"

"I don't blame my mother," she said in a rush. "Jennie didn't know. I'm not sure any of them knew Thoth's master plan. But the way he looked at her.... It made my skin crawl. Walter saw it, too. He gave us money and told us to run, so I took her and didn't look back."

"Mads..." he reached for her hand.

She grasped her mug instead, sipping her tea. "Look, deep down, people just want to believe in something bigger than themselves. A club. A hierarchy. A chance at immortality. It's all the same. I'm not saying there isn't a bigger conspiracy to what happened to you—I've heard some crazy shit from my clients—but I can't believe it's aliens or ghosts or fucking fairies dicking with humans because we're meat puppets meant to serve mythical beings." Her mug landed on the table with a thump. "But if they're real, those gods are *terrible* at being worthy of worship."

Julian had never seen her so vulnerable and raw. Or so beautiful. She had a point. Not one he cosigned, but one he could respect. His heart swelled, and he knew without a doubt his connection with her wasn't about sex magic.

Well, not only sex magic.

The silence stretched.

"Someone should call Roland," she said.

"It's my job," Julian said, surprised he'd rather deal with the asshole personal injury lawyer than the awkwardness in the room.

Thankfully, the call went to voicemail.

"Mr. Hanford, this is Special Agent Worthy. There's been another incident at your mother's house. You need to come right away."

When he hung up, Madeline glanced at the clock. "It's late."

Julian opened his mouth. Closed it again. Drank his tea. What was left of the night seeped through the cracks of Mason's Manor like the steam from their mugs. He should try to sleep, but the thought of Spearman and Madeline in the same room did conflicting things to his already overwhelmed senses.

"I don't think I can go back to bed. Not with Constance..." Madeline mumbled.

This time, when he reached for her hand, she didn't pull away.

"Come sit with me on the couch," he said gruffly. "We'll wait for the cavalry to arrive together."

She squeezed his fingers, but her eyes remained hard with determination. "We're going to figure out what happened to her, right?"

He didn't want to lie to her. He really didn't. But Julian heard himself say, "No matter what, we'll figure this out."

CHAPTER TWELVE

MADELINE

C runching tires woke Madeline from a doze. She'd fallen asleep on Julian's shoulder with both of them slumped against the couch. The intimacy had a comforting, *almost* platonic feel.

"Hey," he whispered. "Someone's here."

"Mmph."

They got up and peered through the living room window. In the driveway, a statuesque woman emerged from her federal issue black sedan and stretched. She looked buff and ready for action.

"That's Special Agent Spearman," Julian said, his voice a flat monotone. "My boss."

An approaching engine rattled the windows, and a boxy freight truck pulled up behind Spearman's car, taking up the whole driveway.

Madeline frowned. "What's with the moving truck?"

Julian ran a hand through his hair and rolled his shoulders as if shaking off a bad dream. "It's the mobile ops center. We use it for crime scenes that need special attention. The compartment acts as a makeshift lab."

While they watched, Roland stomped into view from somewhere behind the semi.

"*Now* it's a party," Madeline sighed.

She wished she'd gotten another hour of sleep on Julian's shoulder, but the half-dozen masked men and women pouring from the back of the truck woke her in a hurry. Dressed in black and armed with utility belts, they moved over the yard like ants harvesting fresh roadkill. A shiver of alarm made her wish she was holding her self-defense baton, but Julian didn't seem worried, just resigned.

Thinking of Constance's body in the basement, she felt a pang for Roland and decided the best thing to do was meet his ire head-on. She and Julian stepped onto the porch, ready to face the proverbial firing squad.

"What's the meaning of this, Agent Worthy?" Roland snapped. "Where is my mother? Why are these people on our property?"

Before either of them could speak, Agent Spearman joined them on the porch. She wore a sleeveless white blouse, simple gray slacks, and sensible low heels. Spearman was shorter and leaner than Madeline, and her bare shoulders and arms were sensually muscular. Instead of making her face look severe, her tight bun of dark brown hair brought out her high cheekbones, the slight bump to her nose, and full pink lips. Madeline estimated her to be in her late thirties or early forties, but the authority in Spearman's expression was of a much older woman.

"Agent Worthy." She nodded curtly in Julian's direction and held out a hand to Madeline. "You must be Madeline Da Vinci. Pleasure."

Roland cleared his throat as if he couldn't bear being ignored.

Julian did the honors. "Agent Spearman, this is Roland Hanford, Constance Hanford's son. We were just about to update him on the situation."

Spearman didn't offer her hand, choosing instead to flash Roland her badge. "Let's go inside and have a chat."

She led the way, the three following like dutiful schoolchildren. When they were settled in the living room, the black-ops workers silently streamed through the door, into the kitchen, and up the stairs, systematically snapping photos and holding out strange equipment as if taking the house's temperature.

Madeline thought they were the government's version of The Ghost Busters meets paranormal reality TV "experts". Hopefully, the technicians were checking for what amounted to genuine science: mold, asbestos, and lead paint. Madeline would welcome a cringy discovery, like there was LSD in the town's water supply, to explain the other-worldly vibe surrounding Mason's Manor and Constance's cause of death.

Anything else would be adding insult to injury.

The workers unsettled Roland so much, he was at a loss for words, not that Spearman gave him an opening to take over. "Mr. Hanford, I'm sorry to inform you that your mother passed away last night."

He covered his mouth with a fleshy hand but said nothing. Spearman switched her hazel gaze to Julian. "Agent Worthy will fill us in on the details."

Roland's face sagged, tears welling in his eyes, when Julian launched into a neutral recall of last night's events. A wave of empathy hit Madeline. Poor Roland. No matter what her feelings about the lawyer, she'd casually disregarded the shock, the horror, at arriving too late to say goodbye to his mother. How could she justify such callousness? She didn't really believe Roland was behind Constance's ghost delusions, even if he did have motive for getting her off the property so he could sell it.

Julian wrapped up the story, adding they'd heard a male voice, but not Constance's animalistic sounds of pleasure, leaving it to, "She didn't seem to suffer in the end. In fact, just the opposite."

"Mother's dead," Roland said flatly. He stood, the paunch of his belly leading the way when he paced. "It wasn't supposed to happen this way."

Madeline watched Julian's eyebrows snap together. "How was it supposed to happen, Roland?"

"You federal types," Roland hissed. "I told you there was something wrong with her. But did you help? No!"

Spearman sat back in her chair, steepled her hands, but didn't keep the tedium from her face.

"And you!" Roland swung in Madeline's direction. "She needed to be medicated, but would you listen? No wonder sensible people don't trust shrinks, much less sex workers."

Julian sprung to his feet, his voice radiating a deadly calm. "That's enough."

Roland's tirade flickered and died. At least he knew when a real alpha was in the room. Avoiding their eyes, he said, "I want you gone. Off my property. Now."

Spearman stirred. "I understand your duress, Mr. Hanford, but that's not possible. Until we determine Mrs. Hanford's cause of death, this is a crime scene, and we have federal jurisdiction."

His face took on the semblance of a swollen sack about to burst. "You can take your investigation and shove it. There is no ghost, and this isn't a haunted house. My mother was old, and she died alone. End of story."

Madeline flinched and fought the rise of tears. She didn't like Roland, but his words mirrored her thoughts.

Spearman took her time standing. "What kind of law do you practice, Mr. Hanford? Injury?" She leisurely planted her hands on her hips, looking very much like a stealthy panther. "You're free to contact the sheriff, and file whatever injunctions you see fit, but that will take weeks. In the meantime, this is the country. If you stay in this house, you're out here alone, cut off from civilization. Just like your mother."

The color drained from Roland's face. "Are you threatening me?"

"Threats are a waste of time. I deal in facts." Spearman didn't blink. "Is your insurance paid up, Mr. Hanford?"

Madeline's eyes ping-ponged between Spearman and Roland, but it was Julian's expression that gave her pause. He stared at his "boss" with something close to worship. Had they not spent the last forty-eight hours in close quarters, she wouldn't have recognized the sensual cast to his lips, the flush of arousal on his cheeks, or the subtle tension making his body vibrate. Madeline didn't blame him. Boss Lady had impressive energy. But a simper of jealousy made her look away.

Roland pointed a finger at Spearman. "I have friends in high places. You'd do well to remember that."

He stomped out of the house like a petulant child.

Spearman sighed and addressed Julian. "Where's the body?"

Madeline found her voice. "Constance. Her name is Constance."

Julian's boss looked like she was going to snap a retort, but her eyes softened. "Yes, of course. Where is Constance?"

Julian shot Madeline a look, who grudgingly nodded, as if she had a say. They climbed the stairs, but when they got to Constance's bedroom door, Madeline hesitated. Julian's head bent toward Spearman, the chemistry between them almost visible.

More jealousy tumbled into the well of her hopes and dreams. Spearman and Julian had history and not just the working variety. He had left that part of his story out.

Well, shit.

To distract herself, she checked her phone. A jolt of shock hit her. During the upheaval, she'd missed a text from Sebastian.

Plans delayed for Brazil. One last fling in Costa Rica?

Was the universe sending her an exit strategy? More important, did she want a fling? The word hurt her—what kind of guy offered a parting fuck?—but she'd be lying if she didn't see the appeal.

131

Constance was dead. Julian carried a decent-sized flame for his boss. What was left for Madeline? In pseudo-paradise, she could put aside her failures and revel in the physical. There were so many techniques, positions, and scenarios she and Sebastian never explored, mostly because Madeline was determined not to scare him away. Nothing to stop her now. She could take her unrequited lust and pour it into ruining him for future lovers. God knew, she had the skill set.

Besides, Julian was busy with his *real* partner, Agent Spearman.

Madeline watched them enter Constance's room, but the thought of going down the hidden stairs, looking at her friend's body, and trying to describe how the past twenty-four hours amounted to nothing more than a long goodbye was unbearable.

Gritting her teeth, she left the duo to play CSI, went to her room, and started packing.

Julian appeared as she was shoving her peach nightgown into her overnight. He had the decency not to ask what she was doing.

"You can't leave yet," he managed.

She shot him a look that said, *You wanna bet?* "Right now, a group of strangers is in the bowels of that clit cavern bagging and tagging a woman I failed to help. What, exactly, is there left for me to do?"

"What about the male voice we heard? Someone–something–was down there with her."

"Julian, we're never going to solve the mystery of Desmond."

"You don't know that."

His confidence gave her pause, but it wasn't enough to make her stay.

Madeline sighed, too tired to think straight. "I have clients. Friends. A life in Virginia."

He scowled. "And a plane to catch, right?"

Madeline's chin came up. "Your boss is here. She is obviously well-equipped to handle the situation. I'll only get in the way."

"That's bullshit. You and I make a good team."

Madeline paused long enough to note the lines of stress around his mouth. He didn't bother to blow his floppy hair back. Resisting the urge to hug him, she rolled her shoulders and scanned the room for leftover personal items. "A team? This isn't Scooby Doo. It's reality. In reality, there are no tidy endings. We will not chase down the bad guy, yank off his mask, and make him confess. The mystery of Desmond is going to be buried with Constance, as it should be. May they both rest in peace."

As if the shadows in the house agreed, four agents walked past Madeline's open door, each holding the handle of a black body bag, heavy with the weight of Constance's remains.

The bottom dropped from Madeline's stomach. She had to leave. Now.

She zippered her own bag and slung the strap over her shoulder, then held out a hand for Julian to shake. "Thanks for not making this terrible. You're..."

She couldn't find the right word. Amazing? Sexy as fuck? Too good to be true?

In love with someone else?

Julian took her hand, not shaking, not squeezing, just enveloping her with touch.

The impulse to drop her bag and stay with him roared to life, similar but unique from the maddening sexual bubble they'd been living in.

If Julian told her he needed her...

But he said nothing.

Madeline let go before she could do something stupid and headed downstairs. She checked the house for anything left behind, but really, her gaze greedily took in the small cottage, it's rose-print décor and bright kitchen, wanting to remember Constance's aura of strength and happiness. Without her, the rooms felt...wrong. Old. Gray in the morning light. As if the march of entropy accelerated without the older woman's force of will to keep it at bay.

In front of the estate, the black truck's door gaped wide. The agents loaded Constance inside and placed her body bag on a gurney. Madeline didn't have the best viewpoint, but she could make out the sterile sheen of surgical instruments and machinery ready to pump, suck, or blow god knows what into trays and jars. Two people in white hazmat suits played with dental drills and long, shiny scalpels.

A sudden breeze gushed over the yard, unseasonably cold. Madeline shivered. The flowers didn't look as vibrant. Even the trees seemed to creak and groan, their limbs swaying in sorrow. There was something very wrong about the situation, but what could she do?

Nothing.

She was about to slide into her RAV4 when Spearman appeared at her elbow.

"Miss Da Vinci. Leaving us so soon?"

Madeline wrinkled her nose. "I'm a sex therapist, not a grief counselor. Even if I had a good bedside manner, Roland made it clear he no longer needs my services."

"There are twats, and then there are twats." Spearman loosely crossed her arms and leaned against the hood. "I'm going to be blunt with you."

Madeline couldn't help but admire her guns. "Do you have another setting?"

Spearman let that go. "This is indelicate, but I have to ask, during your stay on the property, have you engaged in sexual activity?"

Madeline was too shocked to be offended, not that she would have been, given the nature of her confidences, but this was not a therapist-client setting. "I don't see how that's any of your business or relevant to Constance's death."

"On the contrary, I think it's relevant to both."

Wary, Madeline jangled her keys. "What do you mean?"

"Mason's Manor has experienced unusual weather phenomenon, and the reports of increased sexual activity could be a fluke, but in my line of work, there's no such thing as coincidence. Which brings me to you. A reputable therapist with ties to The Disciples of Creation shows up out of the blue to snoop around a haunted sex house? That's a mite suspicious."

Madeline's fist clenched so hard, the keys cut into her palm. "How do you know about The Disciples of Creation?"

Spearman glanced at the mobile ops truck. "Does it matter?"

Swallowing a bubble of bile, Madeline took a calming breath. "Agent Spearman, if you're not going to arrest me, probe me, or serve me a helping of your world famous facts, I'm going to leave now."

"World famous facts? I like that. Belongs on a coffee mug." Spearman shrugged. "Agent Worthy wants to believe there's an paranormal explanation, but you and I both know the power of worldly urges. Humans don't need an excuse to walk on the wild side." She glanced at the house and pursed her lips. "Although, from the look of this place, anyone who wanted to believe in spectral curses wouldn't need much convincing."

Madeline frowned and glanced over her shoulder. Again, the spectral reference didn't fit. The house was old, maybe a little worn down in places, and there were patches of paint peeling she hadn't noticed before, but haunted?

Now that Constance was dead, yes, maybe it would be haunted.

"I just want to go home," she said, sad to her core.

Spearman paused, gave a small nod, and sauntered back to the house.

Madeline's hand was shaking, but she got the keys in the ignition. The temptation to floor it tickled her foot, but she didn't want to give Spearman the satisfaction. Just the same, her eyes found the rearview mirror. Constance's beautiful house filled the rectangle. What once appeared overflowing with life was hollow and rapidly draining of color.

Standing on the porch, his face in shadow, Julian watched without a wave or a word. It was all the evidence Madeline needed to leave Mason's Hole in the dust.

Driving down the blacktop, Madeline tried to focus on the lush forest and how nice it would be to take a break from figuring out other peoples' problems. She even went down the fantasy highway of what she was going to make Sebastian do if they got naked, but nothing stuck.

It didn't help that the exit billboard at the town limits seemed to be laughing at her.

"Come back soon—our ghosts get lonely without company."

"Yikes," Madeline muttered, a spurt of anger focusing her attention. "Who came up with that dark tourist campaign?"

Not that it didn't ring with truth.

The thing that bugged her the most, Constance had died alone. Unless Desmond was real.

No, she couldn't start thinking like that. There was something going on—something dark and twisted—but the black-ops action figures hadn't treated Constance like an intruder-break-in scenario. Which meant Julian could be right, and whatever was going on in Mason's Manor was bigger than mass hysteria.

Had he told Spearman about her past involvement with The Disciples of Creation? Madeline doubted it, but the timing was conspicuous. The cult wasn't a secret; it was more of a cliché according to Wikipedia, and Madeline hated how the media capitalized suffering for soundbites. This applied specifically to Hatty, who was born into the sex-sharing, "everyone exists for everyone else" culture of extreme fanaticism.

Over the years, reporters galore tried to get an interview. Madeline never spared them a comment, and for her family's sake, never would. Innocence and honor were not for sale, nor were they fodder for a warped religion's ideas of sacrifice. The same would apply to Constance's death.

It was past-time for a check-in with Hatty. Madeline's finger lingered over her sister's name on the car's digital display, but right when she would have pushed the button, Peggy Atwood's incoming call popped up on the screen.

Madeline quickly pulled over and parked the car on the shoulder. "Peggy?"

"Madeline! I'm so sorry to interrupt your vacation, but I thought..."

"Are you okay?"

"Yes! Better than okay. I wanted to share with you, I've been doing a lot of soul searching, and, well, I decided it was my turn to call the shots. I let Martin be in charge of initiating sex for years. It never occurred to me how exhausting it was for him, how scared he was all the time of making sure I was pleasured and satisfied." Peggy huffed a breath. "Last night, I booked a room at a nice hotel and told him to meet me there. Then I got dressed up in a sexy secretary outfit. I even put on thigh-high stockings. You should have seen his face!"

Peggy not only sounded inspired, her voice carried a note of power Madeline had never heard.

"Anyway, it's like we stepped into a parallel universe where he was my boss, and I seduced him!" Peggy gushed. "He was wrapped around my finger. We haven't had sex like that in—Well, we've never had sex like that!"

Her reverence circled Madeline in a much-needed hug. "Peggy, that's amazing. I'm so happy for you."

"I know you're out having your own adventures, but you need to know, I wouldn't have had the courage to go through with it if you hadn't set a good example. Thank you, Madeline. Martin and I have a long way to go, but I feel different. I feel whole."

"That's the power of teamwork," Madeline supplied lamely.

"Yes, and I have a brilliant partner. I'm very lucky."

"Very lucky."

"You have fun and come home safe. We'll see you when you get back."

After the call ended, it took Madeline a couple seconds to realize she was crying. Tears for Constance, tears for her lost relationship with Sebastian, tears for everything she wanted to be but knew she wasn't. Streaks of moisture cascaded down her cheeks, but she let the storm pass through her and stayed present, not pushing away or clinging to any particular thought, until a fierce swell of calm replaced the sorrow.

Having a good team didn't come without work. There was always the risk of being wrong or rejected, but the reward offered a bond that couldn't be bought or sold. Madeline could run off to paradise and maybe she'd find momentary distraction from her pain, but could she find a real partner?

Wiping her face with the back of her hand, she glanced around and saw another billboard further down the road. "Still Leaving Mason's Hole? Don't worry. The probe was *probably* just a dream."

Probes. Dreams. Julian.

Frowning fiercely, Madeline angled the rearview mirror down, and met her red-rimmed eyes. The woman looking back at her wasn't perfect, but she didn't back down when times got tough. And she didn't let her friends down.

Julian was her friend.

He'd treated her with respect, asked her opinion, and tried his best to be vulnerable while protecting her when both of them had been horny as teenagers. There was definitely something between him and Spearman, but he hadn't wanted her to leave.

Maybe she was reading too much into it, but Julian offered her the chance to be a part of something bigger than the sum of their parts. It was risky. Dangerous. Sexy as hell. And he had promised they *would* figure out what happened to Constance.

The woman in the mirror sat up straight. Her chin lifted. Madeline was about to fly back into a web of secrets and possibly murder—but there was no way she was leaving Julian alone to handle it himself.

That's not what friends did.

CHAPTER THIRTEEN

JULIAN

Julian wondered if he'd ever hear from Madeline again. Would she check back to see how things turned out? Had she sensed the tension between himself and Spearman? And likewise, had Spearman sensed the tension between himself and Madeline?

The screen door clacked, rousing him from his woolgathering.

Spearman strode across the porch. "Agent Worthy—"

"You brought a lot of fire power for a routine fatality." As soon as the words left his mouth, he realized how passive-aggressive he sounded.

She folded her arms, making her toned biceps look even firmer. "I've lost track of how many times I told you not to take this case."

Their eyes met, sending a pang through Julian. He'd seen those eyes in the throes of passion. Now they were hard, and maybe a little sad. Like she wasn't surprised to be standing on a dead woman's porch. Something clicked into place.

"Son of a *bitch*! You *knew* this was going to happen! Were you watching Mason's Hole? Hoping for another Slate Hill?"

"Don't be an ass, Agent Worthy."

"But you knew?"

Spearman examined her nails. "Suspected."

"You didn't want me to see the goon squad catalogue the house and dispose of the body?"

"So I could avoid this annoying and unnecessary conversation."

Julian brushed back his blazer and put his hands on his hips. "There's an obvious connection to the planetary alignments and ancient relics in the basement. What are you hiding, and why won't you let me in on this?"

"There is no *in*. No *connection*."

"Oh, come *on*."

Her chin jutted out. "You call me in the middle of the night—twice—and tell me there's another Slate Hill happening. I took you at your word, sent the cavalry, and drove my ass down from Washington to find an elderly woman who died of a cardiac arrest while masturbating." She gave Julian a derisive frown. "Some Slate Hill."

Julian pointed a finger at her. "Go ahead. Just leave out the important details. Like Constance was found in a vagina-shaped cave, lying on an altar carved with sex symbols, some of which match those carved into the trees of our fuck-fest."

Spearman's gaze dropped to his extended digit. "Put that away."

Julian did, realizing he may have overstepped.

The steel in her voice was undeniable. "I suggest you gather your things. You're going back to Washington."

He resisted the urge to stamp his foot. "This is bullshit."

"An order is an order."

Julian turned on his heel and went into the house. There was nothing to gather. His go-bag was ready. But he pretended to mess with things while he tried to figure out how to stay a little longer. Nothing came to him.

He brushed past Spearman, got into his rental, and wriggled the black sedan around the ominous trailer. Driving down the long dirt track, he muttered every curse in his vocabulary. Nearing the highway, Madeline's green Toyota pulled into the driveway, blocking his escape.

She slipped from her car and walked over to him, a faint smile playing across her lips.

Something like hope blossomed in Julian's chest. He banged the shifter into 'Park' and got out. "Did you forget something?"

"Yeah," she said. "I forgot a bunch of stuff."

He raised an eyebrow, wondering how a put together woman like Madeline could forget anything. "Like what?"

She held up her hand and started ticking off items of importance. "From day one, you acted like a gentleman when you could have taken advantage of me. You treated me like an equal and sought my opinion. You came here to protect Constance, same as I did, and I bet you're going to fight to save her reputation. In a nutshell?" She took his hand. "I forgot what friends do."

A lump rose in Julian's throat. He wasn't crazy about being in the Friend Zone, but he'd have to be okay with it. "Lousy fucking timing, friend. I just got thrown off the case. I'm supposed to report back to Washington."

She looked at a point over his shoulder. "Put your arms around me."

"Huh? I thought—"

"Shut up. Put your arms around me. Kiss me."

"Wait, I—"

He didn't get a chance to finish.

The weight of her against his chest, her scent, vanilla and spice, felt like home. Strange, though. She moved as if they were making out but kept her lips closed. Julian puts his arms around her, anyway. When she pulled away a few seconds later, he could taste her, peppermint and determination, and his trousers were too tight.

"There," she whispered in his ear. "A whole bunch of black suits saw that."

"I still don't—"

"For a federal agent, you're kind of derpy," she said, not letting go of him. "It's Friday. You have a girl. No reason you shouldn't enjoy yourself for the weekend. When the dust settles, we can sneak back into Constance's house."

Julian let himself smile. "Great idea. But I don't see what good that will do. The house will be crawling with agents."

"There's another way in," Madeline said. "Lots of ways, if the map is accurate. All we have to do is find the clit."

Julian squeezed her before pulling away. "Long way around for that joke."

"Totally worth it." She flipped her hair ironically. "Let's get a motel room and some flashlights!"

He tried to make his smile reflect the warmth in his chest. "With all that's going on, maybe we skip the motel room, *friend*."

"Point taken," Madeline said, without missing a beat. "You're off the case, but we've got to stash that thing." She nodded at his car. "It sticks out like a sore thumb."

"It does sort of scream *federal agent inside!*" He rubbed a hand over his jaw. "I guess we can park it at my motel. I still have my room. Since we'll be there anyway, might as well freshen up and figure out a game plan."

Once at the Climax Motel, Julian did his best not to notice the swell of his friend's breasts. Or the languid way she moved. Or the way her hourglass hips curved into her round bottom. By unspoken agreement, they gave each other plenty of room.

Julian checked his guns, one on his ankle, one in his shoulder holster. Then he checked the batteries in his flashlight. His pulse surged, eager for the adventure ahead.

When they were ready, Julian pocketed the room key and tossed his go-bag on the pile of luggage in the back of Madeline's RAV4.

He'd been so wrapped up in the day's events, he had forgotten his new partner gave up a Costa Rica vacation without protest. He would have, too.

Kindred spirits.

They provisioned themselves at the town's only big box store. An extra flashlight for Madeline, batteries, bottled water, and a meager meal of fruit and protein bars. Back in her car, Madeline rummaged in a crinkling plastic bag of supplies and produced a round red apple. "Let's look at the map."

Julian definitely didn't notice the way she licked the juice from her full lips as he unfolded the paper.

She pulled up her map app and held it next to the parchment. "Remember, we were talking about female anatomy?"

"Vaguely."

"Turn it ninety degrees." When he complied, she zoomed in on the digital topography. "The cave shaped like a uterus is near the library."

Julian squinted at the map. "The uterus could be the portal."

"Portal? I don't know if I'm with you on that." She took another bite of fruit. "But I admit the configuration of the tunnels is fucking weird. Besides, who puts a portal in a uterus? Wouldn't it be near the altar in the vagina room?" She gave him a sly wink. "I mean, a vagina is already a portal to another world."

Jesus. Julian did his best to shrug. Not the time. Not the place. "I didn't see a mine entrance when we were in town—" He stopped when he saw her nose scrunch like a cute little gerbil. "What?"

"First of all, you don't just go stomping into someone's uterus. Second, if it's important, an abandoned tunnel entrance is not going to be in a place easy to locate..."

She trailed off, then suddenly gave a "Shit!" so loud, Julian wanted to reach for his gun. "What?!"

"The librarian hinted there was an entrance under the building. I got the impression she'd been there recently."

"Huh." He sat back in his seat. "It could be a coincidence, but you wanna check out some books?"

Madeline grinned and put the car in gear. "I'm game."

Julian ate his protein bar as she drove, desperately trying to ignore the cloud of invisible energy pulling him toward the magnificent woman at his side. She'd come back. For him. It was enough to swell his ego, dick, and sense of responsibility. Whatever happened, he had to keep her safe.

The concrete lot around the library held a decent number of cars. Strange, since it was after closing hours, and the sleepy town had virtually become a...well...ghost town.

She parked under a stand of oaks, and they approached the impressive ornate wooden doors. Julian tried the latch. Unlocked.

Madeline's hand clenched around her backpack's strap. "Maybe they're holding a special event."

"The mortal portal book club?"

He watched her stifle a peel of laughter, pleased with himself. But it was time for stealth mode. Opening the door enough they could squeeze through, Julian eased it closed behind them, praying the fading daylight didn't communicate their presence to whomever might be lingering in the library.

Dim yellow bulbs cast a feeble glow over rows of dust-choked stacks. Low voices drifted through the tall shelves packed with esoteric tomes. Julian tilted his head. He could place Sarah Dubois's lusty voice. What was she doing here? Were they about to stumble into a sex magic orgy? He hoped not, but a glance at Madeline's cleavage gave him second thoughts.

Bad Special Agent. Bad.

They skirted the perimeter of the shelves, keeping to the shadows, but paused when the small group came into view. Amid the multi-book series and epic fantasies in the Teens section, Sarah sat at a round table with three others. A scattering of hard covers, glass containers of unknown liquid, and leather pouches splayed over the surface. A huge white candle flickered in the center next to what looked like a magician's wand.

"That's Effy, the librarian with the fluffy hair," Madeline whispered. "And Rosamund the baker is next to her."

"I recognize the town clerk and the guy from the convenience store," Julian whispered back.

"What are they burning? Incense?"

Julian shifted, trying to get a better view. "Probably frankincense and myrrh to consecrate the space. See? There's a pentagram for protection drawn in salt on the table."

"They're Wiccan?"

"Who knows."

Unaware he was being watched, Even, sometimes Eve, cracked his knuckles. "Are you guys sure this is a good idea?"

"We all agreed," Rosamund said, "if we want the magic to stay in Mason's Hole, we need to be proactive."

"Desmond's spirit would approve," Effy said with reverence.

Rosamund scanned her list. "Do we have all the ingredients?"

Julian stiffened as Sarah picked up *The Lesser Keys of Solomon* and flipped pages.

"Some of this stuff is so arcane," she huffed. "Might as well say we need the tears of a virgin collected on Tuesday during a full moon. Any of you virgins?"

Rosamund nudged her girlfriend. "As if."

The group gave a collective chuckle.

Effy cleared her throat. "Let's get serious. Who wants to lead the incantation?"

"Let's all do it," Rosamund suggested.

Julian resisted the urge to step from the shadows and tell the group they were looking in the wrong place for answers. Once the stars fell out of alignment, the sex energy would dissipate, if not vanish completely. That is, unless Desmond's ghostly presence offered its own bubble of power, and the celestial alignment magnified its effects.

"This will take a while," Julian muttered to Madeline. "Let's see if we can find a door to the basement."

He backed away from the group, and they edged deeper into the library. The building was old and had been updated over the years. A secretarial office of modern plaster gave way to a glass-paneled storage supply closet, but as soon as Julian opened the door, his groin tingled with arousal.

Almost as good as 'X' marks the spot.

No light came from the outer halls, but a tiny window near the ceiling outlined industrial shelving. Cleaning supplies gave the room an orange-peel twang and masked a hint of musky damp.

He didn't want to use his flashlight yet, but—

"There's another door," Madeline hissed from behind a stack of crates. She'd already opened it when he rounded the corner, and no shocker, this was the beginning of a spiral staircase leading to what he hoped was the basement. Also not a surprise, an eerie green glow illuminated stone steps.

Madeline glanced over her shoulder and did a double-take. Her eyes lingered on his crotch. Lips twitching, she said, "If we get lost, we can always use your dick as a divining rod."

"You're hilarious. As if you don't feel it, too."

"A lady never tells."

Cheeks flaming, Julian adjusted his pants and followed her into the stairwell. How was he supposed to work like this, with Madeline's erect nipples staring him in the face all night? At the bottom of the stone steps, they found a well-swept room with a pallet on the floor and several blankets and pillows piled next to a camper's gas lantern.

"Quite the love nest," Julian said.

Madeline swung around. "There's nothing here. No other doors."

His boot nudged under the thick cushion of the pallet and swept it aside. A steel hatch lay in a disc of cement. On its handle, a padlock. No markings gave any hint at its purpose.

"Are you going to shoot the lock?"

He swallowed a chuckle. "That's not really a thing."

"Well, I don't know," she said. "Unless you keep bolt cutters in your go-bag, how do we open it?"

"The lock looks pretty solid," Julian said. "But the hasp is rusty. We could whack it a couple times with your trusty self-defense baton."

Madeline unzipped her backpack. "How about a tire iron?"

Julian thought she was joking, but his eyes widened when she pulled a compact iron from her bag. "I'm impressed."

"Flattery will get you everywhere."

He took the tool from her hands. It took two good yanks braced against the cement before the rusted hasp gave way. The bang echoed deep below, and they both winced.

"Hope the summoning circle didn't hear that!" Without waiting, Madeline pulled the heavy steel hood aside.

A hazy plume of trapped energy exited the hole. Time slowed, stilled. Julian shivered as if an electric finger had run down his back. He couldn't help noticing the way the sinews stood out on Madeline's arms. The way a wisp of red hair lifted in the draft and waved at him.

The flashlight's beam revealed a ladder made of bent iron bars descending twenty feet to a rocky floor. As he stood over Madeline, he felt the energy wafting past her, sending the cacophony of pleasant scents rolling from Madeline's skin into his nose. He shuddered. Unable to stop himself, Julian reached out, running his fingers over her soft shoulder.

She peered up at him with feline green eyes.

Julian swallowed. "Just to be transparent, you feel that, right?"

"You touching my shoulder?"

148

"The energy...getting stronger."

She licked her lips. "Horny much?"

He nodded.

"Yeah." She scanned him with sultry eyes. "Must be the right place."

"I should go first," he said.

"No way. I gave up a potential hook-up with my ex for this. If there are aliens down there, I want to see them before you scare them off."

He straightened. "Your ex called you?"

"Sebastian texted before I left Constance's house. Something about one last fling in paradise."

Julian gritted his teeth, but put on a sweet smile, waving to the ladder. "Then by all means." The tire iron clanked as she lowered into the opening. "You're taking that?"

"Why not? You going to give me a gun?"

"You know how to use one?" he countered.

Her chin lifted. "I'm no stranger to a firing range."

Because she'd run from a cult and needed to protect her sister. Julian felt a twinge of pride at her resilience but couldn't go against his training. "First thing they teach you at the Academy, never give up your gun."

"Then the tire iron comes with me."

God, the way her eyes shone like green grass, she'd be impressive handling his weapon.

"Focus," he grumbled.

Madeline clanked down the ladder, step by step.

"And you're worried about *me* scaring off aliens?" he hissed down at her.

She dropped the tire iron. It fell with a *bang* that echoed some twenty feet below.

"Malicious compliance," Julian muttered, and climbed in after her. He moved as fast as he dared, eager to make sure nothing unpleasant waited for them in the shadows.

At the bottom of the ladder, Madeline stood, her flashlight illuminating a tunnel hewn from rock. The beam faded into the dark distance, but they both noticed the immaculate workmanship of the shaft. The walls were so smooth, they almost looked polished.

"We're in for a lengthy walk. Let's hope the tunnel points in the direction of Constance's house," Julian said.

"At least I have the shoes for it."

He glanced at her flat loafers and had no idea what he was supposed to do with that.

Madeline scooped up the tire iron. "You can go first, if you want."

"Cool," was all he could think to say. He held his flashlight in one hand and his gun in the other. Pebbles clattered under their feet, throwing tiny echoes into the darkness ahead.

Neither spoke. There were no sounds but their muffled footfalls. Sensory deprivation left Julian hyperaware of the tug in his groin. The magic would only intensify the deeper they went. He needed something to take his mind off the vivid fantasy of pushing Madeline against the tunnel wall and kissing her until the world narrowed to the press of lips and the rush of breath.

"You and Sebastian..." Something hard bumped his head. She'd swung her ready-made weapon to shoulder level. "Watch it with that thing."

"Sorry," she murmured much too close to his ear. "Sebastian's a nice guy, but we weren't suited for each other."

"Were you tempted?"

She snorted. "To do what?"

"Meet him for one last fling."

She was silent so long, Julian readied an apology. Finally, she said, "No."

The word fell on his ears like a caress, but before he could catch the thought, they stepped into a circular chamber the size of a small bedroom.

The walls were carved with honeycomb-like structures, each cavity empty. A faint, organic scent hung in the air—musky, damp, and wrong. Julian swept his light across the room, tracing the bare stone niches. On the other side, the tunnel continued on.

Madeline's light paused on one of the compartments. Her brow furrowed.

"This is an ovary," she said, voice low. "The structures... follicles."

Julian stepped closer. "So what would go in them?"

Madeline gave him a sideways look. "Eggs. Don't you remember any of your high school health classes?"

The word detonated in Julian's mind.

Eggs.

Alien eggs.

His chest tightened. His breath hitched, vision swimming. Near weightless, he slumped to his knees.

"Julian!"

The tire iron clattered to the floor. She crouched in front of him, hands on his shoulders. A second reality superimposed on his consciousness.

"Talk to me," Madeline said. "What's going on?"

He forced himself to give the memories words. "My abduction," he said in a faint whisper. "I made it seem like I was a Special Agent. I wasn't. I was a teenager. Didn't even have my diploma...."

In his head, Julian lay on the curved trunk of the tree altar. He couldn't move, but he could feel the feminine ghost pressing her sex to his mouth. She felt so real. Smelled so real. The moisture of her arousal in his mouth tasted real. He fought the lust and helplessness tearing at his sanity. The ghost sex in his head, and the softness of Madeline's touch, conspired to bring his cock to full attention.

"Keep talking, Julian," Madeline urged. "Tell me what you see."

Julian closed his eyes and focused.

"I lived in Slate Hill, North Carolina. Grew up there, and couldn't wait to leave. The summer before I left for college, the whole place goes sex crazy for a day or so, just like here. I was working as a pizza delivery guy and saw an old teacher go into the woods. She was acting...strange. I followed her, my feet moving like a slow-motion movie, and came to a clearing. I remember...something about lack of light. It was the middle of the day, but it looked like midnight. In the middle of the clearing, a bent over tree formed an altar like the one in the vagina cave."

He could feel the bark on his skin. His fingers tracing the symbols. The things it provoked...

"It's okay, Julian. You're doing great."

Julian sat heavily on the stone floor, flashlight forgotten, hard-on straining against his pants. "When I touched the tree...it...touched me back. It told me to take off my clothes and lay down. Lightning flashed across the sky. And then a woman was on me. She felt so fucking real, touching me, making me feel good. She kneeled over me, riding my face, urging me on."

Madeline straddled his leg, still holding him by the shoulders like she feared he'd turn into a puddle. "Who did, Julian? Who was touching you?"

"She was, I don't know, like a ghost. All shimmery, but I could touch her. She was so beautiful..."

The memory took him over. The warm feeling in his belly. The softness of her skin.

"Don't stop," his past ghost lover commanded.

"Don't stop," Madeline whispered.

"I couldn't help it, I wanted her. She ground herself into my face, bucking through her orgasm. And then...." He tried to pull back, tried not to be disrespectful, but his hips came off the floor, pressing his trapped cock into Madeline's denim clad knee. She didn't pull away. "And then something came out of her, into my mouth. It was egg-shaped." He gulped air involuntarily. "I swallowed. I had to. She made me. Told me I was a good boy…."

"Oh, Julian," Madeline said, running a hand through his hair.

His hips lifted again. Maddening layers of fabric kept the contact from being satisfying. He shuddered and turned frantic eyes in her direction, focusing on the heart outline of her face. "Please let me go, Madeline. It's the energy down here. I can't…. I don't want this for us."

She backed away, but sat close to his hip. "You don't have to keep fighting the memories. We can handle it together."

God, he didn't want to finish the story. She would think him delusional. But she was in real danger now. And Julian refused to let her go another step without knowing the nature of his investigation.

"Later that day, I met Agent Spearman. She asked me to show her the altar. The magic, or whatever you want to call it, took her over. We…. Christ. We had sex on the tree altar." Julian's cock ached for freedom, remembering how Spearman had commanded him to fuck her. "When I entered her, I saw ghost people all around us. There was the lightning again. She was clawing at me, urging me on. She finished, I finished, and…" His hand sought hers on the cold stone floor. "I felt something leave my body, Madeline. It was, I don't know, more than sperm."

She took his fingers and squeezed. "It's okay, Julian."

Why did she keep saying that? It was far from okay. For a long moment, only his ragged breathing punctuated the silence of the stone chamber.

"Afterwards, Spearman was…confused…just like me. But there was this bond between us. I cared for her, and I thought she cared for me." He rubbed a hand over his face. "The black trucks came, same as Constance's house. They surgically removed whatever was in us. Made me go to their shrink. They tried to tell me the hallucination was brought on by a rare plant that grew in the forest. Spearman went along with the program, but I know she knows the truth. Or at least some of it."

The soul-crushing aftermath had softened his erection, but finally remembering what happened to him ten years ago flooded him with determination. "When Spearman left, I went back to the forest to chop down that fucking tree, but it was gone. Yanked out of the earth. Nothing but a compact mound of dirt in its place."

The need to bust the tree with his ax sparked a new recollection. Before he'd been released from the black trailer, he'd seen a tall, powerful man in a dark suit. Shadow Man. He was talking to Spearman. Smiling at her. Touching her arm as she nodded. He'd wanted an ax in his hands then too.

Julian recognized him as the same man he'd seen staring at Madeline near Desmond's statue. But he couldn't tell her about the connection, not yet.

A surge of helplessness made him angry. Madeline had come back, but she wouldn't stay after his confession. "You probably think I'm crazy."

"Why would I think that? I saw them put Constance's body in the black trailer, and I'm sitting in a stone ovary, for Christ's sake." She took a deep, steadying breath. "I believe you."

Those words. Those fucking words. Words he'd longed for anyone to utter, slammed hard as a gut punch. He took a breath. Let it out. Took another one. "Thank you," was all he could manage.

Madeline rose, strong and sexy, clutching her tire iron.

He took up his light and stood. *She believed him.* "Thank you," he said again. "Slate Hill wasn't the only incident. There are others, notably one called Slaughter Beach. Same M.O. I don't know how they're connected, but if my department is trying to cover it up, it must be serious." He gathered himself and donned the mantle of protector again. "The danger is real, but nothing's going to happen to you. Not on my watch."

"I'm a big girl."

"I know, or I wouldn't have let you come with me."

She laughed, dispelling the somber atmosphere. "Like you had a choice."

He managed to smile back. "Ready to go find Desmond, partner?"

She focused the beam of her flashlight under her chin. The light cast her with a scary campfire vibe. "Would Thelma refuse a good mystery?"

They walked a fair distance, hard to tell how far, both lost in their own thoughts, but Julian guessed they covered a mile of tunnel. They had to be getting close to Constance's property. Another ten minutes of darkness, the tunnel dead-ended in a smooth, seamless wall of stone. Pale rocks, bone-white and faintly glossy, formed the faint outline of an arch. There was no visible handle, no doorframe. Just the suggestion of a threshold.

And the etching of the Butterfly Pea insignia, same as on Desmond's headstone, in the center of the stone.

"Huh," Madeline said, drawing up beside him. "What do you think?"

Raw and vulnerable from the ovary room, he needed every scrap of masculinity he could muster. He did his best to lower his voice a register and speak with confidence. "Probably just a run-of-the-mill secret door."

"Oh, yeah. Run-of-the-mill. Because secret doors in a pussy-shaped mine are *sooo* common."

Pocketing his flashlight, Julian flattened his hand against the etching, shocked at how the smooth and supple beveled edges slid beneath his fingertips.

Madeline aimed her light at his hand. "Could this be your magic gateway thing?"

"Could be," he said. "Slate Hill's portal was made of trees shaped by years of what looked like a planned platform. It had symbols carved into the bark. Slaughter Beach's chamber was carved from ancient coral and flooded at high tide. Makes sense this one would be another element. Stone."

"Earth, water, air, fire. Some rituals never die," Madeline said. "Let's open it."

He pulled his hand away. "Wait. If it *is* a portal to another dimension—"

"Let's not jump off the deep end. We found a fancy tunnel entrance, and soon we'll find the magic button, whatever it turns out to be."

He smiled in spite of himself. "This could be the greatest scientific discovery of all time, and all you can think about is your clit."

"Ha, ha," Madeline said. "Seriously, what are we supposed to do? Wait until Desmond's apparition walks through?"

Julian blew at his bangs. "It's a thought."

"We know things happen in the vagina, and this is how we get there."

A smirk curled his lips.

She rolled her eyes. "What do you think is more likely—we end up in another dimension, or another weird-ass room in the cave? Besides, I don't think we have much choice."

She was right all the way around. As much as he wanted this to be a portal, right now it was a dead-end. "Okay," he said. "You're the expert at opening these things."

She stepped closer and brushed her fingertips across the petals and where his fingers lay against stone. "I guess I am."

A soft hum bloomed in the air, low and resonant. The rock didn't move, but shimmered faintly. Julian stepped back, his arm sweeping out to protect Madeline. The surface became translucent—like frosted glass flushed with pink. A gentle, pulsing glow rippled through the gateway.

"That's..." Julian couldn't hide his surprise at how she easily she triggered the hidden mechanism. "I..."

Madeline flashed her light through the opening. "What can I say, I know secret doorways. Look."

Their lights played across an amorphous triangular room. Julian drew up beside her, a little bummed it was empty. "The uterus?"

"The uterus," she agreed.

Along the room's far wall, another archway of white stones glittered. Madeline stepped through the open arch.

"Wait!" Julian reached out to stop her. Electricity crackled, zapping his hand. He yanked his arm back. "What the fuck?"

He tried to pass his hand through the entry again, this time, slowly. Before contact, he felt the delicate force of resistance and the buildup of static like running sock-clad feet around a plush carpet.

"Mads, there's something stopping me."

On the opposite side of the threshold, she frowned. "Maybe the gateway sees your virility as a threat. Like it's some kind of fertility security system." Her gaze landed on symbols carved into the floor of the threshold. "More etchings. Remember when I couldn't pass through from the vagina room last night?"

"Yeah." Tensing his shoulders, Julian tried the direct approach and put his shoulder into the semi-transparent veil. Again, arcs of blue lightning shot out and pushed him back. "Goddamn it! Fuck. That hurts."

"Julian, stop. Look." She pointed her light at the floor. "This spiral symbol is from the Disciples of Creation."

It was a simple spiral, something a child could draw, but it reminded him of a coiled snake. Dread collected in his belly. "The sex cult strikes again."

"Thoth, the dude that ran the cult, used to say it represented harnessing the power of pleasure." She moved the beam to the next etching. "This one with the two interlocking circles means fertility, the female offering." She slid the light along the threshold, landing on the last symbol, three stars in a triangular pattern. "That one is for a male offering." She leaned back. "Put them together, it looks like a lock. Like the room won't open unless the right combination of energy passes through."

"The right energy?"

She stepped forward and tried to re-enter the tunnel. The electricity reached out and grabbed her. "Ow! Shit, that *does* hurt." She stepped back. "Okay, I'm supposed to be here. You're not. But the same way rubbing the clit opened the door for me, sperm might open this door for you."

Julian didn't think he heard her right. "Come again?"

Madeline threw him a playful smile. "That's the spirit."

He rubbed a hand over his face. "I can't come in unless I'm not a threat? Unless I'm spent? You're kidding me."

She raised her hands in a shrug. "Secret doors? Portals to other dimensions? How is this any weirder?"

"Sonofabitch. You're seriously suggesting I unzip and jerk off?"

"You have to cum," she pointed at a receptacle carved into the floor, "to come in."

This was an impossible scenario, but he couldn't protect her from a fucking ghost egg impregnation if he couldn't get into the room. As if all the shit that happened to him before was insane...

Lightning crackled through the archway, briefly illuminating them in its cold blue glow. Their eyes met across the veil. Julian shuddered, his semi growing hard and thick as if she'd reached out and licked him.

Madeline sucked in a breath, and her eyes took on a faraway cast. "Julian, every time the lightning sparks, it's like...being touched." She braced a hand on the wall. The other pulled at her blouse. The top button slipped free, revealing her impressive cleavage. "It was strong in the tunnel, but in here, it's intense."

He couldn't avert his eyes. "I can't just... cum on command. It doesn't work like that."

"I'll help you."

The blood left his head. "What are you—"

One finger traced the creamy slope of her upper breast. It wasn't indecent, just highly suggestive. "Script twenty-two."

"What?"

"You wanna know how I took care of a ten-year-old while putting myself through school? I was a phone sex operator. We had these scripts for certain kinks. Twenty-two was the Dominant Boss Scenario." She touched her neck, leaning back into the wall, as if she were on ecstasy or another mood-enhancing drug. "Given what I know about your background and the fact you and Spearman have a thing..."

Fucking hell. "This is insane."

Blue streaks of electricity crackled through the barrier. Alarm battled with sensual awareness. Could he really masturbate in front of her?

"Close your eyes," she said.

He let out a breath and did as she asked.

"Julian," she began, her slow voice dripping in sultry notes. "I think you know why I've called you into my office."

Was...was she imitating Spearman's voice? It wasn't spot on, but it was close, like she reached into his mind and pulled out the plumb of his desire. His cock threatened to break open his zipper.

Her voice got slower, deeper. "We're laying off some of the staff. If you want to keep working here, there are additional duties you need to perform. Close the door."

In his mind's eye, Julian was back in his office. Spearman was leaning against the wall, close enough to touch. He closed his door.

"What are you waiting for? Get on your knees in front of me."

God, the huskiness of that voice...Julian lowered to his knees.

"Good boy."

If there was any lingering question on whether Julian had a praise kink, here was the confirmation. Between her silky voice, the crackling sex magic, and his desire for Spearman, yeah. She had his number.

"Do you think I'm sexy?" she asked.

In response, he palmed his throbbing cock through his pants.

"Use your words."

"You're very sexy, Ma'am," he said.

"I'm coming around the desk...resting my round ass on the edge...lifting my skirt. You see that small patch of dark hair just above my sex? When I spread my legs, you can see how wet I am. Glistening. Do you know what that means? I'm hot and tight and ready."

"Yes," Julian sighed, nearly inaudible.

"Unbuckle your pants."

Madeline's commands acted like smooth ridges of sound slipping beneath his defenses. Julian did as he was told.

"Unzip. Take that fucking cock out."

Hands shaking, Julian withdrew his erection, thankful his eyes were closed.

Madeline took in a breath. Julian imagined her head tilting against the wall, the luscious arch of her throat exposed. If she kept talking, he wouldn't last long. *Keep talking, Mads...*

"I want to see that beautiful hand at work, Special Agent Worthy. Stroke for your job. Stroke for my beautiful cunt."

Julian broke into a sweat. She never called him *Special* Agent. His hand slid up his thick shaft to the tip, gathering wetness in his palm and smoothing it back down his length. The pleasure was immediate and intense.

"Good boy. Now bring your face to my pussy, but keep your mouth closed. Do you understand?"

"Yes," he moaned.

"Yes, *Ma'am*," Madeline corrected.

"Yes, Ma'am." Julian thought it was impossible for his cock to get any harder, but he was an iron bar. A granite pillar of willing flesh.

"That's right. Now take a deep breath. Relax. Smell my sweet sex while you stroke that cock for me. That's it. That's right. Faster.

160

Good. I'm going to spread my legs wide, and you're going to bury your face in my beautiful pussy. You're going to lick when I want you to lick. Suck when I want you to suck. You're going to pleasure me the way I deserve to be pleasured."

Julian could picture it perfectly. Her desk. Her office. The grit of woven carpet under his knees. The gray briefs gathered around his thighs constricted movement, but it was a delightful boundary. Was it Spearman or Madeline above him? It should be Spearman. But the scent in his nose was Madeline's, remembered from when he'd barged in on her ghost sex dream.

"I didn't tell you to stop!"

He *had* stopped, confused by his dual arousal for the two women. He moved his hand again, a surge of pleasure pushing him toward orgasm.

"Lick me, Jules. Slide your tongue up my slit. Gather my wetness and coat my clit. Yes. Flick your tongue along the sides. Stroke yourself faster!"

Julian stroked faster.

"I'm grabbing fistfuls of your hair in both of my hands, jamming your face into my cunt. I'm riding you. I don't care if you can't breathe. My pleasure is all that matters. You are my fuck toy. Nothing but a tongue and cock for me to use."

Julian's hand pumped. He wanted to please her, needed the command in her voice. Pressure moved from his center, edging toward an inevitable release, building...

"Suck my clit," Madeline commanded. "Harder. Suck it like you mean it. Work your tongue on the underside. Yes, like that!"

The idea of being sensually dominated was all Julian needed to push him to the edge. His orgasm pushed outward. So close. But he needed to hold it. Needed for her to tell him when to cum. Instead, she pushed him higher.

"When you cum, I'm going to make you clean it up," she murmured, voice thick and breathless. "Make you lick it off my leg."

Julian was disintegrating from the delicious torture. Her smooth, soft skin under his tongue. Her pink pussy taunting him. Moaning, exultant, and helpless, his body tightened unbearably. "Yes, Ma'am!" he groaned.

"You're going to give me what I want now. Aren't you, Julian?"

He struggled to retain his last vision of Spearman's sleek thighs and Madeline's temptress voice, but they'd both ended up in his fantasy office. The image spiked his pleasure, and Julian went over the edge, the heat of it breaking him open from the inside out.

"Good boy," Madeline moaned. "Give it to me!"

For long seconds, the grip of climax—and sharing it with Madeline—took his body and mind and wrung them like a wet towel. Pleasure seeped from his skin, jetted from his body, and raced through his muscles like lightning.

The electric shield keeping him out pulsed once, soft and warm, as if acknowledging his offering, and vanished. Almost boneless, he folded over the threshold, giving a silent thanks he had decent aim.

Madeline sank down, leaning on the wall beside him. Concern pursed her lips, but her eyes were alit with passion. Like she wanted to strip off her pants and join him for round two.

Jesus. Give him a two-hour nap and a sandwich, he'd make sure she was satisfied.

He caught her eye. Fire burned in his cheeks. The flush wasn't completely from embarrassment. He opened his mouth to tell her he'd never felt so close to someone, so safe sharing his secrets, and so emptied of his past.

But he couldn't say that. He'd already shared too much. And he had a gut feeling the cave wasn't finished with him. There would be more tests to come, ones that required all his strength, if not his manhood.

CHAPTER FOURTEEN

MADELINE

The echoes of Julian's orgasm rolled around the cave like tribal drums beating at the zenith of a ritual. They shook Madeline's body as if she, too, had been pleasured. There wasn't voice or direction left in her throat, just a slow and heavy throb, a subtle satisfaction of a job well-done.

Who knew script 22 would come in handy all these years later?

Julian leaned against the inside of the archway in stunned relaxation. She shouldn't look, but she looked, and...nice dick. Well-shaped. Stocky. For a brief moment, Madeline let herself consider all the things she could do with that cock. *Sex magic*, she reminded herself, *equals sex-starved. Stick to the plan.*

She knew better than to ask him how he was feeling, but wanted to offer some kind of aftercare. Rummaging in her pocket, she pulled out a rainbow bandana and pressed it into his hand. "On behalf of the female architects, the cave is happy with your donation."

He snickered, then laughed. Madeline joined him, giggling like a guilty teenager.

Julian wiped at his hand. "And I said *you* were noisy."

This prompted a fresh round of giggles.

While Julian righted his pants, Madeline studied the uterus chamber. She barely needed her flashlight; the room glowed a rosy pink. The walls were just as smooth as the tunnel but had been carved into rolling swells and dips. Skimming her hand along the rock, Madeline could almost believe she was in the ocean. Floating, suspended, at home.

"Wow," she murmured.

"You're not bad yourself," Julian said in jest, checking his gun was securely holstered.

Smirking, she crossed the small room and examined the archway. To go by the map, the tunnel from the library had been a fallopian tube, which led them to an ovary. That meant they were in the uterus, and Madeline was surprised it was empty of any relics or altars. The exit arch had the same shimmery force field, but this one was opaque. She squinted but couldn't make out what lay beyond the barrier, and didn't want to touch it, for fear of getting zapped.

"What do you think the next room wants as tribute? Blood?" Madeline trailed her flashlight around the archway and found the next symbol, this one of three interlocking circles. "No time like the present. Ready?"

Julian tugged at the crotch of his pants, squared his shoulders, and nodded. "Ready."

Madeline pressed the carving.

The veil turned transparent. The main chamber, what Julian had deemed the vagina room and where Constance had died, came into view. In the center stood the empty altar. Spearman stood beside it talking with a tall, striking man.

She and Julian dropped into a crouch and clicked off their flash-lights.

The man turned in their direction. Madeline froze, an inner radar pinging in recognition. He had thick black hair and powerful shoulders. Egyptian or Middle Eastern features. Slashing eyebrows were followed by a long, straight nose, and a sensuously full bottom lip. He was dressed like Spearman, but his suit had the flare and cut of old money. Had she seen this guy before? Maybe loitering with the crew outside of Constance's house?

Julian leaned into her ear. "That's Shadow Man, the guy I saw staring at you near Desmond's statue."

The agents didn't act like they'd seen or heard anything, much less become aware they were being watched. Without thinking, Madeline stood and moved in front of the veil.

Julian's hand gripped her wrist, tugging. "What are you doing?" he hissed.

"Watch," Madeline whispered, using his hold to pull him up beside her. She waved at the dark figures, and they continued to ignore her. "They can't see us. The cave wants *us* to be here, not them."

There was a pause, then Julian said, "Just for the record, this time you're the one convincing me of supernatural hooey."

She rolled her eyes and listened, aware Julian pulsed like a heating blanket at her back.

Shadow Man said, "I told you to keep the therapist here."

Spearman's stiff posture suggested she couldn't bear standing next to her boss. "I took Da Vinci's statement as protocol dictates, but she was adamant about returning to her clients. If I kept pushing, she might have gone to the press. I didn't think it was worth the risk."

"The portal closes at dawn. We lost the only viable female who could act as a surrogate." He paused, his velvety voice dripping with menace. "Unless you're volunteering?"

Julian's body coiled into a mass of muscle, ready to lunge through the veil. Madeline clutched his arm, her breath stumbling to a halt.

Spearman lifted her chin. "Da Vinci is a civilian. I thought our directive is limiting exposure until we know what we're dealing with—"

"What you think is irrelevant," Shadow Man said.

Even though she believed they were protected, Madeline edged backwards. The man hadn't moved a muscle, but he was so *powerful*.

Shadow Man tucked his hands in his pockets, but there was nothing casual in his stance. "If I haven't made myself abundantly clear, let me do so now. Your first *directive* was to keep Agent Worthy out of this. Your second *directive* was to keep Da Vinci here so we could monitor the phenomenon now that Mrs. Hansford is gone. You've failed me. Twice."

Spearman wasn't backing down. "Julian is off the case. And Da Vinci is a bystander we're sworn to protect. Neither of those are failures."

"I understand you favor Agent Worthy, Spearman. You've done a good job hiding your history, but don't forget, I know what happened at Slate Hill. What do you think will happen if the incident becomes public?"

Spearman was smart enough to keep her mouth shut.

"Disobey my orders again, and you risk being reassigned." He offered her an ominous smile. "You know what that means."

"It's against regulations," Spearman protested. "You've already blunted enough of my memories. Another brain alteration could endanger me."

"Correct."

The threat hung between them.

Madeline felt Julian stop breathing and squeezed his arm. She had no doubt that if Shadow Man went for Spearman, Julian wouldn't be able to stop himself from attacking.

"Don't force my hand, Spearman." Shadow Man growled. "I have no objection to using deadly force if it means keeping our country protected from danger, both from within and without its borders."

Spearman stood down, but her eyes took on a flat, hard cast.

Shadow Man's smirk returned. "Pity. I was almost looking forward to disciplinary action. It's been far too long since I used my talents. At any rate, we'll make do with whatever information we can gather from the old woman's body."

Madeline gritted her teeth at hearing Constance referred to in such a way, but whoever Shadow Man was, he was playing hardball. He seemed to be following a different set of rules, none of which followed a respectful, law-abiding lifestyle.

Shadow Man's head tilted in their direction, as if listening for rats in the walls. Madeline and Julian froze.

"Sir?" Spearman asked.

Spearman and Shadow Man didn't seem to notice the shimmering veil shielding the nearby room, but Madeline thought the dark alpha knew they were there, and could almost be sure she caught the glimmer of a smile.

A sharp jab behind her eyes made her vision dim, blur around the edges. The stone walls vanished. As if in a dream, Madeline had the image of Shadow Man standing before her, shirtless. Gasping, she tried to turn and run, but couldn't look away from his face, his eyes. She was as naked as a sacrificial offering, and they weren't in a cave. They were in a...cathedral? A huge stained-glass medallion emblazoned them with color.

She didn't know him, much less how he looked out of that tight designer suit, but god, his wide chest was corded with muscle. The sprinkling of black hair made her palms itch with the urge to touch. And his cold, sarcastic expression had changed, become hypnotic with secrets he wanted to share. Nothing shielded his predator gaze from looking at every part of her. She hated being so exposed...but she also loved it.

What the actual *hell*? Now she was hallucinating?

In her vision, he didn't speak, but her name slid like a serpent down her spine.

Madeline...

A wave of weakness—and lust—pooled in her belly. The feeling was mirrored by the heat in his charcoal black eyes.

Eyes that transformed to glowing red embers.

Back in the cave, Shadow Man turned away. The spell broken, Madeline would have stumbled had Julian not caught her shoulder. He opened his mouth, but she shook her head.

"Lock this place up," Shadow Man said, waving a hand at the workers coming down the stairwell. "We'll return in the morning with a crew to collect the artifacts and bulldoze the house to the ground."

Spearman shook her head and followed behind her boss. In a few moments, the vagina room settled into silence.

Julian relaxed behind her. Madeline didn't move, too afraid whatever she'd just imagined wasn't a trick of adrenaline. Julian had gotten his release, but her sex drive was at a record high. The way Shadow Man said her name, like it was a promise, a command, a warning.

"Madeline, you can't stay here." Julian gripped her arm. "As soon as we're sure they're gone, we need to get you off the property."

Her senses staggered with information overload. She caught his sleeve, her fingers twisting the fabric. "Did that creep say 'surrogate'? As in surrogate *mother*?"

The look on Julian's face didn't help.

She swallowed. "There really is a government conspiracy. I didn't want to believe you..."

"I don't blame you. It's a lot to swallow, pardon the pun."

Snorting, she reached a shaking hand to steady herself against the archway. "If it's the right person, swallowing is great."

Julian's body tensed. Aside from his tactical training, his body was as charged and ready to go as if he hadn't blessed the threshold minutes before. Had it only been minutes? His recovery was impressive. She bet he wasn't a speed racer in the sheets. Unless she impersonated Spearman's demeanor and dressed in a sexy skirt.

Not a great thought. Her fingers curled into the stone, found grooves, and pressed the intrusive thought away.

A cloud of green light swirled around them, solidified, and formed an imprint of a tall man with curly hair.

"Holy shit," Julian snapped and got between Madeline and the apparition. His pistol was out before she could blink.

They were still alone...but not really. The man was dressed in old-fashioned clothes much like the picture they'd seen of Desmond in Constance's photo album.

Shocked, Madeline snatched her hand off the archway, and the transparent man disappeared.

Julian turned to her. "What did you do?"

"I don't know." She found the mark in the stone. The etching was vaguely familiar, geometric and celestial, as if it was a representation of a star constellation far away. She touched it again.

The green vapor hologram reappeared. Desmond, transparent but fleshy, spoke to them like a futuristic letter from a dead era.

"Hello, friends." Deep and resonant, his voice was undoubtedly similar to the man they'd heard with Constance. "If you've found this chamber and activated this message, my beloved Constance has left her human body. I cannot tell you everything—my people forbid it—but I can show you the path that led me to this place and how I came to be Desmond Mason."

Madeline was speechless, entranced by the projection. Julian, equally dumbstruck, circled the glowing man. He even reached out a hand and let it pass through the man's back.

"Julian!" Madeline squeaked.

"It didn't hurt. No protective shield."

Desmond's recording didn't seem to mind. Madeline felt like he was smiling directly at her, and for a moment, she remembered a ghostly tongue lapping between her thighs.

First Julian. Then Shadow Man. Now she lusted after a spectral recording? She sighed in resignation. Water everywhere and not a drop to drink.

The apparition shifted into an amorphous cloud. Inside the cloud, Madeline saw an interstellar movie of planets, asteroids, and galaxies.

As if they travelled on a spacecraft, the point of view entered The Milky Way. They sped past the pale blue opal of Uranus. Saturn's rocky rings of glitter made Madeline gasp in delight. Julian passed a hand through Jupiter's unending storm. Finally, they slowed at Mars' iron-colored exterior. Over the red planet's horizon, Earth came into view.

The oceanic magnificence sent a pang of wonder through Madeline's heart. This was her home. But maybe not to everyone on Earth.

Damn. This was not the time to entertain the concept of extraterrestrials.

The galaxy disappeared. Desmond stood in the center of a circle of people wearing the same late 1800s style clothing. He was speaking to them earnestly, but they shook their heads. One by one, their ghost forms vanished until he was a solitary figure looking around a field that would one day become Mason's Hole.

The next image was that of a young woman, Desmond's wife, Lula. She was young and vibrant, smiling and holding out her hand to him. No longer alone, Desmond's fingers curled around hers. The vision shifted, and Desmond was swinging a small boy into the air while the woman sat on a blanket, clapping her hands.

A happy family.

The next projection wasn't of people, but of the house he'd built and the mines he'd opened. The Butterfly Pea symbol appeared everywhere. Figures of employees came and went. A map hovered over the granite floor, and Madeline watched the formation of the town. Tiny beacons of green light shot up from the ground. Mine entrances, like the town hall and the library.

There was pride in the picture. Success. Purpose. And then it came crashing down. Lula and the boy dead, Desmond, standing over their graves. Alone again, he stood in the living room he'd built for his family and lifted a vial to his mouth. Clutching his stomach, he fell forward. His body remained, but another, lighter shade floated above the inert form.

Desmond's ghost.

"No fucking way," Madeline murmured, but it wasn't out of disbelief as much as the engrossing home movie.

Ghost Desmond stood in front of his house, looking up at the night sky. The planets and stars revolved in a kaleidoscope of streaks and tails, showing the passing of time. He was reaching up, summoning the heavens like he was about to levitate off the planet, but a 1970s Chevy Impala came down the driveway.

Constance, her husband, and a young Roland climbed out of the car. The boys didn't seem to notice Desmond, but Constance sensed his presence. She put a hand to her throat, gave a little laugh. She knew she was home.

Madeline jumped when Desmond's voice returned.

"As you can see, my people left, but I could not. There was too much to enjoy, too much to protect. They forbade me from taking another human form, but allowed me to stay with Constance as long as I created a portal."

The home movie lingered on Constance sitting in front of the fireplace, dancing with a young Roland in the kitchen, pulling weeds in the garden.

"If you are watching this, you are Constance's friend, and therefore mine. There is much I would like to share with humanity, with you, as a gift for showing me great love and great pain, two emotions my kind has distanced themselves from by stepping away from their corporeal bodies."

Julian shot her a glance. Was he gauging her bullshit meter? Waiting for her to throw up her hands and declare, *Beam me up, Scotty*? But he just shrugged, as if to say, this was out of his depth, too.

Desmond's voice took on a wistful note. "We hoped to produce offspring, the best of our two worlds, but it was not meant to be. Now that Constance is gone, my time has come to an end. This portal will remain open while the celestial bodies are aligned. It is my hope you make the most of this opportunity."

His body reappeared to stand directly in front of Madeline.

She jumped back, bumping against the cavern wall, but her hand was glued to the etching.

Broad-chested and virile, his maleness transcended her definition of "ghost." The man was hot, and his expression said he knew how to use his powers.

As if reading her mind, Desmond smiled. "We are not so different, you and I. Maybe you will join me and find out for yourself."

The green glow faded and disappeared.

Julian let out a long breath, then his face nearly split with a grin of excitement.

She held up a hand. "This is not the time to say 'I told you so.'"

"Me? Never. But come on, Mads. That was unbelievable. I wish I could have met him, talked to him." He took his cellphone from his pocket. "I'll try to record the message. Touch it again!"

Sighing, Madeline touched the etching. Nothing happened. Frowning, Julian traced the carved stone with a fingertip. No effect.

"He said he knew we were Constance's friends," he grumbled. "Considering the technology, I bet the species could manipulate the conditions of not just the room, but whoever is in it."

Madeline shivered, apprehension dispelling the wonder of the home movie. "There was a moment I thought he was looking right at me."

"All the more reason to get you out of here."

Madeline gave a shaky laugh. "I didn't get the impression Desmond's—" she choked on the word "—ghost wanted to hurt me."

Julian shook his head. "It all goes back to that first night. The dream you had that wasn't quite a dream. I think Desmond was taking you for a test drive."

She cleared her throat. "To see if we were compatible?"

He shrugged. "Stranger things have happened."

"And this is the last night of the planetary alignment?"

"According to what Otto said, yes."

Madeline ran a hand over her eyes. They needed to leave, yes, but the urge to stay kept her feet frozen. "This is so bizarre. Maybe I'm caught in a dream right now."

Julian's gaze was drawn back to the vagina room's arch. His breath came in a quick inhale. "I think I'm going to get my wish."

She squinted, her body going rigid. Whatever she'd wanted to do and thought she understood faded like a cloud of vapor.

"That's Desmond," she breathed, and stepped forward as if pulled by a gravitation field. "He's standing by the altar...waiting for me."

CHAPTER FIFTEEN

JULIAN

Desmond was definitely standing by the altar, and he wasn't alone. Gathered around it were a dozen figures, each diaphanous, incorporeal, and nude. Their perfect human-looking bodies glowed with an inner green light. At the head of the gathering, Desmond chanted in an unknown language, hands raised to the ceiling.

In a trance, Madeline stepped toward the archway.

"Madeline," Julian hissed.

She didn't look at him. Didn't react to his voice.

He grabbed her wrist.

She tried to tug free, and her foot passed through the veil. On the other side, her shoe, sock, and pant leg disappeared, as if the portal had erased her clothes.

Julian tugged harder. "Stop!"

She didn't acknowledge him. Didn't turn. Instead, she pulled Julian with strength he hadn't guessed she possessed, dragging him through the opening.

Over the threshold, his body was slammed with tendrils of sensual energy. He shouldn't *want* to see her body—her glorious, naked body—but he did. His cock sprang to attention with no pants to constrain it. Where was his flashlight? His gun?

Like Madeline, crossing the barrier had melted his clothes away without so much as a tingle.

"This is dangerous. We shouldn't be here."

His words lacked conviction. The sensual vibe in the room was a hundred times more intense than it had been in the tunnels. Time slowed. Julian's cock twitched in sync with his pounding heart. And his heartbeat thumped to the cadence of invisible drums.

Unearthly voices chanted with the spectral music. Music of which Julian's body was a part. The chanting grew slowly, steadily faster. His fragmented resolve vanished as his eyes traced the curve of Madeline's exposed thigh.

Yes. No. But, yes.

The beat throbbing through the rocks shook Julian to his core. It was Slate Hill all over again. The driving need in his center. The irresistible tug of the entities circled around the altar.

The rational part of him resisted, still trying to pull Madeline back. But her naked splendor delighted his eyes. The full globes of her ass bunched as she moved closer to the paranormal beings.

Cool air stirred the hair on his chest, the taut expanse of his belly, and thighs. He should stop. Let go of her. Go back and get his gun. But he longed to caress the soft skin of her arms, her back. The primal part of him allowed her to tug him toward the altar.

He barely glanced at the glowing beings, his attention drawn to the giant slab of stone. The secret part of him that wrestled with wanting Madeline roared in excitement. Maybe he could join her on the altar. Make love to her, tenderly, passionately.

No, goddamn it. *No.*

His voice, shaky and unsure, rang out between the thumps of the cave's heartbeat, this time pleading, "Madeline!"

175

The ghosts circling the altar moved aside for them.

Desmond smiled and motioned Madeline forward.

She shook Julian free at last. Then quickened her steps to reach the apparition.

"No!" Julian shouted.

A flash of movement caught his attention. A dark figure surged through the door leading to Constance's hidden staircase.

Roland ran straight for Julian, his lip lifted in a snarl.

"What the—" was all Julian had time to say before the lawyer slammed into the center of his body, knocking them both to the dusty stone floor.

Pain blossomed in Julian's back and elbows. Their hard-muscled flesh slid against one another as they grappled for advantage. Roland's leg curled around Julian's hip. Julian heaved his body to the side, threw the huffing man off, and rolled to a crouch.

"Why won't you just—" Roland swung wildly at Julian "—go home?"

"What the fuck are you doing here, Roland?" He chanced a glance toward Madeline, but the bodies of the ghosts surrounding the altar blocked his view.

The distraction proved a mistake.

"Meddling government prick!" Roland yelled and landed on Julian again.

Breath rushing from his chest, they tumbled to the ground. Julian's head spun with pressure and adrenaline. The weight of the angry man on top of him, the thrumming of the cave, the sensitivity of Julian's persistent erection, it was as if the cave itself whispered, *Let go. Give up.*

But this time Julian had something he didn't have in Slate Hill, a growing connection with Madeline, and the knowledge of what they'd do to her if he didn't fight.

He worked a hand free and went for Roland's neck.

Roland responded in kind, grabbing Julian's throat. His other hand clamped around Julian's wrist, trying to break the claw-like grip on his windpipe.

Spots appeared at the edge of Julian's vision. He fell back on his training, let himself relax, then used Roland's weight against him, and arched upward in an explosive bolt. Roland flipped over, landing on his back.

Julian was quick to straddle his chest. His fist clenched, drew back, and slammed into the side of Roland's head. In his triumph, he didn't block Roland's answering blow in time. It caught him in the shoulder, sending a spasm of numbing pain down his arm.

But Julian didn't budge from his dominant position. Masculine prowess ignited every spark of his body. He hadn't wanted to hit the guy, but since he was there...

Julian landed another punch to Roland's head, aiming for the sweet spot of his temple.

Roland's eyes went glassy, his head lolling on the gritty cave floor.

Julian climbed off Roland to regroup, panting, hands on his knees.

Dazed but not out, Roland rolled to the side and pushed up to his knees.

"Fuck," Julian grunted. "Why won't you stay down?"

"You didn't try to save my mother." Roland snarled through gritted teeth. "You let this happen to her. Just like you're letting it happen to your friend. You're just like the government goons I had to sneak past to find you. Complicit."

Roland's words hit Julian harder than any physical blow. He *had* let this happen to Constance. He *had* let this happen to Spearman in Slate Hill. He'd tried to stop it. All of it. Now Roland was stopping him from doing his job. Protecting the only person left to protect. Madeline.

"I tried to save your mother," Julian said. "And now I'm trying to save Madeline."

Roland glanced at the circle of ghostly figures. His fists dropped a notch.

Julian could swing now. End the fight. But maybe words could end it too, turning Roland from enemy to ally.

"The things that killed your mother are right there!" Julian pointed. "Fucking her therapist!" It wasn't exactly true. But it might be true enough to turn Roland's anger toward the altar. "Help me stop them."

The confused lawyer looked from Julian to the circle of beings, but his anger was too deep. "And whose fault is that?"

The kick Roland delivered to Julian's chest caught him so completely by surprise, it sent him crashing into the ring of spirits. He bounced off a glowing woman's side. She bumped into the man next to her in the circle. Gasps erupted from the nude figures.

The altar broke Julian's fall. Looking up, he came face to face with Desmond.

The handsome man appeared not to see him. His gaze fixed on Madeline, laying spread eagle beneath him.

"Madeline!" Julian shouted. "It's a trap! Don't let him fuck you!"

He had just enough time to register Madeline's smoldering gaze before Roland crashed into him, yanking him away from the altar. The punch connected with Julian's cheek, snapping his head to the right.

A cry of passion echoed through the room. Madeline's voice.

"Listen to her!" Julian shouted at Roland. "Help her before it's too late. Don't you want to get revenge for your mother?"

Confusion clouded Roland's features as Julian's words penetrated his rage.

"I don't want to fight you." Now or never, Julian had to take a chance. He backed off and spread his hands, palms out. "Desmond took your mom. Not me."

Again, Roland looked from Julian to the alien apparitions.

"They did it," Julian repeated, his voice calm, earnest. "Please, help me save Madeline."

With a growl of resentment, Roland gave Julian a curt nod, then crashed into the circle of humanoids.

Julian did likewise, shoving at the glowing green forms screening the moaning Madeline from his gaze. The thrumming vibration in the vagina room increased, throbbing and insistent. But the apparitions weren't interested in a brawl.

When Julian stumbled punch-drunk between the beings and the stone edifice, the deep sexual energy seeped into his lowered defenses. A wave of erotic pleasure drowned his reason, made him desperate to touch and be touched. To fuck.

The woman beside him, the same one he'd bumped into, leaned into him, running her hands over his back. She slid a hand down his glistening skin, following his happy trail to the confused member swinging between his thighs.

On the altar, Madeline wrapped her long, sexy legs around Desmond's back.

Julian wanted to shout, but his voice came out as a whisper. "Madeline...." Dizzy and aroused, he shook his head. If he could reach the platform, he could throw Desmond aside and climb atop her himself.

To protect her? Make love to her? He didn't know.

Julian's eyes sought Roland. The ghosts ran their hands all over the angry lawyer, stroking his cock, humping his sides. Preventing him from reaching Desmond.

The sex magic, and the glowing woman's knowledgeable fingers stroking his flesh, prevented him from moving. Making the air a thick viscous thing he couldn't swim through.

It was too late. He'd lost.

Just like Slate Hill, Julian couldn't fight the heady delight duping him into believing there was anything he could do but surrender to pleasure.

Chapter Sixteen

MADELINE

How she got into the vagina room and standing in front of the altar, Madeline didn't know. Didn't care. The second she saw Desmond, the dream she had the first night sleeping in Mason's Manor came flooding back.

The man in front of her was as familiar as a friend, as exciting as a rollercoaster. She remembered the broad, well-muscled back. His large hands, strong, yet gentle, handling her as if she were water and he a magician that could change the course of a river. The voice crooning encouragement promised a satisfaction that had no limits.

Her clothes were gone, and she was vaguely aware Julian called her name. It was fine. He could watch. Hell, he could join in.

Naked, free, unashamed, this was her true form.

Desmond glowed a bright, soothing green, and when her eyes met his, they glittered like emeralds. Madeline remembered the pleasure he'd given her and longed for Desmond's weight on top of her, the hot glide of his fingers stroking between her legs. The need to be touched tightened her nipples, then dropped like a spoonful of honey to collect hot and slippery between the plump folds of her labia.

Desmond reached for her, and she glanced at her hand. It was glowing red, pulsing with the same magic that had been swirling around her for days.

What was going on?

That is your power, Madeline, Desmond's voice said in her mind.

Yes. She had feminine, creative, volcanic power coursing through her veins. But what were those distracting sounds in the background? It sounded like a bar fight. Did they matter? No. Nothing bad could happen if Desmond was there. He'd take care of her like he took care of Constance, and she'd had a beautiful life. Hadn't she?

Madeline.

As if reading her thoughts, Desmond smiled knowingly. He didn't need to speak. His mouth was meant for other things.

She was dimly aware of the glowing beings chanting a wordless frequency. Their energy was encouraging, but underneath the praise, they were hungry for the coupling. They wanted to see it, hear it, and share in the pleasure coursing through her. Madeline didn't blame them, but a ripple of unease stilled her hand where it hovered over Desmond's palm.

She was so close to touching him. Being touched by him. Her hesitation lasted half a breath.

Madeline gave him her hand and gasped. Pleasure, bright as a new star, sharp as a honed blade, bloomed where green and red light merged. When he pulled her up the small stone platform, they were bathed by an ethereal spotlight. She didn't want to look away from his eyes, but couldn't help notice the planes and angles of his beautiful body. His dark hair made tight spirals to his shoulders. The width of his chest tapered into a narrow waist. His cock was long and thick, pulsing in anticipation.

Her pussy clenched in helpless want. She'd made him hard.

More than hard, he murmured. *I've dreamed of you, as you have dreamed of me.*

Madeline wanted the dream again. All of it, with no interruptions.

His mouth met hers, soft lips molding, licking, opening. Her breasts nestled against the firm muscles of his chest. One big palm came up to cup her, his thumb dancing along the edge of her nipple. The tight bud tingled but longed for his mouth's attention. He obliged, ducking his head and taking the straining nub to suckle.

Another surge of pleasure had her melting over his arm, drugged but not heavy or helpless. If anything, she was floating. In his arms, they levitated from the cold stone. Their twined bodies flowed over the surface of the altar.

A call came from far away. "Madeline!"

What about Julian? She'd made him cum earlier. Using her voice to arouse him, edge him, she'd wanted to make him lose control. But not in a bad way, never a bad way. The memory of his release made her ache with need. Longing. Dissatisfaction. Where was he? She wanted him with her.

But she was with Desmond, where she was supposed to be. He was going to quench the unrelenting thirst of a lifetime's dissatisfaction at the hands of lesser lovers.

They could not possibly understand what you crave, darling, he said as long fingers slid between her thighs, skimming her clitoris. *But I do. I'll give it to you. I promise.*

Madeline's skin flushed with heat, and her heart swelled with gratitude. Desmond understood. But so did Julian, and she didn't want to leave him out. He'd already been hurt before, and whoever messed with him, they weren't like Desmond.

Turning her head, she scanned Desmond's friends. What was their deal? Voyeurs? Beyond them, two male bodies rolled over the cave floor. At first Madeline thought they were having sex too, and a momentary pang pricked her heart at the thought of Julian being with someone else.

This isn't about him, Madeline, Desmond said, kissing his way down her belly. *In this place, you are the goddess, the mother. Nothing is as important as you. Wouldn't it be nice to forget about those who cannot see your value?*

Dizzy, she nodded and was rewarded by Desmond's fingers slipping inside her. The relief spread, the desire tightened. Her toes curled even as her thighs parted.

You're very wet. I can make you wetter. Hotter. Higher.

One hand slid up her back, and the other over the blade of her hip. It followed the curve of her bottom and dipped between the cleft. His fingers were replaced by the weight of his shaft pushing against her. The tip was bathed in her dew, but he didn't enter.

Do you want all of me inside you?

God, yes. She was going crazy wanting it.

Desmond—ghost, spirit, apparition, whatever he was—wasn't completely solid or completely transparent. But he was fully erect. Hard dick usually led to ejaculate…with ghost cum? The thought of impregnation nipped at her excitement like a rabid dog. Julian had been used in such a way.

Desmond's mouth switched to her other breast, tenderly lapping before drawing upon the puckered berry. Madeline almost lost her train of thought again. This was not the time to worry about conspiracy theories. Or spooky vibes in an imaginary haunted house. Or…Julian?

Was this the time to think about Julian? Yes. He knew about all this paranormal shit, not her, and how to uncover the secrets of Mason's Hole. Most importantly, he knew how to make her feel like more than just a vessel for sexual energy.

Where *was* Julian?

As if he'd heard his name being called, Julian's voice cut through the fog of lust.

"Madeline! Wake up."

But she didn't want to wake up. She'd been on high alert since childhood. Being dragged into a cult, knowing something was wrong, *very* wrong, with the people who called themselves her family, she'd fought like a hellcat to save Hatty. Even now, it wasn't fair to be awake and worried. If she didn't keep her guard up at all times, bad people would steal what was left of her sister's innocence.

Desmond's voice followed in her head. *You can do whatever you want, Madeline. Have whatever you want. If you stay with me here, there will be no more rage, no more loneliness, no more doubt.*

"How?" she whispered.

Shall I show you? I'll give you a taste, just a little, and you'll know what to do.

His cock was right there, sliding against her clit, back and forth, while his fingers did other things to her ass. God, she was empty, so empty! He would fill her completely and then some. "Yes," she breathed. "Please."

His mouth returned to hers, and his hardness passed the swollen folds of her nether lips, sliding inside deep and slow. The coils of tension buffeting her for the last two days condensed. She writhed around him, lifting her hips to take more, and dug her nails into his back.

Desmond offered a husky growl of approval and gave her what she demanded, pulling back, then surging forward and grinding into her wet pussy.

Madeline screamed into his mouth and came hard, her body a greedy, milking fist. It was a good orgasm, much needed, but it only freed her from the feminine hunger living just beneath her rational façade.

Her body squeezed at him, demanding movement, but Desmond gathered her to his chest and laughed softly.

That was only the start, beloved.

She'd always wanted to be teased and made to cum while her lover waited and watched. How did Desmond know?

His body withdrew, pushed in again, and her nerve endings exploded in a cacophony of fireworks. He fit her perfectly, and the gentle thrust of his cock against her clit stirred the need again. Another orgasm rose in tandem with the fantasy of staying in Mason's Manor. She could live in the country, stay with Desmond, and be worshipped every day for the rest of her life. There would never be another lonely night when she woke aching, empty, and twitching from a hunger that seemed more than human.

Yes, Desmond whispered. *I see it.* His hands tenderly smoothed her hair, but his body trembled in excitement. *Do you know how special you are, Madeline? You were meant to be here, with me.*

His hips quickened their pace. Madeline whimpered, clutching his shoulders, wanting more.

Give yourself to me, Desmond groaned. *Le petit mort. I want you, now and forever.*

Forever.

The weighty word pierced her fog of rapture. Forever was a long time. Like, commitment central. Madeline didn't believe in happily-ever-after. Never had. And as much as she appreciated the thought of a 'little death,' fucking in an underground cave was too damn close to real death.

What exactly did her ghost lover want?

Reading her hesitation, Desmond's hand slid between their bodies. His fingers found her clit again. They pulled at her, stroked and circled, as the waves of his hunger made his cock bigger and harder.

The delicious sensation had her wondering if his cum would be smooth as stardust milk. Sweet like pineapples. Sharp as a ceremonial knife. Surely, his seed would cleanse her of the past. There would be no going back to a normal life, dating normal men, always wondering why she couldn't settle down and just be happy. She'd never think of her childhood again, never worry about her sister and what the damn cult did to her, never worry that her deepest, darkest desire was to be the center in which chaos sprang.

And the price for this gift? She'd never have a human child.

Madeline didn't know how she knew, but the knowledge burned like the flesh glowing green beneath her hands. Maybe it was for the best. She wouldn't be a good mother. Couldn't be. Not with her past, what she'd seen, what she'd done.

You can have a child, Madeline, Desmond murmured against her lips. *I can give you my child.*

A tidal pull of pleasure collected in the base of her womb at the thought. She could take Desmond and fulfill this endless void of want. All she had to do was nod, and he would cum. Her power would squeeze him dry, and inside her, a new world free of pain and starvation, terror and war, would form.

CHAPTER SEVENTEEN

JULIAN

J ulian ached from the hand-to-hand with Roland, but adrenaline kept the real pain at bay. The ghost woman in Desmond's
entourage placed his hand on her breast. An erect nipple solidified
under his palm. How could she be both corporeal and not? Ghosts
were supposed to be just an impression of psychic energy left behind
from a tragic death. So this woman wasn't a ghost? She was something else. A demon, an alien?

Julian spared her a glance, met a smiling, nearly transparent face,
but her details didn't sink in. Conflicting emotions, intensified by
the walls of the vagina room, illuminated the passion on the altar
in waves of pink light. Madeline was obviously enjoying herself. She
floated in Desmond's muscular arms and was anything but passive.
Moaning, arching, her legs wrapped around Desmond's svelte hips,
her body was a glorious instrument of pleasure. Any other time,
Julian would have been cheering her on simply because Desmond
was...well, a force to be reckoned with. Two hundred years of lovemaking evidently perfected pacing and prowess.

The ghost woman—wait, alien species?—God, he didn't know, but she was reaching between his legs, stroking the skin of his belly and down his happy trail, to tease his cock. Pulsing desire rose inside him, threatening to take him over, but Julian could not give in.

"No," he said aloud. "Desmond, don't do this."

He couldn't seem to free his hand from the ghost woman's breast. His fingers pinched the taut skin of her nipple without his brain sending the command. A tingle of pleasure tightened his own nipples, like they were being plucked. Were the aliens capable of telepathically sharing pleasure?

Cool. But no. Not the time.

With a supreme effort of will, he reached out with his free hand, pushing through the thick air. If only he could grab Madeline's shoulder and let her know this was wrong. It wasn't beautiful lovemaking, but an alien impregnation.

No amount of pushing or grasping allowed Julian's outstretched fingers to penetrate the invisible barrier surrounding the ritual.

"Madeline! He's going to put it inside you!"

She turned her face, meeting his eyes. A slow dreamy smile spread across her plump lips. Madeline's tongue swept her bottom lip, leaving it glistening in the dimness. She nodded, as if to say, *Finally*.

Julian shook his head. "No. He's going to put an embryo inside you. Don't let him."

Another alien woman flanking Julian's side took his chin between her strong fingers. She barely had to touch him, the magnetic force of her power was so great. His gaze landed on the succulent lips leaning into him, parting, brushing his gaping mouth with hints of moonbeams and electricity. Julian shuddered as the hand around his cock began to stroke him.

Oh Christ, he was almost at the edge, and didn't know how much longer he could resist. Madeline. Think about Madeline. He was responsible for her. She was in danger. Where was Roland? Maybe he could help.

Julian drug his eyes to the other side of the sex circle. Nope. Roland stood locked in the embrace of ravenous beings. The glowing specters ran their hands over his body, squeezing, cupping, caressing. He was getting the full work-up just like Julian.

The first ghost woman he'd knocked into moved in front of Julian, blocking his path to Madeline. He could only catch glimpses of her over the apparition's shoulder.

Lost in the sensation of two pairs of hands stroking his shaft, cupping his balls, and exploring the cleft of his ass, Julian ground his teeth together. He was so fucking hard. Moisture leaked from his tip and expert hands spread it over his length.

A moan escaped his lips.

Focus. He had priorities. What were they? The fucking altar was a portal to another world. A clandestine government conspiracy kept them from the truth of Constance's death. Madeline was getting properly railed, and he wasn't the one doing the railing.

Julian managed to turn his head and look at the writhing couple. Glimpsed through a gap in the wanton flesh in front of him, Madeline's soft skin rippled as Desmond drove into her. A beatific smile played across her full lips.

But she was stretching out her hand to him.

"Julian..."

Her voice cut through his ecstasy like a knife. It seemed to have the same effect on his welcoming committee. They paused and pulled back, as if Madeline's needs were more important than anyone else's.

Whether by her word or her will, the invisible curtain between them lifted, allowing Julian to reach out and take her hand.

"Yes," she moaned, turning her eyes back to Desmond. "Yes."

Madeline's body writhed in quick waves. She arched her pelvis up to meet each of Desmond's thrusts. Julian heard her exultant "Le petit mort!"

The use of the French expression for orgasm cut him. The little death. Anger washed away some of Julian's lust. Desmond wasn't fucking her for love, or even desire. He didn't know who Madeline was, not really, and one thing Julian had learned over the past few days was that his partner was anything but an empty vessel.

His hand tightened around Madeline's fingers, willing her to focus on him, acknowledge—

The ghost women wouldn't be deterred. They crowded against him, stroking, guiding his free hand to their wet clefts. The scent of arousal filled his nose and emptied his brain of rational thought. The woman closest to him bent over, hands gripping the altar, presenting herself to him.

Madeline moaned her encouragement like she wanted him to be fucked the way she was being fucked, thoroughly and with great skill. And why not? Why shouldn't Julian have his pleasure, too?

The alien woman smiled over her shoulder while the others pressed their hands against his hips. The tip of his cock brushed a hot, wet entrance.

Julian froze, every muscle trembling, his attention splintered between the need to give in to the maddening lust and his promise to protect Madeline. She gripped his hand in the throes of ecstasy while her handsome lover drove deep to plant an alien seedpod.

Julian's haze dissipated. Dammit, it wasn't going to happen again. Not to him and not to Madeline. He simply wouldn't permit it. Not on *his* watch.

Shaking off the sensual hands, he sidestepped the willing feminine form in front of him. His pleasure didn't matter. He must save Madeline from the agony of having an inhuman thing cut from inside her in the back of a black truck.

"Mads, look at me."

She blinked dazedly, but a part of her sharp awareness flared to life.

His voice echoed around the room, loud, strong, and commanding. "Ask him about the egg."

"Mother of life...." she whispered, a frown marring the radiant glow of her face.

"Whose life, Madeline?" Julian asked.

That got Desmond's attention. He froze over Madeline, and his blazing emerald eyes scanned the length of Julian's body, measuring him.

Julian braced himself and twined his fingers tight with Madeline's. They'd have to rip his arm off to pull him away. Hopefully, it wouldn't be necessary. Julian didn't know what Desmond was, but he wasn't like the beings at Slate Hill. He was a protector, a creator. Maybe he could be reached.

"Is this what Constance would have wanted?" Julian asked him. Okay, maybe not the best question to ask under the circumstances, but the spell enveloping the vagina room didn't leave room for deep introspection on shared lovers.

Julian tried again. "Does she know what you're about to put inside her? Constance didn't prepare her. No one did."

Desmond's confident stare flickered with unease.

Madeline looked up at him, questioning.

"They're using you. Both of you," Julian said. "This isn't adoration. It isn't empowerment. The people who were in this room, who took Constance's body, will take whatever you put in Madeline."

Desmond's features went from sensual to fiery god. Julian seized the moment. He let go of Madeline's hand and shoved Desmond backward... or tried to.

Electricity crackled between Desmond's shoulder and Julian's hand. A vision came unbidden to his mind.

Madeline was sitting up in a pristine white bed. In her arms, she held a baby. The beautiful wriggling bundle had strange, alien eyes, glowing green and slit like a jungle cat. The visceral nature of the image stunned Julian. His mind reeled. Madeline wasn't just a surrogate, she was the *mother*.

Whatever Desmond had in mind, it wasn't the same as Slate Hill.

Julian had no time to work that out. Desmond grasped Julian's hand where it lay on his shoulder and squeezed.

An alien consciousness entered Julian's mind, seeking, questioning.

The full weight of memories surfaced, the veil blocking his mind blasted into tatters. The sensation of the egg entering Julian's mouth from a ghost woman's body. The bursting forth of his climax inside Spearman and the endless sensation of filling her with seed that was partially him, partially something else. The surgery truck that came to remove the implant from inside him and his altered seed from Spearman.

Desmond knew what the Slate Hill creatures were. He gave Julian the image of the object he'd swallowed. Inside the implant, thousands of tiny lifeforms squirmed, waiting for the horny eighteen-year-old Julian to splash them into every female in Slate Hill.

No words flowed through the connection between his mind and Desmond's, but clarity descended. Julian felt Desmond's disapproval of the events of Slate Hill, and his shock that there were other entities trying to use the Earth as some sort of incubator. On the same scale, Julian understood Desmond and the people in the circle weren't the same species as the ones who captured Julian.

Minds still connected, Julian and Desmond shared the intelligence that Madeline was innocent. She was meant to be a part of this but hadn't consented to birth a hybrid baby any more than Julian had consented to spread the embryos implanted in him.

Ultimately, no matter what he or Desmond wanted, the choice was hers.

CHAPTER EIGHTEEN

MADELINE

Madeline's hands relaxed their grip on Desmond's shoulders and started stroking the swollen muscles of his chest and neck. "Desmond, you're delightful. I love everything you're doing to me, but what is Julian talking about? What egg?"

Desmond's eyes found hers. The emerald depths flared bright and pure, his attention focusing beyond the wild rush of sex. The longer he looked inside her, the more Madeline got the impression he was seeing her as a person—an individual—for the first time.

I have seen your memories, Madeline. The fear. The trauma. The sacrifice, Desmond said. *I can take your pain away. Permanently.*

A ripple of pleasure cascaded from where their bodies were joined. With it, Madeline had access to his thoughts like he'd flipped a switch and let her into a sacred room. She saw them together as they were now, joined and exultant. But Desmond wasn't just talking about giving her mind-blowing sex. He meant to cleanse her like he'd done for Constance.

He continued, *Our kind do not have the same limitations as humans. If you take my seed, if you bond with me and produce an offspring, our combined power will elevate your mind to such a level, you will never doubt your cosmic significance. Our species can co-mingle. We will bring a new era to your planet.*

Never doubting her cosmic significance sounded lovely, and tempting, but she wasn't sure she even wanted children.

"No, Desmond," Julian said between his teeth.

Madeline shifted her gaze. Poor Jules. He sounded half-tortured by the hands that teased him, the mouths that licked and nibbled. But he kept a hand pressed to Desmond's pecs. If she could hear Desmond's thoughts, the skin-on-skin contact must let Julian hear the ghost alien's thoughts.

Julian said, "Our kind won't let it happen. They'll take the embryo from her. Then they'll erase her memories. And you can't stay here to protect her, can you?"

A frown marred Desmond's noble forehead. Madeline saw flashes of his long-dead wife Lula, felt the hope for a child they could never conceive, and heard the echo of Constance's voice healing him from the worst of his wounds with love and understanding.

He sighed and ran a hand through her hair. *Thousands of years ago, my kind was like yours. Flesh and blood. Bound by time. Stuck in the ravages of war, consumed by abundance, never at peace. We thought we left it all behind, and when we found Earth, we pitied you. But I met Lula and Constance. They showed me what our species sacrificed to touch immortality.*

He'd wanted a child, a living, breathing blessing joining the two species, but he could only use the portal during the planetary alignment, just as Julian had predicted. He'd been allowed to stay with Constance all these years, but after tonight, he would have to return to their world.

This was his last chance at a child of his own, and with Madeline's denial, he was losing it.

Sorrow welled up in Desmond's heart, dulling the vibrant green glow. Madeline felt the ache like it was her own. Hot tears flooded her eyes, but her hands came up and cupped his cheeks.

"I'm sorry," she whispered out loud, more herself than she'd been since she entered the chamber. "Desmond, I'm so sorry."

He seemed entranced with her tears, his eyes lingering on the tracks of silvery liquid wetting her cheeks.

Your species has never been more vulnerable. His lips brushed away the moisture. *But your partner is right. I can't stay to protect you.*

Madeline wasn't sure what they needed protection from—other than their own impatience and avarice—but she had the feeling Desmond was talking about something far beyond her scope of vision.

A flash of Shadow Man appeared in her mind.

Desmond's eyes widened, and he stiffened over her. The members of his party had the same reaction, and their hands fell away from Julian.

How do you know this man? Desmond asked.

Madeline wet her lips. "He was here, earlier. In the chamber. You didn't see him?"

Desmond took a deep breath and tenderly withdrew from her body. The murmur of anger from the green beings thrummed like a sonar ping through the cave.

Without the connection, Madeline lay naked and alone on the stone table. Desmond stood next to her, one hand on her shoulder, one hand on Julian's arm.

Looking to Madeline, Desmond picked up her palm, pressed his lips to the center. *I must leave you, beloved. I'm truly sorry I could not give you the gifts I promised.*

Madeline managed a shrug. "It's for the best. I'm not ready to become the mom of a super baby."

Desmond smiled and stroked her cheek. *You have a beautiful mind and the body of a goddess. I'm privileged to have been inside you.*

At her shoulder, Julian grumbled.

I do have one gift to share, Desmond said.

He clapped, and the others formed a circle, linking hands. The energy swirled around the chamber, and their auras brightened. Like a halo of lightbulbs experiencing a surge of electricity, intense green light blanketed the room.

When it dimmed, Constance's ghost stood in the center.

CHAPTER NINETEEN

JULIAN

Julian's mind reeled. A moment ago he'd been naked, hard as blue steel, inches from Madeline's luscious body and ready to ravish her in Desmond's stead. Now he stood fully clothed and staring at Constance's spirit. Gone was the leeching stillness of death. Her translucent form was light, inner peace radiating from her edges like a beacon.

She beamed a smile in greeting, then turned her ghostly gaze on Madeline.

Tears stood out in Madeline's eyes. "I meant to protect you."

"From what? Desmond?" the ghost asked. "He protected me. Now I'm going with him."

A thunderous crack of massive stones reverberated through the room.

Julian shot a look at the ceiling, fear rising when he saw the jagged crack. He shook off his surprise—and horniness—and cupped Madeline's arm. The back of his mind registered the fabric under his fingers. She was dressed again, too.

"Mads, this is awkward timing, but I think we've overstayed our welcome."

Madeline wasn't paying attention to him. Her eyes were riveted to Roland as he struggled to his feet outside of the circle of aliens.

Roland shook his head as if waking from a dream and focused on Constance's apparition. His voice wavered with a mix of longing and hope. "Mother?"

Constance sighed. "My sweet boy. I'm so sorry. I could have done so much better by you. I should have paid you more attention when you were a boy, but I was so lonely...." She trailed off, her eyes shifting to Desmond.

Roland rushed forward, reaching out. "I wanted to protect you from father, but I didn't know how to stop him from hurting you." He shot a look filled with confusion and bitterness at Desmond. "Then you came. You killed him."

Desmond skipped the telepathy and spoke aloud. "I did what I did to protect you and your mother. Your father's rage. His drinking. His violence. He would have killed you both in the end."

"You don't know th—"

Desmond grabbed Roland's arm.

Roland's eyes widened, and his mouth fell open. Julian was pretty sure he was getting a dose of Desmond's memories, complete with the live-action flashback of Thomas beating his wife.

"He was going to murder us," Roland mumbled, horrified.

Desmond nodded. "The night I crushed his heart was the night he planned on poisoning all of you."

Roland's eyes swung back to his mother. "Mama..."

Pebbles and dust rained down from the ceiling, dancing like pink glitter. The stone room shook as if trying to cast off its occupants. A fist-sized chunk fell, knocking Roland unconscious.

Julian winced. Roland wasn't having a great day, but it wasn't time to wallow in the feels. "This is all very touching," he said, lifting Madeline from the altar, "but we really have to go!"

"Take Roland," Constance's apparition implored. "Take my baby boy with you."

Julian hesitated, knowing Constance was right. They had to take Roland. He rushed to his erstwhile opponent, kneeled beside the man, and managed to drape the lawyer's slack weight over his shoulders in a fireman's carry. Damn, the man was heavy, and the shaking floor didn't help Julian's balance.

"Madeline, say goodbye," he said through gritted teeth.

"Constance," Madeline whispered, reaching out a hand.

"Go on," Constance made shooing motions with her diaphanous fingers. "There's nothing more I can share. Nothing you don't already know. Seeing you two together, it's good. It's *right*. You'll find the truth, and you'll help others. This is the way it's supposed to be."

An unnatural keening filled the chamber, as if some cosmic whale called for its mate from across the veil. Constance and Desmond led the procession of apparitions toward the clitoris portal. It shimmered as it had when Julian passed through after his oh-so-embarrassing orgasm. This time, though, it glowed with green energy like the alien apparitions themselves. Julian could make out nothing on the other side. It was like looking through a heavy downpour of rain, if the rain were iridescent green.

The moaning music in the chamber became discordant and cloying as the procession of ghostly figures crossed the portal's threshold. Waves reverberated through Julian's body, pooling in his stomach, making him feel sick. The light pulsing through the walls turned bloody crimson.

"Jesus, we're going to get buried alive," Julian hissed and staggered under Roland's weight.

The crunch of breaking stone thundered across the chamber. In front of them, the altar cracked and splintered. Another report of mass splitting at the seams sounded in terrible rhythm with the music.

The altar crumbled further.

Julian risked taking a hand from Roland's limp leg and grasped a chunk with a familiar symbol carved in the rock. It was the same one Madeline pointed out earlier as being part of The Disciples of Creation. He pocketed the shard of stone.

Madeline was frozen in front of him. She couldn't turn aside until Constance's form entered the portal and disappeared. A chunk of debris the size of a toaster oven fell near Julian's shoulder.

"GO!" he shouted.

Jolted into action, Madeline raced for the exit. Julian was right on her heels, lumbering for the stairwell that led up to Constance's house. The crash of a heavy boulder hitting the floor behind them broke the floor into uneven, jagged slabs.

Madeline yelled over the cacophony. "This place is coming apart!"

"No shit, Sherlock!"

More dust sprinkled down on them from above, making the air a choking hazard. Lungs heaving, Julian mounted the stairs leading to Constance's bedroom, doing his best not to drop Roland or bash the man's head on the wall for a third concussion.

The bloody light filtering through the vagina room went out, leaving them in darkness. Slowing its beat but becoming more sinister, the tribal music continued as if the otherworldly drummers had been replaced with malevolent monkeys playing a melting organ.

The stairs took forever, especially in the darkness, and Julian's legs burned like he'd run a marathon with a weight vest. Energy draining at an alarming rate, he burst through the back of Constance's closet and squeezed Roland's dead weight through the narrow opening, no longer caring if he beat the guy up a little on the way out.

He ran into Madeline's trembling back.

"Holy shit," she gasped.

Moonlight filtered through the now tattered curtains and revealed a decaying room. As Julian watched, the once-pretty floral wallpaper frayed and yellowed. Pictures fell from the walls. Glass shattered on the floor. The boards creaked and buckled underfoot. Black mold crept across a bed crumbling into ruin.

Whatever spell held the house in a perpetual state of storybook beauty was breaking along with the altar. Julian had a terrible feeling, if they stayed, they'd start decomposing, too.

"No time for sightseeing," he panted, nudging Madeline forward with Roland's limp foot.

The house shuddered, and the sickly stench of rot filled his nose. They made it to the second-floor landing, and the disintegrating handrail leaned dangerously away from safety. Lightning arced through the windows, momentarily flashing the rapid decay a ghastly blue-white. Then, an impenetrable, malevolent shadow crept along the edges of the walls.

As Julian descended the second floor, strips of wallpaper peeled free of the plaster, the moldering edges curled even as they fell onto the treads, making the stairs treacherous. Finally, they made it to the living room. The comfy couch he'd slept on the night before was a mess of lumpy, dirty stuffing. Spiderwebs covered the light fixtures. The hearth looked black and hungry, charred from unfriendly fire.

Madeline shot him a horrified look over her shoulder. "What the fuck is happening?"

Julian didn't answer in his haste to get to the front door. He nudged her aside and grasped the handle.

It came free in his hand.

"Fuck!"

The lace curtain covering the door's window shrank, yellowed, and fell. Cracks appeared in the glass, chasing the ruin across a dusty surface. Julian cast his eyes around the hall. They alighted on an umbrella stand. "Grab that and bash the window," he commanded.

Madeline scooped up the rod, slamming it through the glass. She reached through the shards and opened the door from the outside.

"Dammit," she yelped, retracting her scratched and bloody arm.

Echoes of splitting wood resounded from deep within the bowels of the house. The floor shook.

"Go, go, go!" Julian shouted.

A chunk of plaster narrowly missed Madeline's head as she made it across the threshold. Coated in dust, Julian exited, bent double under Roland's weight.

Madeline dashed down the suddenly crooked porch steps. Julian collapsed to his knees and half-rolled Roland in the driveway. His chest heaved. Rivers of sweat poured from his face. He placed a finger on Roland's neck, checking his pulse. Strong.

Good.

Lightning flashed soundlessly through the night. Julian couldn't hear the discordant music from the stone chamber, but the rumbling and creaking of Constance's home continued.

On shaky legs, he rose and joined Madeline. She stood in the driveway staring at the house, hand to her mouth, blood dripping down her arm. The cottage's flowerbeds lay dead and filled with weeds. The quaint clapboards hung askew like broken teeth. A paint-peeled shutter dropped, planks of wood cluttering the ground.

"Julian?" She limply tugged on his sleeve. "It's like the townspeople said and the newspapers reported. Mason's Manor is a *haunted house*."

He spoke unconsciously, his mind forming the conclusion as the words left his mouth. "The portal is closing. The magic that held things in stasis is ebbing. The planets are moving out of alignment."

Madeline shook her head. "I don't believe in magic...."

At her words, the rumbling faded away. The night went deadly quiet. No crickets. No birds. Nothing.

Julian whispered, "A sufficiently advanced technology is indistinguishable from magic."

"What?" Madeline asked without taking her eyes from the ruined spectacle of Constance's once fine home.

"Clark's Third Law."

Madeline turned wide eyes to him. "Who?"

Arthur C. Clark, renowned author. He didn't want to explain it. "How's your arm?"

"Huh?" She looked down. "Oh." A gash split the pale skin on her upper arm. Moonlight turned the crimson wound black.

Julian pulled the flashlight from his pocket and aimed it at her cut. "Don't see any fragments," he said. "You'll need stitches. I'd give your handkerchief back, but...."

"You used it."

He shot her a look of chagrin and caught the slight mischief playing on her haggard features. Madeline talking him to orgasm was the hottest experience he'd had in some time, but it didn't prevent the flush that burned his cheeks.

Clearing his throat, he tried to match her teasing mood. "If that was script twenty-two, how many are there?"

"You don't want to know."

"I think I could take it." He rolled stiff shoulders. "When I've slept for a week. How are you feeling?"

"Aside from the creepy, crumbling house scaring the blue balls out of me?" The smile slid from her face. "What happened down there? Who was Desmond, really?"

"You know," Julian said. "He showed you. Spoke to you with his mind, as he did with me. Didn't he?"

Madeline shook her head. "Just because I remember it, doesn't mean it happened. If he..." She faltered for a moment, swallowed thickly, and carried on. "If *they* had the power to make this house look beautiful, to come here through some portal, then they had the power to make me believe things happened that didn't. The whole thing could be some kind of psychotic delusion. They could have sprayed something in the air...."

Her words trailed off, accompanied by a look of child-like confusion. With the pale moonlight playing across her vulnerable expression, Julian stifled the urge to reach out and caress her cheek.

"I was there," he said softly. "I saw you making love to him. I felt the house shaking."

Fuzzy half-remembered images crystalized in his mind. The tree altar. The ghost woman putting the egg in his mouth. Fucking Agent Spearman like a man possessed, which, he supposed he had been. The memories rushed back, full and complete, like it happened yesterday.

Truth turned his exhaustion into confidence. But how to convince Madeline?

Julian felt the bulge in his pants. The hard lump pushed against his thigh. He pulled it free. "I grabbed a souvenir."

Madeline's piqued face tightened into what looked like nausea when she recognized the shard with the ancient fertility etching.

"The symbol is from your childhood," Julian said. "From the cult you told me about, isn't it?"

Before she could respond, the sweep of headlights lit their faces. Crunching tires broke the eerie silence. A black sedan pulled to a stop just short of them. Behind it, the big black truck, which had received Constance's body the day before, idled. Its air-brakes moaned, then sighed. The tang of diesel exhaust bit Julian's nose.

He pocketed the stone just in time for floodlights to pierce the predawn gloom of the front yard. "The goons are back."

Spearman got out of the car. From the passenger side, Shadow Man emerged.

"Damn it," Julian muttered.

"Special Agent Worthy," Spearman said, her voice cold and stern. "I thought I removed you from this case."

There was no good response, so Julian made none. He pointed to Roland's still body. "That man needs medical attention."

Shadow Man took Madeline's arm, inspected the wound. His thumb swiped at the blood seeping down the gash before letting her go. "So does Ms. Da Vinci."

"I'll take her to the hospital," Julian said, stepping in front of Madeline. He cast his eyes to the black truck. If they took her in there, they'd likely give her the memory drugs they'd used on him after Slate Hill. He could not permit that.

"That won't be necessary. Luckily, we have a medical suite on-site." Shadow Man said, his words dripping with menace. "We'll handle her."

Julian's fists clenched. His breath came in ragged gasps. "Like you handled me?"

Dawn's first rays lit Spearman's hard features. She stepped close to him, almost nose-to-nose, and whispered, "Tread carefully, Jules. By coming back, you've put us both in a very tricky position."

Madeline stood motionless behind him. He sensed her confusion morphing into angry rebellion. This was his chance to tell Spearman his memory—and their power dynamic—had changed. In a low voice, he said, "I failed to protect you in Slate Hill. I'll always be sorry about that. But Madeline isn't a part of this. Let me protect her now."

Something in her expression softened, but Shadow Man shifted, and Spearman looked at him. His menace expanded to block out the light. When she turned back, her eyes glinted like they'd never been lovers. "Step aside, Agent Worthy. I'll handle this."

She reached for Madeline's arm.

Julian blocked her. "No."

"Stand down," Shadow Man called lazily. "We wouldn't want to have to take you to the truck and sedate you."

Julian searched Spearman's face for any sign of warmth but found nothing but a blank slate.

"It's okay, Julian," Madeline said, putting her hand on his shoulder. "It's just a scratch. They can give me a couple of stitches."

Shadow Man's smile was as icy as his voice. "Once again, Agent Worthy, your contemporaries are ahead of the curve while you lapse behind."

Spearman gestured to Madeline. Together, they walked toward the truck.

"Madeline," Julian called after her. "I'll be right here."

She flashed a smile over her shoulder. "If the doctor gives me a lollipop, I'll ask for two."

Fear twitched down Julian's spine. How could she be so glib? So lighthearted? Moments ago, she'd been exhausted and dazed. She was shining it on, he realized. Considering her background, she was used to staring the devil in the face and spitting in his eye, but he had the feeling her bravado was for his benefit. As he was trying to protect her, she was trying to protect him.

A lead weight replaced the panic in the pit of Julian's stomach. First Spearman, now Madeline. He hadn't felt this helpless since Slate Hill.

He marched up to Shadow Man, shaking with rage. "I don't know *who* the fuck you are—"

Shadow Man's gaze raked Julian from head-to-toe. "No, you don't, and I guarantee this is not the time to get to know me."

At Julian's feet, Roland groaned but didn't move. If he couldn't help Madeline, he could keep his promise to Constance.

Kneeling by the prone man, Julian glared at Shadow Man. "I don't see you rushing to help your accomplice."

Shadow Man shrugged, not bothering to deny their association. "Mr. Hansford didn't fulfill his part of the bargain. All he had to do was report his assault, get his mother out of the house, and he'd be half a million dollars richer."

"So you *were* the intruder."

The dark man scoffed. "Agent Worthy, Roland should be grateful I only knocked him out. If I'd attacked him for real, he wouldn't be alive."

The house behind Julian creaked and groaned, an eerie wind leaking between the fault lines as if the ghosts trapped inside couldn't wait to join the lawn party. Shadow Man's smile returned.

Julian's eyes widened. Against his will, he stepped back. For a second, Shadow Man's eyes had glowed as red as any demon from hell.

CHAPTER TWENTY

MADELINE

B lood ran down Madeline's arm in a warm, slippery trickle. Following Spearman to the van, she put her palm over the gouge made by the shattered window and winced at the burning pain. At least she had a focal point. If she didn't ground herself, she'd snap, scream, or throw a kick at one of the black-suited men streaming across Constance's front yard.

The pretty cottage filled with basket ferns and floral-print wallpaper was no more. What existed was *not* the house she'd slept in. Or had a breakfast of pancakes and bacon. Or been fucked by a ghost who was more like an alien. From another planet.

Behind her was a proper haunted house, complete with dead bushes, cobwebs, broken shingles, and a penetrating darkness that leeched into the woods on either side of the property.

Madeline should be freaking, but a resolute calm settled over her. Probably because she'd hallucinated the whole damn thing. That was the only explanation.

Sebastian had left her, and to avoid dealing with her failed relationship, she'd created a fantastical escapade filled with a wise woman, a knight in shining armor, and a villain who screamed Bad Boy.

A headache pulsed in her temples as she followed Spearman to the black truck. Madeline kept her gaze glued to the semi-dead grass in the once-verdant lawn, but in her periphery, the dark stranger loomed.

Shadow Man hadn't moved from his stoic position against the sedan's side, but his presence followed her like a...well, a shadow. Spearman hadn't introduced him, and Madeline didn't want to know his name or anything about him. He'd been a spooky addition to the underground chamber, but seeing him exposed to the light of dawn made him too real.

Raven-black hair long enough to curl swept a strong, angular face. He was over six-feet tall and wore his designer suit like it was lovingly sculpted around his muscular body. Power emanated from him, but the guy seemed to absorb energy like a black hole. Light did not reflect from his face and broad shoulders, not like it did Julian, who seemed to pull sunshine around him like a shield.

Madeline, Shadow Man's dream voice said in her mind much like Desmond's.

She stumbled. Great. More hallucinations. But she peeked over her shoulder as if someone had called her name.

Shadow Man was staring at her, and was he...? Yes. Licking his thumb. With her blood on it. She should have been disgusted, but a wave of sensual promise swelled through her exhausted body.

Did you like your little adventure down in the tunnels?

Keep moving, she reminded herself. Do not listen to strange voices, do not pass go, do not collect two-hundred dollars. She wasn't crazy, Mason's Hole wasn't a sex cult, and her adult self could kick the shit out of Shadow Man's subliminal games.

But hadn't she always had a thing for bad boys? God knew they were easier to predict than the guys who enthralled with sweet words and promises of happily-ever-after. Even Sebastian had the aura of no-shits-given when it came to making it known he was the top of his priority list. But what about Julian? He was definitely a rebel, and he had his own agenda, but not once had he forgotten she was there. And he'd been adamant she *not* get in the medical truck because of what happened to him at Slate Hill.

Was Madeline going to be experimented on?

Too many questions, too many unknowns. What she wouldn't give for a glass of Constance's lemonade, the older woman's gentle hand on her shoulder. If this was a mind-fuck, Madeline wanted to keep Constance. And Julian. If she could just talk to him alone, they could argue about the haunted house, the stupid sex magic, and about what was going to happen in the black truck. Hallucination or not, together they'd figure out what to do next.

Don't be ridiculous. You don't believe anything Agent Wonderbread says. It would be better to talk to me. Only me.

She squeezed the wound on her arm. Sharp pain flooded her system. Shadow Man's voice—his energy—abruptly disappeared, completely blocked from her mind. Madeline's headache dissipated. She stopped at the ramp of the truck, turned, and looked at the dark stranger, staring at him boldly.

Shadow Man frowned and directed his attention at Julian, saying something about sedating him. At their feet, Roland lay motionless.

Madeline opened her mouth, heard herself ask Spearman, "What about Constance's son?"

Spearman didn't look at her, just walked up the ramp. Strips of thick plastic obscured the inside, reminding Madeline of the entrance to a butcher's shop. In the background, a rumble of timbers and tiles brought a segment of Constance's roof collapsing into the first floor. For a moment, Madeline hoped the earth would open and swallow it whole. Leave no trace behind. Whatever magic had lived there was gone and would never return.

"Madeline," Spearman said. "Let's get you checked out."

Inside the truck, bright fluorescent lights attacked Madeline's eyes. She blinked rapidly, trying to process the white-on-white sterility of a hospital bed, stainless steel sinks, trays of instruments, and hanging surgical tools. Fucking-A, she had stepped from *The Haunting of Hill House* to medical porn.

They'd brought Constance's body in here.

The thought had her turning around, but Spearman's hand firmly gripped her uninjured arm, pushing her to sit on the cushioned gurney. The agent pulled up a rolling chair and sat next to the bed. She looked fresh and hard, but she spoke softly, as if aware of Madeline's tumultuous night. Her fingers were gentle as they assessed the wound on Madeline's bicep.

"How are you holding up?"

Madeline winced but wasn't so tired she felt the need to drop her guard. "I've had worse nights."

"Right. You managed to escape a sex cult when you were—how old? Thirteen?"

"Fifteen."

"In the bloom of womanhood. Brutal." Spearman slipped on a pair of surgical gloves and grabbed a tray of antiseptic spray and gauze. "This will sting."

Madeline didn't flinch as Spearman washed her cut. The dark blood liquified and spread in an inkblot over the cotton squares. Was her younger face in the macabre shape, hiding from the realities no child should have to deal with?

A flash of hot pain flared behind her eyes, momentarily blinding her, but Madeline pushed it away.

Spearman inspected the wound for debris. "About what happened in the chamber, I don't have time to be delicate. You had sex with the visitor?"

The visitor? What a politically correct way to talk about Desmond. "Yes."

"Did he ejaculate inside of you?"

Heat flooded Madeline's neck and face. "No."

"If you lie to me, there will be serious repercussions."

"We—stopped," Madeline said bluntly. "I didn't want what he was offering."

Spearman's shoulders dropped a degree, and she gave a curt nod. "Your arm has stopped bleeding, and there are no glass fragments." She probed the edges of the wound. "The cut isn't deep. I think you can get away with butterfly sutures, but you'll have a scar."

Madeline turned her attention to the other woman's features. Strong lines. Sharp nose. Full lips. Tiny wrinkles on the sides of her eyes and mouth she doubted were from laughter. Spearman had seen her share of hardcore shit and had the scars to prove it. "Physically or mentally?"

Spearman's brows rose, but she nodded in acknowledgment. "Depends on if you can be an adult and play the game."

"Your boss seems to have plenty of rules," Madeline countered. "Is threatening to sedate people a secret government thing or just kinky shit he's made up to pass the time?"

Spearman stiffened, a muscle in her jaw twitching. "You've witnessed things that would have other people questioning their sanity."

A dry snort left Madeline's throat. "I won't be running to the tabloids with an alien abduction story, if that's what you're worried about."

"I'm worried you won't know how to process the experience."

Spearman finished taping the sutures and stripped off the gloves, tossing them on the white linoleum. Her chair rolled to a locked stainless-steel cabinet where she punched in a code. The cabinet beeped, and a drawer slid open.

Spearman reached inside and extracted a vial of yellow liquid. "It's not company policy, but Homeland Security has a protocol for—diluting—the worst of your memories."

"The worst of my memories?" Madeline mocked, pushing down her instant panic at the sight of the vial. "Like the CIA did to Charles Manson? Little somethin'-somethin' acid trip extraordinaire?"

"You're an intelligent person, Madeline. Intelligent people want answers to their questions. Answers you won't get." Spearman's lips thinned as she reached for a sterile syringe. "I'm talking from experience when I say the need to know will eat a hole through your sanity. I'm offering you a chance to go back to your life and never think of this place again."

A wrenching pang struck Madeline's heart. Never think of Constance or Julian, again? "Thanks, but no thanks. Besides, I bet your trucks and black-ops crew are busy erasing what's left of Constance's life. What difference does it make what I believe?"

Her blasé assurance didn't stop Spearman's hands from opening the needle's protective plastic sheath. Madeline tensed, her mind flitting through a series of self-defense moves, should the need arise.

Spearman took a quick look at the entrance of the truck and lowered her voice. "Just so we're clear, what exactly do you think happened in Mason's Hole?"

That was easy. If Madeline put secret tunnels, horny townspeople, and memory-erasing drugs on a Bingo card, she could scream cover-up. And why not make a stink? This was Madeline's chance to confront Spearman about the questionable circumstances surrounding Constance's death. Not that Madeline thought she'd actually seen a portal to another universe, but she did believe Mason's Hole was the tip of a government-sized iceberg.

The needle in Spearman's hand froze her tongue.

Taking a deep breath, Madeline chose her words carefully. "I think Mason's Hole is a little town with a big imagination. Too much time on their hands, too much late-night TV, it's easy to project subconscious fears into a myth."

Spearman's lips twitched. "A myth?"

"Everyone likes a good ole-fashioned ghost story."

Spearman brandished the needle like it was a magic wand. "So you don't believe any of it?"

Madeline's eyes flashed. Whatever was in that vial was connected to Julian's memory lapses. She was sure of it. But if Spearman wanted to drug her, wouldn't she have done it? The agent was testing her, giving her an opportunity to see a bigger picture.

At least, Madeline hoped that's what she was doing.

Leaning back and crossing her ankles, she went for nonchalant. "I have a busy practice back home. Clients to see. Relationships to heal. To be honest, if I had to face everything I've seen and heard, I'd probably go blind, so like I said, divulging details about this trip isn't in my best interests."

"What will you say if anyone asks you?"

Bile rose in her throat, but Madeline forced herself to lie. "That a lonely woman suffering from untreated delusions died quietly in her sleep."

Spearman jabbed the needle into the rubber vial and filled the syringe with the potion. Madeline got very still, wondering whether she should punch Spearman in the throat or go for her eyes first. Like Julian, she was probably packing a pistol and a boot knife.

"Don't try it." Spearman's tone was hard, but her touch gentle as she grasped Madeline's wrist.

The needle drew close.

A flush of rage coursed through Madeline, as familiar as an old friend. Definitely a throat punch.

Spearman tightened her grip on Madeline's arm. "Listen to me very carefully. We don't have a lot of time."

Madeline stopped breathing.

"My boss isn't the only one who can play games, and I have my own set of rules. Can I trust you?"

She scanned Spearman's face. Urgency and anger glazed her hazel gaze, but under the hard façade, Spearman glowed with the same stalwart justice Madeline saw in Julian's eyes.

Slowly, Madeline nodded.

Spearman pulled herself close to Madeline's side and shot a look over her shoulder. A tiny camera stared at them. They were being watched. When Spearman tugged at Madeline's arm again, she pushed it forward, the needle hovering over the pulsing blue vein on her wrist.

Spearman pushed the plunger on the syringe. But instead of jabbing Madeline's arm, the needle shot a stream of yellow poison harmlessly into a sink beside the gurney blocked from view by Spearman's strategically placed back.

"My boss has secrets he'll do anything to protect, and he wants your memories scrubbed," Spearman whispered. "But you know how to lie, how to tell people what they want to hear. Play the game and don't give him a reason to question your recall."

When the syringe was empty, she placed it back on the tray and picked up a rolled bandage.

"You're fuzzy around the edges right now," Spearman explained and wrapped Madeline's arm. "A little confused, but calm. You barely remember Constance Hanford or her son. Her death was an unfortunate accident you heard about in passing, and since she isn't your client, you came to Mason's Hole to see a haunted house and tool around a quaint town before heading home."

Licking dry lips, Madeline said, "I'm supposed to be headed to Costa Rica."

"Your flight was delayed. I can handle the details." Spearman finished the dressing and pushed away from the gurney. "There you are. Good as new."

"What about Julian?"

Spearman tilted her head in consideration, but her eyes grew hard, immovable. "You met him on a ghost tour. Had a couple drinks. It was a fun one-night stand in a sad motel room. Nothing to write home about."

Madeline rubbed the heel of her hand against her sternum. The pain in her arm was nothing compared to this impending sense of loss. "I'm supposed to lie to him about everything? He's not going to believe me."

"Make him believe you." Spearman rose from the rolling chair, her stance suddenly vibrating with tension. "Like I told you, my rules. If Julian acts like he's solved this case, and he's got a witness to back him up, not only will my boss be pissed, he'll go after all of us."

Madeline found her feet. She didn't want to be in the truck anymore. In fact, she wanted to be as far away from Mason's Hole as possible. But before she could leave, she had to ask. "Why are you doing this?"

Madeline didn't think Spearman would answer. Conflict dug the grooves beside her mouth into trenches, but the agent surprised her.

"I met Julian ten years ago. He was young. Smart. Full of potential." She shrugged. "Shit went down. Shit I regret. I can't change it, but that doesn't mean I have to let it keep happening." Spearman gave her a thorough once-over. "A word to the wise, I wouldn't pursue a personal relationship with Agent Worthy if I were you. He's got baggage. Skeletons in the closet, some of them real, some not so real. To put it in your terms, he's highly susceptible to worshipping powerful female figures."

Madeline gave Spearman a knowing look. "To put it in my terms, people project their insecurities onto those they secretly desire."

Had Madeline not been watching, she would have missed the widening of Spearman's pupils, a sure sign the older woman was remembering something she longed to forget. Or, in Julian's case, something she longed to experience again.

Spearman straightened, drawing her professionalism around her like a dented but sturdy shield. "Our agency is like an extended family. We protect each other, because at the end of the day, family's all you have. You know what that's like, don't you, Madeline?"

The agent plucked a card from her pocket and placed it gently on the tiny table next to the empty syringe. "My number. In case you ever run into family troubles."

CHAPTER TWENTY-ONE

JULIAN

Minutes ticked by, but to Julian, it felt like hours since Madeline had disappeared into the black trailer. Roland was slowly coming around, much to his relief, but dawn drove a wedge of pale gold into the sky behind the trees. It silhouetted Shadow Man, making him even spookier.

When Julian couldn't stand it anymore, he reared up, staring into cold, dark eyes. "Who the fuck do you think you are? I don't have your name, your affiliation with DHS, nothing. For all I know, you're some wacko Spearman picked up at a bar."

Shadow Man leaned in, putting his nose a hair's breadth from Julian's cheek and gave it a loud, lingering sniff. "Your naivete is delicious, but self-righteousness gives it a bitter tang."

Julian stepped back. "What the fuck!"

"We could work together, Agent Worthy." Shadow Man pursed his lips. "It would be...uncomfortable for you at first, but it would be worth it to have the answers you seek. Given enough time, you'd learn to like my ways."

Julian could see the whole thing. Shadow Man pointing him at the cases that served his interest. Or, keeping him away from them. "With you holding my leash?"

"Yours. Spearman's. The Da Vinci girl might be fun, too." Shadow Man winked.

"You're sick."

"Oh, come *on*. I know what you had to do to get through Desmond's special security. Good thing Miss Da Vinci was there to help. And I know exactly what went on in the altar room. Don't play the prude. It's unbecoming in such a comely young specimen." The playful smile vanished. "You've interfered in my business, but you're persistent, and I admire that quality. Here's a nibble for your troubles. Desmond Mason's kind are called Xraptics. Beings from a higher dimension. They like Earth girls. And of course you met the Copulus Souls in Slate Hill."

Julian stood firm as Shadow Man leaned in again, but mentally, he reeled. This time, Shadow Man's lips brushed his ear, sending an involuntary shudder down his spine.

"I know what they took from you. I know what happened to it."

Julian shoved at his chest, but it was like trying to move a marble statue. "Tell me."

"Tut-tut. You get more flies with honey than you do with vinegar." He looked down at Julian's hands gripping his black suit jacket.

Julian let Shadow Man go.

"You seem overcome. Just as you were in Slate Hill. Perhaps you need a trip to the medical truck after all."

Julian tried to keep his face an impassive mask, but Shadow Man's reference gave him a nasty jolt. The image of a syringe filled with yellow liquid flashed in his mind's eye. "Who. Are. *You*?"

Shadow Man tucked his hands in his pockets, suddenly pensive. "I'm an archeologist. I know where all the skeletons are buried and how to dig them up." He paused. "And I know where to bury a few, should the need arise."

"Are you threatening me?"

"Believe it or not, I'm on your side. Team Worthy, rah-rah-rah."

Julian's hands clenched into fists.

Shadow Man glanced at the gesture. "Lighten up, *Special* Agent Brian Julian Worthy." He smiled and snapped his fingers. "I just got that. Your name is BJ Worthy. I'll keep that in mind."

Julian stood with his mouth open as Shadow Man turned his back and walked toward the crumbling house. Xraptics? Copulus Souls? Was the asshole pulling his leg, or confessing the existence of extraterrestrials knowing Julian couldn't confirm or deny the statement?

The plastic flaps of the medical trailer parted, breaking Julian's trance. Spearman stepped from the trailer, and she looked grim. Rage burned through his paralysis, and Julian marched up to the ramp, trapping her.

"Where is she?" he demanded.

Spearman placed her hands on her hips, adding a superhero quality to her powerful countenance. "Finishing up her treatment."

"Just what would that treatment entail?" Julian spat, adrenaline singing along his nerves.

"You know damn well what I'm talking about. It's protocol for civilians who become entangled in the S.E.X.D. files, as you've been warned."

Spearman was talking about chemically induced memory loss, the same treatment he'd been given when he was eighteen. He hadn't wanted to believe she could do such a thing to Madeline, but Spearman was right. She had warned him. On several occasions.

Julian wanted no part of it anymore. It was a shame to lose the resources of S.E.X.D., but he didn't want to be party to non-consensual brain tampering. He'd find his answers another way.

He fished his badge from the inside pocket of his blazer and held it out to Spearman. "I'm done. It's over. Bring Madeline out."

Her hazel gaze turned to ice. "You'd quit your job for this woman?"

"She's had the shot, so no, not *for* her." Julian scowled. "*Because* of her."

Spearman made no move to accept his badge. The disappointment in her eyes bored into Julian. She made a curt nod, almost to herself. "Julian, I tried to stop this at every turn. I even *kicked* you off the case. You knew the risks, but did she?"

Julian pressed his lips into a hard, thin line.

"What happened in that trailer is entirely your fault. Not mine. Not hers. *Yours.* Giving me your badge won't change the results. Quitting your job and running off to join the circus won't change it, either."

Julian opened his mouth to protest.

Spearman held a finger to his lips. Something in her face changed, softened. "Giving up now means you can't learn from this. You can't stop it from happening to someone else. You can't help people no one else believes. Give me that badge now...and it was all for nothing."

Julian's heart pounded. Heat bloomed in his cheeks. All these years later, she could still have this effect on him. After everything she'd done. As if there were still a chance for them.

She was manipulating him, and he was letting her do it.

Spearman withdrew her finger. "When was the last time you slept?"

Julian shrugged. He was still pissed, as much at himself as at her.

"Ate?"

He said nothing.

"Talk to me Monday. If you still want to quit, we can discuss it then. Now, can I get off this fucking ramp?"

Julian moved aside, the brown leather badge-wallet still clutched in his hand.

Spearman stepped down and stretched. "God, I don't miss the hours in the field."

She could pretend everything was fine. Settled. Back to normal. But Julian was beyond angry. Disgust roiled in his belly. Never before had he thought Spearman could break their bond, their friendship, but it lay in tatters around his feet.

The med van's flaps rustled again. Madeline stood in the doorway. The thin lines of her eyebrows drew together in a question.

Spearman turned. "How are you feeling?"

"A little fuzzy," Madeline said in a small voice.

Rage replaced Julian's disgust. It had nowhere to go. He could direct it at Spearman, but she wasn't the cause. Not really. And it was too much to point inward. He'd go back to work—but only to plan his next move taking her and Shadow Man down.

Shadow Man appeared from around the corner of the trailer. "Ah, Madeline." He made an approximation of a warm smile. "How are you feeling?"

"A little fuzzy. Wait. I just said that, didn't I?" She paused, searching Julian's face, and grimaced awkwardly. "Julian? What are you doing here?"

Julian let out a little breath of relief. She remembered him, but the bond they'd forged was gone. It was almost more than he could bear. They had been survivors with a common goal, and she'd come to mean something to him. Something more than a friend or potential lover. He couldn't name it. He dared not. Loss rushed in to fill the void.

He was alone again.

Spearman spoke before Julian could. "There was an accident last night during your ghost tour. You two are lucky to be alive. The house is collapsing. Rotten foundation." Though she'd been answering Madeline's question, her eyes drilled into Julian's, cautioning him not to contradict her.

"Oh," Madeline said. "Right."

When Madeline stepped into the driveway, Shadow Man went up to her, still wearing a phony, beatific smile. It didn't reach his eyes. "My name is Detective Right. I'm investigating the collapse. What do you remember about last night?"

"I...." Madeline frowned. "That's funny. I don't remember anything."

Shadow Man's eyes narrowed. "Come, Miss Da Vinci, surely you can give me something to go on?"

"Mmm. I remember being in the car with Julian, and then, waking up in there." She indicated the trailer.

"You're sure?" Shadow Man stared at her.

Julian silently willed her to say nothing.

Madeline sighed. "I'm sorry. It's like... it's like last night never happened. That's weird."

"It's common among victims of traumatic events. Accidents. Things like that. Completely normal," Spearman said. "Isn't that right, Agent Worthy?"

Julian restrained the urge to choke Shadow Man or shake Spearman like a rag doll. "Right."

"Can I take you somewhere?" Shadow Man asked Madeline. He leaned in, as he'd done with Julian, and whispered something to her.

Julian didn't hear what the asshole said, but he saw the flush in Madeline's cheeks. It made his blood boil.

"Oh, no. Thank you," Madeline said, touching a hand to her chest. "I don't want to miss my flight to Costa Rica. I'm meeting my boyfriend Sebastian there."

Disappointment flickered across Shadow Man's face as he straightened. "Of course."

"I'll take you to your car," Spearman said. She glanced at Julian. "You too. You've done *quite* enough here."

Julian followed, glancing over his shoulder at Shadow Man, who stood rooted to the spot, frowning at them.

Ahead of him, the two women walked side-by-side. Spearman, with her trim figure hidden by her suit, and Madeline's curves, accentuated by her tight jeans and t-shirt. Despite it all, he wanted them to know he saw them for who they really were, and he remembered *everything*.

CHAPTER TWENTY-TWO

MADELINE

M adeline sat in the backseat of Agent Spearman's sedan. Julian sat in the front seat. The scent of sweat, dust, and failure circulated with the arctic air conditioning. No one spoke, but the energy zipping between him and Spearman was so combustible, Madeline felt like a kid caught between squabbling parents.

She sighed and leaned her head against the faux-leather seat.

Radical honesty was key in her therapy, and now she had to do the one thing she spent weeks, sometimes months, helping her clients overcome: keep a secret from a loved one.

Her mind screeched to a halt. A loved one? She barely knew Julian. But he'd become dear to her in a short time. She respected him. Trusted him. Genuine affection warmed her heart, but love? Maybe not of the romantic variety, but yes, love between two people traveling the same path of discovery. She could own that.

Which made her task harder.

Lying sucked, and she loathed playing games, but a part of her was proud she could still pull off doe-eyed innocence to odious characters. Believing the lie was part of the deal. Julian's safety, and possibly her own, were at stake. Madeline could keep up the charade in front of Shadow Man—or Agent Right, what a shitty fake name—to spite his arrogance, but Julian was another story. What would happen when they were alone?

She closed her eyes and let the friction of rubber tires over asphalt lull her. Hadn't she known at some point this would happen? A product of growing up in a cult, secrets were the root of suffering, and her childhood had loopholes and conspiracies woven into the fabric of "rational" behavior. She might have run from dogma, but it was always there. Waiting. No one wanted the truth, not all in one sitting, but they sure did demand it from everyone else.

Spearman looked at her in the rearview mirror. "How are you feeling, Madeline?"

"Tired," she said. It was the truth.

"Once you're in Costa Rica, this will seem like a very strange dream. No harm, no foul."

Madeline glanced at Julian's profile. He stared out the side window, but she could see his jaw muscles working, and that floppy bit of hair was in his face again. He didn't bother to brush it aside. Her heart ached for his palpable loneliness.

When they reached the library where they'd left her car, he got out of the sedan without a word. Madeline followed suit.

"Agent Worthy—" Spearman warned.

"Her stuff is at the hotel," he snapped. "I'm making sure she gets there safely."

He promptly closed the door.

"Can you drive?" he asked Madeline.

Madeline patted her jeans, giving a silent prayer of thanks her key fob hadn't been lost in the cavern's missing clothes orgy. "I can drive."

Inside her car, they buckled their seatbelts, the awkward silence muffled by another blast of air-conditioning, this one pine-scented.

She was surprised Julian wasn't quizzing her about their adventure. He hadn't even mentioned Constance. Maybe he wanted Madeline to forget. The thought was painful, but a necessary possibility she had to face. As were all the events of the last twenty-four hours.

Julian cleared his throat. "Can I ask you something?"

"Sure."

"What did Shadow Man say to you back there?"

Madeline opened her mouth to respond, but they were playing a different game now. "Uh, you mean Agent Right? He insinuated he'd be available for a chat in a less official setting if I had follow-up questions." She grimaced. "Rather tactless for a government employee, but better the asshole you know than one who thinks they can mind-fuck you, right?"

Julian muttered a curse under his breath.

Comfort had to get in the backseat of the forgetfulness façade, but there were other ways to let him know she cared and didn't consider their adventure a one-night stand. "Julian, we're okay. I mean, I don't remember the details of last night, not really. But I remember you and I were...good together. I know I'm safe with you."

He jerked like she'd slapped him. "I didn't keep you safe, Madeline. You should never have been in the situation we were in. Never been at Constance's house. Never been in the back of that truck."

Despite her promise, Madeline felt her hackles rise and tightened her grip on the steering wheel. "Oh please. It's better to let the big strong man handle the hard stuff? I'm all for men being men, but sometimes a feminine touch does a better job. I have a mental filing cabinet full of scripts at my disposal."

His surprised glance was full of hope. Which he quickly concealed. "This might not mean anything to you, but I still can't afford your rates."

"I give a great government employee discount."

The side of his mouth twitched, and his eyes searched her face. "You're really okay?"

They pulled up to the motel room. Madeline turned in her seat. "I'm really okay. Are you okay?"

His mouth opened. Closed.

She reached out and brushed his hair back. "It really has a mind of its own, doesn't it?"

Julian took a deep breath and said sadly, "You have no idea."

They exited the car. He unlocked the motel door and pushed it open for her to enter. The room was everything Madeline thought it would be. Bland, beige, and dated enough to calm her scattered emotions.

Julian rubbed the back of his neck. "Did you want to, I don't know, take a shower, rest a minute before heading out? I know you have a plane to catch, but I can arrange a late checkout. No pressure."

Julian looked storm-cloud angry...and boyishly vulnerable standing thoroughly dirty and rumpled in the middle of the drab motel room with his hands hanging at his sides.

Madeline juggled her car keys. She could feel whatever heightened energy Desmond's power cast over the town waning with each passing minute, but her body responded with tingling languor. So the attraction between them wasn't just a product of weird atmospheric events. Thank God.

Julian stared at her as if sensing the spark of renewed chemistry. His eyes took on the heavy-lidded sleepiness of an aroused man.

Ghost cock, aliens, haunted houses, it was a clusterfuck, but better than the empty bungalow she'd left in Virginia. They'd agreed not to engage in sex magic, but her amnesia could come in handy. Madeline could reach for him. Finish what they'd both been longing to do, sex magic or not. But if she seduced Julian, she'd be doing it to spite Spearman and give a middle finger to the heavy-handed tomfuckery of the week. Then what?

Spearman's warning came to mind. *I wouldn't pursue a personal relationship with Agent Worthy if I were you.*

Biting her lip, Madeline turned away before she could see if Julian was disappointed or relieved at her rejection. "Actually, a shower would help clear the cobwebs."

The bathroom was nothing special. Chipped off-white tiles adorned the floor, but at least the shower wasn't held together with duct tape and super glue. A lax plastic shower curtain with tiny blue flowers made her heart long for Constance's cabbage rose décor.

She stripped off her streaked, stiff clothing and turned on the shower, praying for decent water pressure. Stepping under the fall of hot water, a rush of comfort washed the grime from her hands and shoulders. Her body ached from exertion...and the touch of a lover's strong embrace.

Madeline shuddered. Remembered emerald eyes appraising her face. A smile of warmth and brilliance that held no ill-will, the body of a god pressing into her loins, a pulsing promise of mutual satisfaction just out of reach.

No. Don't think of that.

Desmond certainly felt real, but the vision of an alien child was the stuff of science fiction. Possibly horror. If anyone found out the details of her weekend, they'd be pushing to quantify her experience. It was easier to believe in werewolves, mermaids, and vampires than face reality.

Which was what?

The most logical conclusion was hypnosis combined with mind-altering drugs. Now that Madeline had seen the back of that trailer and felt Shadow Man's ominous presence, disregarding chemical interference was foolish. If this was a real investigation, Julian could get the townspeople tested.

Hell, *she* should get a blood panel.

Would that explain Constance as a ghost, transparent and happy, joining hands with Desmond and sending her a wave as she stepped into the unknown? Probably not. The farewell had been an unexpected gift. A necessary suture over a deep gash.

And it was a deep gash. She'd loved being with Constance, feeling like she had a maternal presence grounding her, sharing wisdom and truth. Constance's country house had been beautiful, packed with safety, cabbage roses, and home-cooked meals. Madeline could have stayed, could have had a real home...

But the house she and Julian had run from was the epitome of gothic lore, just like the townspeople and ghost hunters reported. The memory of rotting walls and creaking floors made Madeline crank the heat a notch.

Fuck. It was all too much to process.

With the last of her adrenaline leaching down the drain, Madeline crumpled to the shower floor. The tears came, and she didn't fight the urge to cry. It was the second time she'd unraveled in the last twenty-four hours, but she didn't stop the stress exiting her body in heaving spasms.

When was the last time she had let herself be so open, so vulnerable? Not since she'd escaped with Hatty, and they'd huddled together in a bus station in downtown Santa Fe. She'd cried then, quietly, trying not to wake her sister.

As much as Madeline tried to push the memory away, the fear of not knowing where to go, who to trust, or how she was going to take care of her sister rushed at her from the haunted corners of her past.

Her vision blurred, the light dissolving like a shroud swallowed her body, and it wasn't from her tears.

Gasping, terrified, Madeline clawed at the shower curtain. She couldn't see!

No, Madeline, Desmond's voice boomed through her mind. *Relax. Open your eyes.*

Startled, Madeline blinked under the shower spray, her vision completely normal, and noticed a faint red glow coming from her hands.

She yelped and adjusted the temperature dial, panicked she'd burned her skin and was too dull from a cortisol-dump to react. But touching herself, there was no pain. Even the gouge on her arm felt warm and tingly, like it was healing.

"What the hell," she sniffed, turning her hands over.

The ingenious, child-like part of her psyche didn't question the mysterious glow. If anything, it proved Constance had been real, Desmond—whatever he was—had been real, and Julian's endearing attention had been real.

She was exhausted, angry, and a little sad. Constance was gone, the house was gone, and her connection with Julian was on its way to being buried like the corporeal timbers of a historic relic. But as the glow faded, and Madeline was left staring at her hands, she couldn't help but feel steady. Calm. Stronger than she'd been before. Another vision, another mind-fuck, what was the difference? The answers Madeline craved were out of reach. Par for the course. But she was alive and well. And Julian was on the other side of the bathroom door.

She climbed out of the shower, not bothered by the postage stamp towel that barely covered her breasts. As she wearily slipped into a fresh t-shirt and slacks, a knock sounded.

"Your phone's been ringing," Julian called. "I'm not trying to pry, but your sister's name popped up."

"Thanks!"

Madeline opened the door and was hit again with how sexy Julian looked covered in gritty haunted house debris. She was halfway tempted to tell him about the weird red glow. He'd be thrilled she finally copped to a paranormal connection. How ironic she couldn't tell him.

Lying sucked, and so did being a grown-up.

To distract herself, she looked at her phone. Hatty had called and left a message. She also had a text from an unknown number. It said: *Remember our deal. –S*

Spearman.

No rest for the deceptive.

231

"Shit," she mumbled, evading Julian's eyes. "I better call my sister back. The bathroom is all yours."

Julian hesitated. "Don't leave before I get out, okay?"

Madeline looked into his eyes. Had they always been so blue? "Okay."

Like a zombie, she made her way to the bed and stretched out. Sleep was what she needed. Sleep and time to think. When Julian got out of the shower, she could ask him what he planned on doing next. Tell him she wasn't going to Costa Rica, with or without a lover. Maybe see if he wanted to grab dinner.

Exhaustion closed her eyes, but Madeline's heart refused to go quietly into the less than gentle darkness. She and Hatty never went longer than a week without a text or message telling the other they were okay, but since being in Mason's Hole, Madeline had felt a disturbance in their connection.

Resigned to the inevitable, she listened to her sister's voice message.

"Mads, hey. How are you? Look, I've got something I want to talk to you about. It's—well—about The Disciples of Creation. I know I told you I didn't want to talk about Thoth or the cult, but I keep having this dream. We're back in the commune, and there's this giant snake. It's weird and scary and I need you to help me make sense of it. I'll be in class the rest of the afternoon, but call me, okay?"

Madeline stared up at the ceiling. The sound of the shower cut off. Any minute Julian would emerge half-naked from the bathroom, and she'd be thrown into the tumult of lies and unrequited lust.

Remember our deal.

She'd told Spearman it didn't matter what she believed, she wouldn't risk everything she'd built, but Madeline knew better than anyone, a secret could only stay buried for so long.

There was only one thing to do. Leave before the temptation to tell Julian the truth took over.

Chapter Twenty-Three

JULIAN

No amount of flimsy hotel soap could scrub the guilt from Julian's heart. He'd failed to protect Madeline from Spearman and Shadow Man's memory-erasing drug. She was just in the other room, but she'd never been further away.

Damn it, they were a great team. And despite the danger, he'd had fun solving this case with her. Madeline kept him grounded. Her skepticism made him examine each hunch and supposition, making him think hard to justify his leaps of logic. She'd taken a chance, going along with his theories, and held the space for him to be vulnerable. Now their connection was all but erased.

At least she didn't remember making him come with script twenty-two. There was that. His secret desires, Spearman among them, were still secret. There was hope there could be something between them.

As Julian dressed, he imagined them getting coffee, holding hands, staring into each other's eyes. With his travel and her living in a different city, hell, a different state, it would be a juggle, but they could find other things in common besides Constance, alien abductions, and sex magic.

Like...

Julian couldn't come up with one thing except their affinity for Scooby Doo jokes, and even that was suspect.

Frustrated, he gathered his soiled pants from the floor. His hand bumped over a lump in the pants' pocket. Fishing out the rock he'd snatched from the crumbling altar, Julian traced a finger over the carved symbol Madeline recognized from her youth. The urge to march out of the bathroom and present her with the irrefutable evidence was tangible. And selfish. All it would accomplish would be to make her angry and confused. If she remembered, despite the drug, it might put her back on Shadow Man's radar. Might put her in jeopardy again. Then he'd have failed to protect her twice.

What he should do is let her go gracefully. Let her walk out of the motel room and never see her again. That was his best option for protecting her. Julian absolutely could not let his need for validation, for someone else besides himself to believe, to hurt her any further.

God, he hated the lies. The dishonesty. It left a pit in his stomach. He *should* just tuck the shard into his dirty pants and pack it away. But he didn't.

When Julian opened the door, a cloud of swirling steam and emotion went with him. One sentence after another formed in his mind. Sentences about last night, about how good they were together, how tough she was to survive her childhood and help others, how the future was less colorful without her in it. None of which he could say.

Instead of quietly recuperating, Madeline was stuffing her belongings haphazardly into her bag. It took several moments for the scene in front of Julian to filter past his thoughts. Unease joined the milieu. The way she was packing...

"Is everything all right?"

234

"I've got to go," she said without looking up.

Her words were a downed electrical wire dancing around on wet asphalt, throwing sparks. God, if he could just catch a spark, hold it out to her. He cleared the emotions rising in his throat, but "Of course" was all he could manage.

She was going on vacation, he needed to remember that, but fuck Costa Rica. And fuck what was his name? Sebastian?

Julian tried again. "I had fun, uh, hanging out with you."

She met his eyes and gave him a wan smile. "Me too."

She seemed to mean it. But there was something else. An urgency that didn't exactly match a tropical vacation. Or maybe it was his fatigue, and the comedown from a rough case, coloring his perception.

One more try. "I'd like to see you again."

Christ. He sounded like a bad Tinder date, asking for another try.

"Yeah," she said, slinging her bag over her shoulder. "We should have coffee sometime." Meaning, of course, we *should, but we won't*.

The hurricane force of her blow-off nearly rocked him back on his heels. Julian clutched the altar shard in his pocket like a buoy in a stormy sea.

"Can I help you with your bag?"

Something in his voice made her pause. Her stunning green eyes held his. There was something there. Something she wanted to say, but couldn't. Probably about Sebastian. What kind of asshole name was that, anyway?

"Julian...."

"Right." He nodded. She'd thrown out enough clues. You couldn't become a special agent without the ability to take a hint. "You've got to make your flight."

A flicker of confusion crossed her face and disappeared. "Right," she agreed. "My flight."

Fuck this macho bullshit. The leash Spearman and Shadow Man had slipped around his neck threatened to strangle him. He'd tried to hold it all in, but that wasn't how Julian was built.

"We were good together," he blurted.

Color rose in her cheeks. Her expression softened.

There was something there! Something she remembered! He could *feel* it.

"I'm glad you were with me," she said. Then added quickly, "On the haunted house tour from hell."

"Not Sebastian?" Fuck.

The silence stretched.

She shifted her weight, glancing at the door.

"Don't let me keep you." Well, if *that* didn't sound passive-aggressive. He forced a smile. "Costa Rica awaits."

"Yeah." She smiled. It didn't reach her eyes. "Big vacation!"

The shard in Julian's pocket bit into his fingers.

She walked up to him and threw her arms around him.

Julian released the stone and returned her surprise hug.

"Thank you," she whispered. "For *everything*."

The way she said it, packed with emotion, made Julian think maybe it was more than the false memory of a ghost tour.

Her hair tickled his temple. The scent of her, vanilla and cinnamon, washed over him like a spring shower. God, she felt good in his arms.

She released him, giving him a deeper, more genuine smile. "Special Agent Brian Julian Worthy, it's been a pleasure."

"The pleasure was all mine." There was so much more he wanted to say, but he focused on her eyes and not the lump in his throat.

Madeline gave him one last smile before closing the door behind her.

Fucking Sebastian. Julian would go back to Washington, get on the database, and find out all about this guy. Warn Madeline if he found anything....

"Okay, stop it," he muttered to the empty room.

The sound of her car starting filtered in from the parking lot. The thin motel walls did little to mute the crunching tires on pavement.

Muscles straining, Julian stared at the door. He could still run out and present her with the altar piece in his pocket. Demand she remember.

He had never been to Costa Rica, but he hated it now. "Let her go, man."

The engine noise of her car receded.

Madeline was gone.

He took in a breath and let it out. He should take a power nap or listen to his chakra meditation, but the thought of staying in the Climax Motel without Madeline was a joke. Best be on his way.

Being herded onto a plane, surrounded by strangers, was anathema. No. He'd drive. Return the rental in DC. Let the government pay for it. It was the least Spearman could do.

Tossing his go-bag into the passenger seat, Julian immediately started to sweat in the mid-morning heat. The long stretch of highway worked its magic and cleared his head, but instead of figuring out what to put in his field notes, Madeline's behavior when he came out of the bathroom nipped at his mind.

Normally, Julian had an amazing memory for details. But he'd been up for more than twenty-four hours after thwarting a sex-crazed alien and dragging an unconscious man from a collapsing house with a beautiful woman at his side. He should let it go, but his brain, so accustomed to zeroing in on abnormalities, refused.

He replayed every word Madeline said. Every gesture and pause.

The night Constance died, Madeline told him she had just broken up with her boyfriend. Now she was meeting him on vacation? She could have been lying to Shadow Man to fend off an unwanted advance.

Plus, her attitude had been all wrong. Anyone hurrying off to a tropical rendezvous would be happy. Giddy even. Madeline hadn't been happy; she had been worried and hiding it.

Then there were her parting words.

Special Agent Brian Julian Worthy, it's been a pleasure.

Julian nearly drove off the road.

Post memory-drug Madeline only knew him as Julian.

Had Shadow Man used his full name that morning? Had Spearman?

Julian knew how well the drug worked. His fogginess and confusion had lasted...years. Only a trip to Mason's Hole had managed to rend the veil obscuring his recollection.

Without thinking, he patted his pants' pocket. The shard was warm, almost pulsing, even with the layers of cloth insulating it. Madeline had been hiding more than one secret. He couldn't ask her about it now, but so help him, there would be a time in the near future when nothing came between them.

CHAPTER TWENTY-FOUR

MADELINE

Three days later, Madeline sat in her office and watched the hands of her Georgia O'Keefe clock measure the endless accounting of time. She used to find the labial likeness of the flower's folds calming. Now they reminded her of butterfly peas. Underground caves. And script22.

Waiting for the Atwoods to arrive, she was forced to admit, everything had changed in the forty-eight hours she'd spent with Constance Hanford and Special Agent Julian Worthy.

When she'd come home, she'd dropped her overnight bag and surveyed the bungalow. Her house had been eerily silent. Wandering the rooms, the missing bits of Sebastian's books, clothes, even his toothbrush in the bathroom should have pierced her like brambles in a sticker thatch. Madeline felt nothing but vague relief. She'd told her clients she was home, but the office, a once sacred space, felt claustrophobic.

Nothing felt right. Not her work, not her habitual haunts, not her routine of self-care. Even her dreams were a roiling conundrum of disturbed affect. Twice, she'd woken in the middle of the night with a start, hearing not Desmond or Julian's voice, but Shadow Man's seductive whisper. She hadn't been able to remember the words, hadn't wanted to, but knew they were sexual. Intense. Demanding. Her body had responded willingly and with alarming speed. It was enough to make her question her sanity.

She closed her eyes. Imagined the summer heat rising off the asphalt as she drove away from Mason's Hole. Dense woodlands and craggy mountains yelled for her to stop the car. Virginia might be for lovers, but in North Carolina, Constance found a connection that lasted the rest of her life.

Madeline wanted the same for herself, just in a more corporeal form.

A notification on her phone asked if she wanted to re-book her trip to Costa Rica. She waited for a spurt of purpose, but again, her heart remained unmoved. Eventually, she'd call the airline, get credit on the tickets, and if they gave her hassle, throw Spearman at them. Friends in high places and all that jazz.

As for Sebastian, she hadn't called or texted her ex. There would be no "last fling." If they never spoke again, Madeline wasn't bothered. She didn't wish Sebastian harm, but they wouldn't benefit from hashing out what went wrong in their relationship. Some people were better off gone. How was that for closure?

Frowning, Madeline drummed her fingers on the desktop. She'd called Hatty on the drive home, left a voicemail, and gotten a quick text: *Super busy. Will call when I get the chance.*

But Hatty hadn't called or texted, and Madeline couldn't discount the rise of anxiety. Her sister was incredibly kind, not naïve, but innocent. Her artwork was just starting to take off. Madeline didn't want to impede Hatty's progress, but neither could she stifle the undercurrents of fear her sister might attract the wrong attention.

The intercom buzzed. The Atwoods were in the waiting room. Madeline geared herself to be unflappably serene. She had a plausible excuse for why her vacation was cut short—a death in the family. It wasn't a lie. Roland had called that morning to inform her Constance's memorial would be the following day. Madeline was tempted to jump in her car in hopes of seeing Julian, but the ploy reeked of desperation.

She could see him, give him an awkward hug, then what? What did she want from him? Friendship? Sex? Another dash through a haunted house with a portal to an unknown dimension in the basement? Not that she believed it was extraterrestrial, more like high-level stealth technology or mind control, but if Julian could hear her now, a 'Told-ya-so' smirk would be all over his face. Oh, the irony.

Martin and Peggy opened the door and entered the office hand-in-hand. The cloyingly sweet luster of newlyweds clung to their shoulders.

"Well, well, well," Madeline mused. "It looks like you've been busy."

Peggy giggled, and Martin's face turned red.

Madeline folded her hands in her lap. "Tell me what's new."

Martin was the first to speak. "I have to be honest with you. When we first started therapy a year ago, I didn't think we stood a chance of making a dent in the wall between us. The more we dug, the more it hurt to talk about the past. We were so different from the two kids who got married thirty years ago. I wasn't sure we had anything left in common. But then, I don't know, something shifted." He glanced at Peggy, who nodded. "Somewhere along the line, we decided to start over as the people we are now."

Peggy's smile made her translucent with happiness. "Martin took me on a first date! Dressing up. Coming to the door—our front door—with roses. Pulling the chair out for me at the restaurant. He sat across from me and asked me what I liked as if we were strangers.

And I told him so many things I assumed he knew. My hopes and dreams, the longing I had for him to know *me*. Then it was his turn to share, and I sat there, stunned, feeling those butterflies in my stomach. I was falling in love with my husband." She nestled into Martin's shoulder. "But you want to know the best part?"

Peggy and Martin exchanged a look filled with secrets shared between two people who had each other's back, no matter what. Madeline's heart swelled. "What's the best part?"

"We didn't have sex that night!"

Martin cleared his throat, but he was smiling too. "I stayed in Jackson's room, and the next night, I took Peggy on another date. By the end of the week, we couldn't wait to sit next to each other. Hold hands. Kiss and make out like a couple of teenagers on the sofa."

Madeline clapped. "That's brilliant."

"After all this time, I had no idea I could like sex this much," Peggy confessed. "I really thought, after menopause, that stage in my life was over. But it doesn't have to end."

Martin kissed his wife's knuckles. "We still have stuff to work on, but it's a beginning. For both of us."

Madeline let her pride shine through. "I can't tell you how happy I am for both of you. Excellent work, star pupils."

They spent the remaining time talking about next steps, how to deal with inevitable setbacks, and what tools they could use when old habits came knocking, but for the first time since meeting the Atwoods, Madeline no longer worried about the fate of their relationship. The work of maintaining love was a lifetime commitment, but they were reaping the rewards. Momentum would carry them forward.

When their session concluded, Martin headed outside, but Peggy paused, straightening her floral cardigan.

"I don't suppose you want to tell me what's going on with you."

Madeline turned her smile up. "What do you mean?"

Peggy scanned her face with an eagle-eye. "You're a professional, but I was wondering..."

"You can ask me anything, Peggy."

"You've been my guardian and Martin's champion when we barely bothered to put up a fight. I think it's fair to say you're a love warrior." She gave Madeline an open look of concern. "I just hope you have someone that fights as fiercely as you do for the things that really matter. More than anyone I know, you deserve a partner who's got your back."

With a squeeze of Madeline's arm, Peggy shut the door softly behind her.

Madeline didn't know what to say. Or think. Or feel.

Life—and her time as a therapist—had taught her the strongest bonds were formed during high-stress situations. You either pulled together or fell apart, regardless of good intentions or relationship fantasies. The test of compatibility thrived in the heart of struggle.

Without thinking, she picked up her fertility totem. The goddess's smooth contours gave her strength while reminding her, every fear and anxiety Madeline had, billions of women had already experienced and survived. Given her background, she should abhor any symbol of religion or deity worship, but the truth about sex, love, and intimacy didn't live in the hands of twisted, power-hungry zealots.

It lived in the hands of lovers and friends.

The luscious figure might not have had a face, but she seemed to stare at Madeline, offering a loving. "Well, duh."

Madeline decided then and there to ask Julian for a do-over. It wouldn't break any rules, and she wouldn't have to confess she remembered what happened in Mason's Hole. He had emotional baggage with Agent Spearman, but the older woman didn't feel like a jealous rival.

If connecting with Julian pissed off Shadow Man, well, they'd deal with it. Together.

Flush with excitement, she dialed his number and didn't smother the smile that spread across her face when he answered on the first ring.

"Madeline?"

He sounded as excited as she felt. Her shoulders relaxed. Everything was going to be all right. "Hey, stranger. I was wondering, if you're not buried in Homeland Security cases, maybe you'd like to have dinner with me."

CHAPTER TWENTY-FIVE

JULIAN

After the bright sunshine and fresh-cut grass smell of country living, Julian's tiny office squeezed in on him.

He tapped away at his keyboard, significantly expanding every detail he could remember about Mason's Hole, not that anyone would see his notes. The official report would go to Spearmen, or as Julian had come to think of her, Shadow Man's lapdog, but he'd save *this* version on his personal air gap computer. No Wi-Fi. No modem. No federal database. Illegal, it was true, but if truth was the objective, he couldn't take the risk his data would be redacted or deleted.

Spearman's betrayal soured his already questionable zeal for government work. Adding insult to injury, he'd gotten a company email celebrating her promotion to Assistant Deputy Director. Julian had no doubt the office would be collecting for drinks at Stucky's, a smoky G-Man dive bar, but he'd rather chew off his own arm than pat her on the back for a job well-done. It was muggy and oppressive in the nation's capital, but the arctic climate between Julian and his boss made him want to wear a parka rather than a suit.

He needed a vacation.

What were Madeline and Whatshisname doing in Costa Rica right now? Probably sitting on the beach sipping drinks from coconuts. Or fucking in a tiki-themed cabana.

He backed away from the laptop and growled. God damn. It should be him with Mads, laughing together, walking hand-in-hand as the salty surf lapped at their ankles.

Something bit into his palm. He'd reached into his coat pocket and gripped the shard of altar. The stone had a strange heat to it, as if it were still cooling from the events of Mason's Hole. Julian took it out, squinting. Was there a faint glow to the rune? It seemed to shimmer with an odd green luminescence.

Julian shook his head. Closed his eyes. Looked again. It was just a stone. A stone with an arcane spiral carved into it. Probably a trick of the terrible lighting in his office.

A tap on the door interrupted his thoughts. Julian's head snapped up like a kid who'd been caught with his hand in the cookie jar. Or a federal agent woolgathering with a piece of stolen evidence. He hid the stone in his fist.

Spearman stood outside the office door, peering through glass and reinforcing wire. Normally she'd just come in, but since Mason's Hole, her attitude was uncharacteristically conciliatory.

Julian was having none of it. She could wait in the hall and rot for all he cared.

Five seconds later, Spearman opened the door and stepped into the room. Her eyes scanned the papers strewn across his desk before locking on him. "You should have wrapped up your field notes on Mason's Hole by now."

Julian choked down a dozen angry responses. All he could manage was, "Don't *should* on me."

She sighed. "It's time to put this case behind you. Move on to the next."

He sucked in his lips, making his mouth a hard line. "I know how to do my job."

Spearman rested her bottom on the edge of his desk. "This was a tough one." Gazing down at him, her eyes turned soft. "And though you don't believe it, I *do* have your best interests at heart."

His bitterness bubbled over. "Who are you kidding? You didn't want me to take this case because you knew it would be harder for you and Agent Right to cover up."

"That's enough," she snapped. "We've got to get past this, Julian."

That much was true. He didn't want to quit his job and lose what little access he had to the cases or the phenomena. Someone had to get to the bottom of mysteries no one wanted, thinking it would besmirch their rise to the top, and Julian didn't trust anyone else to handle the dossiers. He couldn't stop. Wouldn't stop until he knew the truth. And he was far from done with Mason's Hole.

They stared at each other. The shard bit into the flesh of his palm. If she wouldn't let him track down more portal locations, he'd have to do it on his own. He couldn't keep at it with another assignment in front of him.

Julian sat back in his chair. "I've got some vacation time saved up."

Spearman let out a breath, her shoulders relaxing. "I think that's a great idea. Go someplace warm and sunny. Do some parasailing or spelunking. Come back when you're refreshed."

Julian had no intention of visiting another set of creepy caves unless they were connected to the shard. He nodded anyway. "I'll start right now."

"I'll put in the paperwork for you."

Her smile held genuine warmth, but Julian didn't acknowledge the tentative bridge. He turned back to his desk, the hunk of altar clutched in his hand.

She rose, crossed the office, but hesitated with her hand on the doorknob. "Will I see you at Stucky's after work?"

If she wanted congratulations on her promotion, she'd be waiting till hell froze over. Julian didn't look up. "I'm on vacation."

Spearman huffed and closed the door. Hard.

When she'd gone, Julian relaxed his grip on the shard. It left sharp red points in his palm, and the stone was definitely warm. Not just from his hand.

With no clear space in the sea of papers on his desk, Julian set the rock on his phone. A tiny green spark danced at the point of contact.

"Do you believe in magic?" started playing.

Madeline's ringtone!

Julian nearly jumped out of his seat. He brushed the shard aside. Her smiling profile stared back at him. He'd never hit 'accept' faster in his life.

"Madeline?"

"Hey, stranger."

Her sultry, modulated tones asking him to dinner played in his head like a choir of angels. Even if he were buried in a mountain of cases proving ghosts and aliens were unequivocally real, he'd set them on fire for the chance to spend time with her.

Courting rituals demanded he play it cool.

"I, uh, wow, yeah, of course," he sputtered. Smooth. So smooth.

"Great!" Her easy laughter crackled through the ether, penetrating his heart chakra.

His mind reeled as they hashed out the details, unable to believe this was happening. Maybe her vague memories of their supposed one-night stand had left a lasting mark, but wasn't she supposed to be in Costa Rica? It was possible she'd only gone for the weekend. If so, she would have just returned home. Calling him and making a dinner date on the heels of a whirlwind vacation with a lover didn't add up. Unless she and Whatshisname were done for good.

No. Don't even think that. Let it be what it is.

By the time they hung up, Julian's mind was on fire, and not at the thought of having dinner with an incredible woman. That was great, to be sure, but the altar shard. The warmth. The green spark, and at that exact moment, the phone call from Madeline. It was no coincidence.

The Mason's Hole portal might be closed, the planets no longer in alignment, but something was still happening. Madeline was a part of it. She might be in danger. He needed to confide in someone he could trust, someone who could keep a secret.

Otto.

Julian gathered the Mason's Hole paperwork, enclosed it in a manila folder, and locked it in his filing cabinet. He didn't need it. He had everything on his laptop, which he slid into his bag.

Moments later, he stepped out of his office. He gave Spearman a curt nod as he passed her open door.

"Agent Worthy," she called.

"I'm on vacation," he said again, not slowing his stride.

Julian marveled at the dichotomy of DC as he approached Otto's place. Gentrification came to the district block by block. Heavy concrete stanchions guarded outdoor bistro tables set on faux grass. Across the street, squat graffiti-covered buildings featured boarded-up windows behind locked iron gates.

Miracle of miracles, Julian found a place to park. He walked along 4th for a bit, stopping now and then to make sure he wasn't followed, knowing Otto was sure to ask. Then he turned into the alley, swerved around an overflowing dumpster, and found himself at a nondescript steel door covered with the tags of local miscreants. In the lower corner, white, poorly defined letters on a green background read 'the deep end.'

Julian smirked. It sure was. He pounded out a complicated rhythm on the door and waited.

"What?" Otto's muffled voice came from inside.

"It's Julian!"

The door opened a crack. "Jesus, BJ. Don't shout your name," Otto hissed. "Might as well announce you're a federal agent and wave your badge around. What do you want?"

Julian huffed at his bangs. "I've got something you'll find interesting."

The door opened another inch. Otto, hair sticking out in wild directions, black horn-rimmed glasses askew, stared wild-eyed at Julian. "Anyone follow you?"

"No," Julian chuckled.

"You checked?"

"I checked."

"Get in here." He waved Julian into the darkness with urgency.

Julian squinted under the dim industrial lights hanging in round metal cages overhead. Machines of every description lined the hall, narrowing it to a walkway that Julian had to squeeze through sideways to get to Otto's inner sanctum.

They stopped at an iron-mesh gate. Otto fished a key from the pocket of the lab coat he wore over plaid pajamas.

"Did I wake you?" Julian asked. "It's almost eleven."

"No talking until we're in the faraday cage," Otto admonished.

Julian couldn't imagine being so paranoid that you wouldn't even talk until you were in a locked cage in your own house...or warehouse, but given Otto's exile, he couldn't blame the scientist.

Set in the middle of the cavernous industrial space, the cage was the size and shape of a suburban living room. Swing-arm lamps lit tables ringing the room. Some held computers, others featured machines and lab equipment whose function Julian couldn't guess.

Otto locked them in, pocketed the key, then folded his arms across his chest. "Speak."

Julian pulled the shard from his coat pocket. "This."

Otto took the shard, turning it over in his hands. "It's warm. What is it?"

"A piece from the altar of Mason's Hole. The symbol is—"

"An ancient spiral depicting life and rebirth, used most recently by the Disciples of Creation cult," Otto cut him off. "So what?"

Julian sighed, then explained the green spark, and Madeline's phone call at the moment his phone touched the rock. He told Otto about the last moments of the altar's existence, leaving out the racier parts of the narrative.

"I'll want to take some samples. Run some tests," Otto said, never raising his eyes from the hunk of stone.

"How long will that take?" Julian asked, doing the mental arithmetic necessary to get him down the Beltway in time to meet Madeline. "I've got a date tonight."

"As long as it takes," Otto said. "Don't worry, I'll get you to the church on time."

Julian opened his mouth to protest, then shrugged.

Otto waved. "Coffee's on. Get yourself a cup."

The red tub of cut-rate coffee squatted next to a pot that obviously hadn't seen a good scrubbing since the days of J. Edgar Hoover. "I'm good."

Otto didn't seem to hear him, already lost in his subterranean world of science.

Julian paced. Then sat. Then took out his phone to look at the restaurant's menu for this evening's date. No service. Of course. Faraday cage. He put the phone away.

Otto scraped at the rock. The resulting powder fell onto a slip of white paper.

"What are you doing?" Julian asked.

"Preparing samples for the M-S two-fourteen forty-five," Otto muttered.

"The what?"

Otto glared at him. "I don't have the time or the crayons to explain it to you. This will go a lot faster if you shut up and let me work."

Julian raised his hands in mock surrender. "You don't have to be a dick about it."

"Sorry," Otto said. "I'm in the zone. I'll explain later."

All Julian could do was watch as Otto tipped the rock scrapings into a vial, added fluid, and sent the sample through a variety of machines. He weighed the rock, took its temperature—repeatedly—and performed countless esoteric tests, muttering to himself the whole time.

At last, nearly two hours later, Otto placed the altar stone next to his computer.

"Okay, Jules, come take a look."

"You know I hate when you call me that," Julian said.

"First you have a problem with BJ, then Jules. Relax, it's a metric of energy, a term of endearment. Anyway. Look."

Julian bent over the desk. The periodic table appeared on the computer screen. Red dots indicated the presence of various elements.

"This thing radio-carbon dates to the Precambrian period. Specifically, one point seventy-six million years ago. And the mass spectrometer revealed more interesting data." He pointed to the red dots. "This baby has traces of gold, copper, and clay. That combination of minerals is found in these amounts, and in rocks of this age, in only one place on Earth."

Otto, ever the drama queen, paused.

Julian waited.

Otto's face curled into a thin, mischievous smile.

"Well?!" Julian asked, exasperated.

"Taos, New Mexico."

"Home of the Disciples of Creation," Julian breathed. "Begging the question—"

"What the hell was it doing in a cave under a North Carolina basement?" Otto finished. "That's not all. The first temperature reading was twenty-six point six degrees—"

"It's not that cold," Julian cut in. "Are you sure your machines—?"

"Celsius, Jules. Celsius. This is science, not a—"

"Okay, okay."

"Point is, it's heating up, and it shouldn't be. The ambient temperature in here is only twenty-two point one three degrees. It should be cooling down. Whatever the hell was going on in Mason's Hole is still going on. Probably in Taos, New Mexico."

Julian frowned. "That's quite a leap."

"Have you ever heard of quantum entanglement?"

"I've heard of it but...."

"It's a well-documented phenomenon. A group of particles initially share a spatial proximity, but the quantum state of each particle can't be described independently, even when separated by enormous distances."

"I kind of follow you," Julian said.

Otto pinched the bridge of his nose. "Let's say all the particles in your body are part of a quantum entanglement group."

"Okay."

Otto held up the sharp-edged tool he'd used to scrape the rock sample. "And I cut off the tip of your finger."

"Jesus, Otto."

The scientist held up a hand for silence. "I take the tip of your finger to Antarctica and poke it with a pin. Hypothetically, you'd feel it here in DC. No time delay. No accounting for the speed of light. Instantaneous, you understand?"

"But nothing can travel faster than light."

"Quantum theory doesn't agree with relativity. It's the greatest quandary in modern physics."

"Shit," Julian said.

"Well spoken, sir." Otto looked at the rock. "Can I keep this?"

Julian shook his head. "Evidence in a federal case."

"Yet you're carrying it around in your pocket. I'm willing to bet if I checked the evidence log on the Mason's Hole case, I wouldn't find an entry for this baby." Otto smiled. "I'm surprised at you, BJ."

Julian smiled back. "I don't know why, but it's still important. Like it's some kind of key. Like I'm supposed to have it."

Otto frowned. "Not very scientific."

Julian shrugged. "Just going with my gut."

"I'm keeping the data," Otto said.

"Of course."

Out of Otto's lair, Julian sat in Beltway traffic, trying to make Virginia for his date with Madeline. Movement was down to a crawl, so he booked a flight to New Mexico. Crazy? Maybe. But the evidence from Otto's tests was too compelling to ignore. Besides, Washington, DC, was the antithesis of Taos. Not the sandy beaches one usually thought of when planning a vacation. But there was sun, art, fine dining, and, well, that was all Julian knew about the place. He was eager to do a little snooping regarding the local rock formations...and cults. One in particular.

He wondered what Madeline would think of his plan, but mentally put it on the "Do Not Mention" list.

Julian made it to the restaurant with a half-hour to spare. As he pushed his way through the posh glass doors, thoughts of the altar stone in his pocket, Taos, and the Disciples of Creation fell away. All he could think about was Madeline. Her feline emerald eyes. Her fiery hair. Her sharp mind and easy laugh. The way they'd worked together in Mason's Hole.

Julian asked for a table where he could see the street through the windows. He wanted to watch her walk up. Wanted to see the expression on her face. Maybe get an idea of her intentions for their dinner.

From minute to minute, Julian didn't know if he wanted to pursue a romance or a friendship. He was leaning toward romance, if he was honest with himself. After all, the best love stories were based on friendship, weren't they?

But what about his job? Always traveling. Hardly ever home. What kind of woman would put up with that? Plus, there was the element of danger to contend with. If everything worked out like it did in the storybooks and they eventually tied the knot, there was the possibility he'd widow her.

He shook his head. No use thinking like that. And no matter what his intentions, or hers, it would be damn good to see her again.

Julian remembered her heat as she slept against him on Constance's couch. Her softness. How damn comfortable they were together, like old friends, not two people who just met. And that meant, no matter what the circumstances, there was hope.

He checked his watch, looked out the window, and waited.

CHAPTER TWENTY-SIX

MADELINE

Madeline deliberated over what outfit said, *I know what I want and how to ask for it*, while still remaining tasteful. A clingy black V-neck blouse with sheer panels at the waist paired with a dark green pencil skirt did the trick. Emerald and gold earrings with a matching statement necklace completed the ensemble.

Looking at herself in the mirror, she smiled. If Julian was battling DC traffic to spend time with her, she wanted to give him a show. The bandage on her upper arm where a piece of Constance's front window had taken its pound of flesh gave her pause, but best to ignore the kinky magic, Desmond, and what she had or hadn't experienced in the basement of Constance's house.

There was a word for her condition in therapist jargon: denial. But that was a problem for Future Madeline.

All dolled up, she decided to head to the restaurant early. She'd catch up on emails in the parking lot. Journal. Give herself a pep talk. It was going to be tricky navigating the amnesia-game, but she'd bullshitted her way out of much tougher situations.

Fluffing her hair in the mirror, she muttered, "Fake it till you make it, baby."

The cold, unfamiliar shape of the rental car fob snapped her back to reality. Her trusty RAV4 had barely limped home from Mason's Hole before demanding a trip to the shop. So much for reliability. Now she was in possession of of a dull gray sedan that smelled like lemon cleaner and regret. Still, it had a certain thrill—like she was undercover, playing spy with her favorite federal agent.

She grinned and slid into the driver's seat, adjusting the too-stiff steering wheel. The engine purred to life with a low hum. Not her car, not her life—but maybe it was time for a Julian-shaped change.

Casa di Amore was a favorite Italian spot among the locals. A converted Victorian, its gables were covered with climbing ivy. Madeline would insist they get a table outside. It wasn't too hot to enjoy a glass of red wine, maybe an antipasto platter, if Julian's picky stomach could handle its unknown origins. When the sun fell, the servers would light candles on the back patio, and depending on the night, they'd hear Mr. Di Amto sing old love songs from the kitchen while his hostess wife teased her man about being tone deaf.

Yep, a perfect first date setting.

She found a parking spot under a sweetgum tree, turned off the engine, and rolled down the windows. A glance at the digital clock told her Constance's memorial was getting under way. Even though Shadow Man's wrecking crew had leveled the house, she imagined Roland, Effy, Rosamund, Even and Sarah Dubois standing in the family cemetery, tearful but glad to have known the vivacious character that was Constance Hanford.

Madeline had sent a bouquet of pink and white roses and hoped wherever Constance was, she could see them, but she had a feeling those who'd embraced Desmond's special form of protection didn't need sex magic or arcane rituals to keep them connected. They had each other and the legacy of Mason's Hole.

Leaning back in her seat, Madeline was surprised to feel excited and content for the first time in a long time. Soon, she'd be with Julian, playing the get-to-know you mating ritual.

She knew far more about him than she could let on, but hell, she might as well have fun with it. He had the hots for older women. Check. He was fiercely protective but didn't strip others of agency. Double-check. Last but not least, he gave off Golden Retriever energy, but under the surface, there was a powerhouse alpha waiting to take charge. Check, check, and check.

What if she let it slip she liked a bit of roleplay and could bring out her inner boss? His face would flush under his tan, and his bright blue eyes would darken—

The passenger door opened, jarring Madeline from her fantasy. Shadow Man folded his imposing form into the car and closed the door.

Madeline didn't jump or scream, but every alarm bell rang through her body. She instinctively reached for a small canister of mace in the pocket of the driver's door, wishing it were her self-defense baton.

"That won't work on me." Shadow Man nodded at her hidden hand. "But I appreciate your self-control. Most women scream, run for the hills, or freeze like a scared rabbit."

"If they're dealing with you, that doesn't surprise me," Madeline hissed.

He gave her a look of mock affront. "On the contrary, I've spent decades studying human nature and believe I give off a calming influence. Goes with the job title."

"Special Agent Asshole?" She paused, the reality of why he was in her car hitting her in the chest. "What are you doing here? Is Julian—?"

Shadow Man rolled his black eyes like a shark before they bite. "I assure you, Agent Wonderbread is fine."

"Then why..." Madeline bit her lip hard enough to make her eyes water. She'd never called Julian Agent Wonderbread in Shadow Man's presence. The fucker was trying to catch her out.

"You're a quick study, Madeline. I like that about you." His eyes raked her body. "There's several things I like about you. Would you like to hear my list?"

A not-unpleasant thrill tingled down her spine. His size swallowed the passenger side of the car, and his hair was thick and black with a tinge of red in the fading light. Shadow Man carried himself with an air of superiority that set her teeth on edge, but she couldn't discount his masculine appeal. Here was a man who, when he chose a path, didn't ask permission to walk it.

Madeline suppressed a heated flush and looked away from his knowing eyes. She chalked up her response to past attraction to bad boys, a quirk of hormones, and repressed anger from Constance's handling.

Sniffing, she gave him her shoulder. "I'm not interested in anything you have to say."

"Really? You don't want to know how I knew you'd be here?"

Madeline stared unseeing out the windshield. "You bugged my phone. Put a tracking device in my car. Something nefarious."

"None of the above. My methods are far more venerable." He stretched his legs out and smoothed a long, tapered hand down the front of his expensive black suit. "How have you been sleeping?"

A flash of her previous dream, his voice coming out of the darkness to whisper her name, threatened her composure. "Cut to the chase."

"You're no fun." Shadow Man sighed dramatically. "Our meeting in Mason's Hole was not a coincidence. Nor is my presence today. Since you're so delightfully set against believing in the paranormal,

I'll let you in on a secret. I have abilities most of your kind do not possess."

"My kind? As in, human?"

He smiled. "As in therapist."

Damn, his old-fashioned speech made him sound like a Dickensian villain, but his tone was warm wax, thick and painful if not given the chance to cool. She felt herself soften and tried to resist. "Fine. I'll play along." She gave him a thorough once-over. "Tell me what I'm thinking right now."

You're a pushy creep.

"Nothing I haven't heard before." His eyes grew heavy and slumberous. "Since you're being a good girl, I'll share a thought with you."

Fuck her praise kink, Madeline itched to spray him with mace. "Not necessary."

"You know how nagging thoughts can burrow under your skin like a tick? They itch and itch until you have to suffocate them. Such is my dilemma with you." He planted an elbow on the center armrest and leaned into her space. "I don't like how closed your mind is to me, but it made me wonder. Roland summoned you to Mason's Hole for a reason. He and Desmond were never on good terms, but that doesn't mean Desmond couldn't influence his dreams."

She pinched her lips tight, trying not to react. It hadn't stopped bugging her why Roland had called her of all people. If she believed in the whole dream transference thing, it was reasonable Desmond might have nudged Roland to find a new participant in his weird mating ritual. Not that she could ask Shadow Man. *Desmond* was the one person she wasn't supposed to remember. He was also the only one who believed Shadow Man was as dangerous as he looked.

So Shadow Man knew she was faking her memory lapse or fishing for gaps. "I don't know what you're talking about."

Shadow Man didn't blink. "How is the cut on your arm healing?"

Her hand lifted, skimmed the flesh-colored bandage. Another memory she was supposed to forget. Shadow Man lifting his blood-smeared thumb to his mouth. Fuck if she'd let him know she had a thing for blood sport. No one knew about it, least of all Shadow Man. He was just good at reading people. "I'm not losing sleep over a scratch."

"You have an amazing mental block, but that doesn't work in dreams," he murmured, staring at her lips. "What is a dream, anyway? A reconstruction of past events working themselves through a complex filtering system? Such a limited perspective. Ask me what I think about dreams."

"No," she said in a clipped voice.

"I think dreams are a way to travel through space and time without the frail limitations of a fleshy vehicle. Not that there isn't flesh involved." His gaze settled on her bandaged arm. "You have very lusty dreams, Madeline."

To hell with his cat-and-mouse game. Madeline went for the door handle, intent on getting far away from him.

"Your sister is in grave danger."

Her hand froze, and she swung around to face him. "Don't talk about my sister!"

His nostrils flared as if drinking in the scent of her anger. "How quickly you revert to your primal self when I touch old wounds. I'd be careful with that. You don't want to give away too many weaknesses. It'll spoil the chase."

"Fuck you, Agent Right."

"Maybe. We have other business first." He held up a long finger. "Wait for it."

Madeline jumped when her cell phone rang. Hatty's golden visage appeared on the screen.

"How bright and carefree your sister looks. Quite your opposite. Personally, I prefer *your* fiery personality." Shadow Man waved at her phone. "Better get that."

Against her better judgment, Madeline angled her body away from him and answered the phone. "Where have you been?"

"Mads?" Hatty said in a low, urgent voice. "Don't say anything. Just listen. I'm in Taos."

Had a bucket of ice water cascaded over her head, Madeline couldn't have been more shocked. "NO."

"I was having nightmares about...you know. And I'm tired of them. Tired of running from what happened." She took a shuddering breath. "Then Walter called me."

Walter. The man who'd helped her and Hatty escape from the compound. Another name she didn't want to think about.

Hatty's voice dropped again. "He said he has information about Thoth, but I had to meet him in person. I got to Taos three days ago, was supposed to meet Walter last night, but he never showed. Mads..."

Madeline squeezed her eyes tight. Reminded herself to breathe.

"I think I'm being followed," Hatty whispered. "I think Thoth found me."

Panic threatened to choke Madeline. "Hatty—"

"Listen, Walter gave me an address. I'm texting it to you. If I don't call you back in one hour, you need to come. You need to help me."

"Yes," Madeline said. "Always."

"Sissy?"

Hatty's voice was small, scared. The same voice she'd had when Madeline woke her in the middle of the night and told her to grab whatever she couldn't live without. Hatty, bless her heart, had reached out and taken the only thing that mattered to her: Madeline's hand.

"Don't do anything!" Madeline nearly yelled. "I'm coming right now."

There was a pause as Hatty collected herself. "I have to," she said with steely resolve. "I want this to be over."

The line beeped three times. Hatty had hung up.

Looking for a target, Madeline faced Shadow Man. "Goddamn you, you're behind this."

"I have nothing to do with your sister's crusade, but I am aware of the situation in Taos." His angular face held nothing but apathetic contemplation. "Picture a slew of farm animals running into a burning barn. Thoth, as you call him, is ready and waiting to padlock the door behind them. That's what's left of the Disciples of Creation."

Madeline no longer wanted to mace him. She wanted to punch him. The glint in his eyes said he knew her intention...and he liked it. Her passion was a part of his game.

The desire to inflict harm was cut short by another call. This time, Julian's sunshine hair and sleepy smile popped up. Madeline had taken the photo the night they fell asleep on the couch. It was silly, but after Constance's death, she'd needed something stable, something real to remind her there was goodness in the world.

Julian can help.

"I see the wheels turning in your head," Shadow Man said quietly. "Shall we game it out? Option one, you confess your sister is in trouble, and Julian drops whatever he's doing. But will his mind be on finding your sister...or his other obsession?"

"Shut up," Madeline growled. The phone continued to ring.

He continued, unfazed. "You were right about him and Spearman. He might be mad at her, but they still want each other. The dog-eyed boy chasing his older female boss? It would be amusing if it wasn't so pathetic."

Ring. Hurt slithered around Madeline's heart and contracted with muscular conviction.

Shadow Man paused. "Then there's option two. You go it alone like you've always done. No one to question your logic, your intuition. No one to get in the way of doing what must be done." He pushed a hand inside his coat. "I see the appeal, but if defending Hatty means taking Thoth down, you can't bury him in the desert without being caught. You'll lose everything you've worked so hard to build."

Madeline's chest squeezed again. Fucking Thoth. Who says she'd get caught? She could almost feel the handle of a shovel in her grip.

"There's a third option, Madeline."

The ringing stopped, went to voicemail. She didn't want to look at Shadow Man. She wanted to yell and knock out a couple of his teeth. But he was holding something out to her. A padded yellow envelope.

"What is that?"

"An untraceable phone loaded with every scrap of information I have on the Disciples of Creation and a direct flight to Taos." He checked his watch. "Which leaves in two hours."

She glared at him, fighting the flare of hope. "Why?"

Again, he appraised her, but this time it was devoid of sexual intent. "When I began studying human nature, I enjoyed the nuance. The passion. The ingenuity of life. But over the years," he shrugged, "it's clear humans are meat puppets going through the motions. Eat. Sleep. Propagate. At times I think I'll be bored to *death*. Then I met you and thought, maybe it's not completely pointless."

Had it not been for his midnight eyes sucking the light from the car, Madeline might have believed him. As it was, her hand curled to prevent snatching the envelope. "What do you want from me in return?"

"I don't want anything from you, Madeline. In fact, I'm willing to stay out of your hair." His smile flashed bright and predatory. "Until you call upon me to assist you. Then I will come before you can question if you're awake or dreaming."

He meant every word.

Unbelievably, Madeline took the envelope, but she hated her hands for shaking. Did she have time to tell Julian?

Shadow Man opened his door and stepped out. "The clock is ticking, Madeline, and Agent Wonderbread will only get in your way. Call *me* if you need help."

She'd had enough of him telling her what to do. Glaring at him, she lifted her phone.

Shadow Man leaned back into the car and pierced her with his dark eyes. "If you contact him, even to apologize, he'll suspect something's up. Then he'll start digging. If he follows you, I will not be pleased." He paused. "Julian Worthy has gotten in my way twice now. The next time, I will remove more than his memory of The Disciples of Creation. I'll remove his memory of *you*."

Madeline felt the blood leave her face. "Who the fuck are you?"

"Call me Atum." He gave her a wink. "Shadow Man is so comic book villain. We both know you can do better."

He melded into the shadows as abruptly as he'd appeared.

Madeline weighed the envelope in her palm. Looked at the restaurant's lovely façade. Glanced at the clock. She was five minutes late meeting Julian, but everything she needed to protect Hatty and nail Thoth's crooked ass was within reach.

She slammed her fist on the steering wheel. "Dammit!"

Chest heaving, she backed out of the restaurant's parking lot, her jaw set in a grim line. There was no time for self-pity or doubt. As much as she wanted to convince herself the Disciples of Creation lived in her rearview mirror, the ghosts of the past never stopped licking their teeth for a taste of the living.

Speeding down the highway, resignation turned to anger. Anger turned to determination. No matter what, she believed Shadow Man, Agent Right, Atum, whatever his name was, wasn't lying to her. Getting to Taos was her priority. Standing Julian up was wrong on so many levels, she didn't have time to list them. But if she involved him, Shadow Man would take Julian's memory of her away for good. It was almost as painful as pretending she didn't know *him*.

When she could think straight, she'd text Julian. Make up an excuse. It would be something innocuous. She had a migraine, car troubles—that was a semi-truth—and could they reschedule?

Maybe Julian would forgive her. Maybe he'd cut his losses. Maybe she was crazy to believe she could help anyone, ever. But she'd come too far, and deep down, she agreed with her sister. She wanted the ghosts of her childhood to stop haunting her.

Hatty was her blood, her responsibility, but the way she felt now, Madeline might as well be cursed to be alone for the rest of her life.

CHAPTER TWENTY-SEVEN

JULIAN

J ulian sat in his chair in the restaurant, shock and anger taking turns poking him with hot irons. He couldn't believe what he'd just seen through the window. Shadow Man skulking around the parking lot. This parking lot. When the creepy agent climbed into a generic gray sedan, Julian had strained to see what was going on inside. His eyes fell on Madeline.

Julian had snatched his phone and called her, muttering, "Pick up, pick up." He wanted to rush outside, confront Shadow Man and save Madeline.... From what? She didn't look like she was in trouble.

He made himself sit still and watch.

Madeline hesitated, phone in her hand. Shadow Man shook his head. She let his call go to voicemail. A pit formed in Julian's stomach. It threatened to suffocate him when Shadow Man handed her an envelope, and she took it.

The clink of plates and smell of garlic faded into the background. Dismay kept him immobile. Shadow Man left, but Madeline wasn't getting out of the car.

She was driving away. What the actual fuck.

Julian stared at the retreating sedan, carrying Madeline—and his hopes of a new beginning—away.

As the hurt of being stood up cooled, Julian's ire boiled. He caught the waitress's eye and held up a finger.

Cute and bouncy with a playful blond pixie cut, she took out her pad. "Do you want to wait a little longer for your friend, or are you ready to order?"

"Scotch," he said, voice curt. "Neat. Oban, if you've got it. And make it a double."

Her smile faded. She gave him side-eye and left him to his thoughts.

Julian had questions. So many questions. Where was Madeline's RAV4? What was in the envelope Shadow Man gave her? Why hadn't she taken his call?

The waitress set his Scotch in front of him without a word.

Good.

The sharp twist of betrayal lapped at his heart. Again. He raised the glass. The amber liquid bit his taste buds and burned pleasantly going down, warming his belly and whetting his mind for the work. No jumping to conclusions. Just the facts. This wasn't a date, anymore. Madeline and Shadow Man's liaison was another part of the case. Mason's Hole, part two? No. Mason's Hole was just another dot on the graph. Slate Hill, Slaughter Beach, and however many cases Julian had yet to uncover, this was the spectral seduction of Agent Wonderbread.

Not anymore.

What did Julian know?

Shadow Man had directed Spearman to waive him off the case, but Julian had refused, leaving the crooked agent scrambling to protect his interests in Mason's Hole. What were his interests? From Shadow Man's point of view, Julian had to be distracted so

Desmond could work his magic with Madeline. In that, Shadow Man had almost succeeded.

But if Madeline was working for Shadow Man, why hadn't he told her how strong the sex magic would be? Then again, why would he? Shadow Man could kill two birds with one stone. Using Madeline as a shill, he could distract Julian with his exact type—an intelligent older woman—and gain a surrogate to study later.

Then there was Spearman. How much did she know?

Julian tried to recall the conversation between her and Shadow Man in the vagina room. They'd called Madeline a civilian. Spearman had been pissed but went along with monitoring the paranormal events.

Another sip of Scotch.

And another.

Julian *knew* Spearman. Her emotions in the cave were real. Maybe she was on his side. If he left now, he could still make her promotion party. Maybe after a couple rounds, he'd get her to talk about what happened to Madeline in the back of the trailer. If that didn't work, he could talk her into going back to his apartment. Or hers.

No. That way lay madness.

Just because Julian couldn't trust the woman who'd jilted him, didn't mean he had to go running to his literal runner-up.

That thought led back to Madeline.

In Mason's Hole, she'd seemed so genuine. Her concern over Constance, her anger at Roland, her sexual attraction to Julian, felt real. But the facts didn't support his *feelings*. Clearly, he didn't know her at all, and he hadn't done his due diligence. He was a federal agent, and not once had he looked into her background to corroborate what she'd told him.

Not that Shadow Man would have sent her undercover without an impeccable fake profile, but who was Madeline Da Vinci, really? Had she been in The Disciples of Creation? Did she really have a sister? Was there such a thing as script 22?

Which left the envelope. If Shadow Man put Madeline on his payroll, she'd gotten a fee for leading Julian on a wild goose chase while he and Spearman set the stage for Madeline's alien encounter.

Julian had beaten him at his own game, almost by accident, and only just. With the game over, there was no need for Madeline to keep up the ruse. Shadow Man had called her off at the last moment, handed her the payout, and sent her on her way. No need for her to take Julian's call. No need to have dinner with the dupe.

The mysterious villain had expertly played them against one another. If Madeline was an award-winning actress, Shadow Man was the most gifted director in history.

Rage burned hotter than the Scotch in his belly. Hotter than his disgust at Spearman for giving Madeline the memory drug. Thinking back on it now, what did he care? So the shill got her mind wiped. So what?

Did Spearman know Madeline was on Shadow Man's payroll? Probably not. He'd like to think after all these years he could tell when his boss was putting on a show. But he'd also thought Madeline was the real deal. Clearly his instincts couldn't be trusted.

As a lawman, his confirmation bias was problematic on so many levels.

More Scotch.

He raised the glass to his lips and found it empty.

What the fuck was he doing? Sitting around wallowing in self-loathing. Eating his heart out and destroying his stomach lining. No. He was on vacation, damn it. A va-case-tion. God, he really shouldn't drink.

The waitress came by again. She looked as if he might bite her. "Another?"

To be fair, he had been kind of a dick earlier. He could be hurt and angry and maybe changed a little for the worse, but he wasn't that guy. If he turned into a bitter asshole, Shadow Man won. And

Spearman would be right; he was too emotionally invested to bring about much-needed justice.

For all the negativity swirling inside him, what he hated most, was losing. Losing the case. Losing himself.

"Sir?"

Julian pasted on a smile. "I'm sorry," he said. "I'm having a bit of a day. Stood up, and other stuff."

"Are you sure I can't get you something to eat? Might help."

"You know, you're right. Low blood sugar isn't helping my mood, and I'm here after all...."

"Exactly!" she beamed, leaning forward.

Julian scanned the menu. He'd barely glanced at it since he sat down. He didn't recognize half of the food, and didn't exactly trust what he did know. "Umm...."

Pasta and chicken. As long as they cooked the chicken long enough, it should be alright. "Chicken parm, please."

"And another Scotch?" The server's bright eyes held a hint of her returning smile.

Julian liked her. "No-oh," he chuckled. "I'm not that guy. Or, I'm trying not to be." His hair chose that moment to fall in front of his eye. He puffed it away. "Sparkling water?"

"You got it."

Nothing to do but wait for his food and plan his next moves. His flight to Taos wasn't until morning. He could change that. His go-bag was packed and in the car. Why not leave tonight? Julian called the airline. He could change the reservation online, but he liked talking to a real person. A commodity that suddenly seemed in short supply.

The next flight out was booked, but he could catch the red-eye.

The waitress returned with his fizzy water.

"I'm sorry," he said. "Can I get my dinner to go?" He didn't want to hang out in the place where Madeline had stood him up for Shadow Man.

271

"Of course." She hesitated. "I shouldn't say this but..."

"What?"

"Your friend." She nodded at the empty chair opposite him. "I think she's an idiot. Any woman would be lucky to share a meal with you."

Julian smiled at her, but the compliment couldn't penetrate his hardening shell. "Thank you."

Madeline was a lot of things in his estimation, but she wasn't an idiot.

Neither was he.

No more playing Agent Wonderbread.

As if picking up on the fire in Julian's belly, the altar shard in his pocket burned hot against his leg.

The heat grounded him. Brought his thoughts into sharp focus.

They'd underestimated him? Good.

They thought he was down—maybe even out? Better. It gave him room to move.

He didn't need Spearman or Madeline's help. What he needed was an edge. Now he had one. And in Taos, he'd use it to cut straight to the truth.

Turn the page for a preview of
Spectral Seduction Book 2

THE DEMONIC DEBAUCHERY OF VIPER'S CLEFT

The Demonic Debauchery of Viper's Cleft

Chapter 1

M adeline barely made the flight out of Dulles to Santa Fe, New Mexico.

She collapsed into her seat, chest heaving as she drew in shallow breaths. Her strappy sandals had carved red marks into her feet, and a headache pulsed behind her eyes. None of that mattered. She was on the plane—finally leaving.

Her baby sister was in trouble. She knew it in her bones.

On the outside, Madeline projected the veneer of a calm, if rumpled, thirty-something sex therapist. But on the inside, her patience was a ragged fingernail, gnawed to the quick and oozing blood.

Anger boiled in the pit of her stomach, fed by a fear she could never vanquish. Frustration made her want to punch the headrest in front of her. Cramped spaces, creepy-crawly insects, heights—none of that bothered Madeline. But her sister calling her out of the blue, confessing she was tired of hiding from The Disciples of Creation and letting the past dominate her future? That was enough to coat the back of Madeline's mouth with an acidic tang.

Droplets of sweat slid from her fiery red hair and ran down her temple. The rumpled date-night attire of her sleeveless black blouse and emerald pencil skirt made her look like she'd had one too many cocktails. She probably smelled like old perfume and panic. Nothing she could do about it now.

As the plane pushed away from the terminal and began its taxi down the runway, Madeline checked her phone for the hundredth time. Hatty said she'd call her back in an hour.

That hour had come and gone.

Settling back into the chair, Madeline tried to make her heart rate settle as the turbojets thrust her into the darkening sky. The flight would take a couple hours. She needed to relax. Decompress. Think. But the other phone, the one Agent Atum Right gave her in DC, burned a hole in her skirt pocket.

"It's everything I've collected on The Disciples," he had said. The intensity of his black eyes promised answers to her past, and something else, something on the darker side of sensual.

She didn't believe Agent Right would show all his cards. Not all at once. He'd mysteriously appeared at Mason's Manor shortly before her client and friend Constance Hanford's sheet-covered body had been rolled away. Had Madeline been alone, maybe she would have leaned into his authority. But she hadn't been alone. Julian had been with her.

Julian.

Madeline closed her eyes, wincing at the vision of Special Agent Julian Worthy waiting for her. He was the lead investigator of Homeland Security's paranormal sex crime division, because of course, every government needed a tall, blond hunk of masculine goodness keeping tabs on spooky encounters with ghosts, glowing green aliens, and spectral portals. And she'd stood him up to head out on this rescue mission.

She'd been with him, what, two days? Their chemistry hit like lightning, singeing the air between them. She hadn't been able to wait a week. Called him. Asked him to dinner. Even though his superiors warned her not to get involved.

As it was, Madeline doubted he'd ever speak to her again. Standing a man up—even one with Golden Retriever energy—tended to leave a bad aftertaste. She had good reason to ditch him, one Agent Right made blatantly clear: involve Julian and his memory of her would be erased.

The thought of Julian looking at her like a stranger caused her stomach to clench like she was about to be squashed by a lead piano. For now, Julian and their tentative romance were off limits.

And wouldn't Julian's boss, the svelte, dark-haired Agent Nina Spearman, be pleased? Madeline was no fool. The older woman looked at Julian with the possessiveness of one who'd tasted his passion and was hungry for more. In the medical trailer, when Spearman had the memory erasure drug poised inches from her arm, Madeline had clocked the depth of secrets behind those hazel eyes.

Secrets that might be on the phone.

Retrieving the device from her pocket, Madeline placed it on the empty seat beside her. The sleek rectangle looked innocent enough. But it could be a serpent of unknown breed, asleep until she turned it on. Once awake, it could strike, puncture her, fill her veins with its venomous riddles.

The dull throb behind Madeline's eyes bloomed, grinding at her already depleted senses. The pain was always there, sometimes accompanied by nausea when she thought about the Disciples of Creation cult, but now it grew acute, like a warning bell for an incoming air raid.

And why not? She *should* be in pain. It was her fault Hatty was MIA. If her sister knew how dangerous Thoth and his inner circle were, she'd never go back. Madeline had kept that from her—to protect her. Now, all these years later, that move had backfired big-time.

Sneering at Agent Right's phone, she scooped it up and pressed the power button so hard her fingertip went white. Whatever he collected, regardless of his intentions, could give her the ammunition to keep Hatty out of the cult's clutches—for good this time.

The screen held one icon: an Ouroboros.

The sight of the snake eating its own tail made Madeline shiver, as if something cold and rippling with scales slid across her feet. The sense of foreboding didn't stop her from clicking the icon.

A neat set of folders appeared starting when the founding members purchased the land near Taos in 1989. The first folder held nothing revelatory. Grainy photos captured the commune in simpler times. Men in work shirts, women with braids, kids running barefoot after goats. There were aerial maps, deeds, and building permits, but nothing hinted the co-op wanted to go cult-ish.

Madeline zeroed in on Thoth's younger picture. Twenty years ago, he didn't look like a charlatan. He looked like what he was, a used car salesman named Daniel, his body lanky, his shoulders relaxed. Madeline vaguely remembered a time when he was kind and soft-spoken, a good leader. A warm smile and sandy flyaway hair welcomed the curious, lost, and lonely. Then he'd started taking nightly visits to the desert, and things had changed. He'd changed.

The next folder contained the official birth of the cult and its name adoption in 1995. A fresh set of photos showed the same suntanned faces, but cosmic calm replaced their shy friendliness. Behind them, new members vied for a spot of recognition.

Madeline blinked, squinted. There—tiny in the background, so small she almost missed it—was her mother, Jennie, hair loose around her shoulders, one arm around a younger, sharp-hipped Walter. Jennie's smile was exhausted, but real.

Madeline's throat tightened. Where had she been? Where had Hatty been when that photo was taken?

Bailing on the visual time capsule, she searched the folders for legal actions taken against The Disciples, missing person reports, and the holiest of bottom lines, the money trail. An hour passed. Two. Drinks were served and snacks eaten. As far as cults went, The Disciples' business model was innocuous. Revenue came via resort-class healing ceremonies, selling essential oil blessed by "high priestesses," and tax-exempt donations for the weekly sermon Thoth broadcast on his satellite station.

Apparently, two hundred people could make a decent living off Thoth's stewardship. Madeline wasn't surprised. He'd become a master storyteller, commanding his audience with tales of affirmation, a slice of fear-mongering, and the promise of salvation, usually rebranded from whatever religious texts he cherry-picked. The Bible, Torah, Quran, Bhagavad Gita — it didn't matter when the sentiment was the same: *Put your trust in me. I know the way.*

All of this Madeline knew, but where were the records of criminal activity? The Disciples grew the psychoactive Sacred Datura or western jimsonweed, which could act as a poison if used incorrectly, but they didn't sell it. Dirtier drugs—meth, cocaine, and heroin—were also off limits. Taos had too many chakra chasers to risk endangering the tourism trade.

So how could Thoth afford to build the new-age compound and adjoining vacation suites? According to the files, there were five missing persons reports, none of them women or children. In fact, the missing and recovered were men in their mid-twenties. Those that were found suffered from thirst, sun exposure, and what was loosely called "mental impairment." In the attached photos, they looked...emaciated. Like something had sucked the life out of them.

Inquiries had been made, but nothing substantial connected the cases to the Disciples.

Another dead end?

A swipe to the next file and the tone changed. A report from the 1930s said, *A woman in white, speaking in tongues, appeared near the canyon at dusk.* Missionary diaries describing "visions" of a desert bride. A yellowed clipping from the *Taos Gazette*: **MIRACLE OR MASS DELUSION?**

Madeline's eyes narrowed, the ice she'd been chewing forgotten in her mouth. Desert bride. Yes. She remembered a bit of lore circulating the compound about a woman in the desert, but she'd had no clue it related to a real case from the 1930s.

The next file made her flinch. She almost dropped the phone. It showed folders organized by name: "Walter," "Thoth," "Madeline," "Hatty."

Gritting her teeth, she opened Hatty's file. It held the usual information: time of birth, mother, sister, and a slideshow of her sweet sister in the blush of infancy, the buoyancy of youth, the budding of adolescence. And then the heart-wrenching tag: *father unknown.*

Madeline grimaced, scanning the document. Where was the missing person alert? Either Thoth hadn't reported their escape to the authorities. Or he'd known all along where they were. Which was, in some ways, much worse.

Opening her folder, Madeline stared wide-eyed at photos of herself from years ago, in places she never knew were under surveillance. Swallowing her ice chunk, she concentrated on the cold burn making its way down her throat and read the end of the report: *Ceremony delayed. Surrogate denied. Potential successor female.* They'd blacked out with redaction bars.

Madeline dropped the phone and shoved her fingers into her hair. *Surrogate.* Agent Right had used that word in the tunnels under Constance's house. And then Madeline had...well...been intimate with Desmond. And what the hell was Desmond? A ghost? An alien from another planet? Not that she totally bought into Julian's conviction he'd been an extraterrestrial visitor, but what the actual fuck?

The plane rumbled, dipping toward the ground. Madeline flinched. They were descending into Santa Fe. She automatically squeezed the phone between her legs, lest it become a real snake ready to go for her jugular.

Enough research. Enough recall. The greater conspiracies of the day could wait until she'd found Hatty.

But as the plane landed and Madeline made her way into the dry desert heat, dread collected in the base of her belly. No texts. No calls. No communication of any sort from her sister.

It was late, after midnight. No news was supposed to be good news. Madeline kept herself under control and headed for the rental car counter while typing a harried, *Hatty, you can't disappear on me now. Call me the second you get this.*

She checked in at the rental kiosk and stared dumbly at the selection. A Camaro and a Prius. Madeline longed for a muscle car, but no one remembered a Prius, and it was quiet compared to the roar of a powerful engine.

Out into the cool desert night, a sleepy-eyed clerk handed her a set of keys, and Madeline trudged down the numbered rental car slots. Her Prius was parked at the end of the aisle...and it was lime green.

"Fuck," she muttered. So much for keeping a low profile. If Julian were here, he'd get a kick out of—

"Stop it," she said aloud. "Julian doesn't know where you're at, and if he did, so what? He probably thinks you're a terrible person."

Madeline plunked into the seat and adjusted the mirrors. The thing was, maybe he was right. The cult had barely tolerated her, she couldn't keep a boyfriend, and her spotted past in the sex worker industry didn't make for a glowing resume. But when she'd confessed about her background, Julian hadn't closed down. He'd leaned in.

So why hadn't he left a message asking why she wasn't at the restaurant? Or texted her, demanding to know why she'd ditched him? Or...anything. Madeline knew it was best they went their separate ways, but why hadn't he asked if she was okay?

Didn't he care?

Maybe he didn't want the drama. The mess. The cat-and-mouse of a woman who had her memories erased in the back of a trailer while an octogenarian's haunted house got bulldozed. Baggage was a bitch.

Her phone buzzed in her pocket. Madeline let out a cry of relief. Finally, Hatty was contacting her! But it was the wrong phone. And this message was from Agent Right.

I trust you had a productive flight.

Her hand clenched around the phone in helpless aggravation. She typed back, *Do you know where my sister is?*

Negative... But in case you're having second thoughts about contacting Agent Wonderbread, I'll give you an incentive.

A flash of the dream she'd had the week before—Atum shirtless, leaning over her, stroking a hand along the blade of her jaw—overrode her waking mind. Madeline's insides liquefied, and she let out a curse. Jesus. She got off on danger—nothing new—but right now? And what was she expecting—a dick pic?

The photo appearing in the chat was not of Agent Right's anatomy. It was a beat-up neon sign. *The Sagebrush Inn.*

A chill numbed Madeline's fingers. *What am I going to find there?*

Hopefully, your sister. Room 15.

Relief washed away a layer of dread. Despite herself, Madeline couldn't help responding, *Thank you.*

Of course, Madeline. I'm at your service.

Firing up her less-than-energetic steed, Madeline headed into the dark desert.

The Sagebrush Inn was a dump, half the letters on its sign burned out. Madeline did a double-take as "RUSH IN" flickered on, then disappeared. Goddammit, this was not the time for her mind to play tricks.

The U-shaped building featured drab clapboards, beige paint peeling like lizard skin. Hard-packed dirt faced motel doors the shade of dried blood. Madeline circled in the Prius, her dread ebbing. Or maybe it was spiking? She couldn't tell anymore. Her eyelids were backed by sandpaper, and the caffeine keeping her going was long gone.

At one o'clock in the morning, a battered Coupe DeVille and a dusty pickup were the only vehicles in the lot. Madeline didn't know who was watching her and wasn't taking any chances. She didn't park in front of Room 15; that would be too conspicuous. A remote motel off the interstate with the incessant rumble of eighteen-wheelers wasn't a palace of intrigue. Just the opposite. This was where people came to be left alone. Or be erased.

She got out of the car and approached Hatty's door. A yellow bulb cast nicotine shadows across the knob.

She knocked.

Nothing.

Her knuckles rapped on the metal again, harder this time. "Hatty!" she hissed, her volume trying to draw the line between hysteria and discretion.

Still nothing.

The lock wasn't modern; no plastic keycard, no swipe sensor. Just an old-fashioned tumbler.

Muttering a silent prayer, Madeline slid the edge of her American Express into the jamb. Gave the handle a jiggle. Nothing. She tried again. It had been over a decade since her last break-and-enter, one skill among many she'd learned from the working women who'd sheltered her and Hatty after they left the cult. If those ladies of the night could see her now...Hell, if her patients could see her now...

Click.

The latch gave, the pathetic excuse for a lock surrendering like a drunk spotting a six-pack of cold beer. Madeline braced herself, waiting for the gut-punch: a wrecked room, signs of a struggle, the stench of rot and decay. The one possibility for Hatty's silence she hadn't let herself consider was the simplest: her sister, dead.

But the room looked normal, even in the low light, and only the faintest trace of Hatty's unique perfume of jasmine and clean cotton met her at the threshold.

Madeline slipped inside, checking over her shoulder. No one lingered outside. No eyes followed her. Closing the door gently, she reached for the nightstand lamp, then froze. If Hatty hadn't returned and someone was surveilling the room, a crack of light through the curtains would give her away.

She flicked on her phone flashlight, sweeping the beam across the dim corners. The single window facing the rear lot was shut tight. She slid the curtain back an inch. Nothing but the dark shapes of cacti and sage glowing blue under a milky night sky. She clicked on the bathroom light, letting the faint light spill into the space.

The double bed sat neatly made, hard and unyielding under her palm. On the floor, an open duffel bag held jeans and socks. A fluffy, oversized sweater. On the bedside table, Hatty's beat-up copy of *The Princess Bride* partially covered her sketch pad.

The bedsprings creaked as Madeline sat on the mattress, slowly, so as not to disturb any potential clues. She eased the pad onto her lap. Another stone of dread dropped into the well. Hatty never went anywhere without her sketchbook. But maybe there was a clue to Hatty's whereabouts, her state of mind, in the lines of charcoal.

What she found didn't assuage Madeline's worries.

Angels with jagged wings. Hungry, lascivious gargoyle faces. Nymphs drowning in their own blossoms. A snail shell swirling with hypnotic galaxies. And on the last page, an unfinished sketch of a figure with Madeline's silhouette, but blurred and erased, as though Hatty couldn't decide how to draw her sister.

Underneath the sketch, a phone number with a jagged name. *Walter.*

Madeline didn't consider the time or the consequences. She dialed the number. Walter answered on the first ring.

His voice was rough, suspicious. "Hello?"

"Walter, it's me."

There was a pause, a spark of recognition. "Madeline?"

She closed her eyes at the familiar voice. "Please tell me you're with Hatty."

He coughed, the garbled sound phlegmy and harsh. "She was supposed to meet me, but she never showed up."

Madeline bit her tongue against the urge to scream.

Walter cleared his throat. "I might know where she is."

"The compound?"

"No," Walter said quickly. "I'll show you. I'll take you there."

"Where?"

"It's not on a map but... You remember, don't you? The rock formation close to Viper's Cleft. There's a cave..."

Viper's Cleft...a scar in the desert's flesh, carved from red sandstone and ending in sheer, lightless drops.

An icepick of pain speared Madeline's temples. She gasped and heard Walter's breath quicken. "Madeline, don't leave the motel. I'll fetch you in the morning."

He hung up.

Drooping with pain and fatigue, Madeline reached out. Her hand found Hatty's sweater, and she laid down with it, using it to cover her face. The scent of jasmine swam under her nose. She would have cried if sleep hadn't reached out its comforting, lethal fingers.

But before it could claim her, Madeline had one last desperate thought.

How had Walter known she was at the Sagebrush Inn?

More Spectral Seduction

Want More Spectral Seduction?
Get the free prequel *Julian*, at spectralseduction.com
Before Julian could protect the world from paranormal sex magic...
he had to survive it.

*Before the agents, before the sex
cults, before Mason's Hole —
there was Slate Hill.*

Julian Worthy just wanted to deliver pizza, save for college, and avoid getting sucked into his sleepy hometown's endless weirdness. But when a strange sexual energy sweeps through Slate Hill, arousal turns dangerous... and irresistible.

Women are behaving strangely. Lightning crackles from cloudless skies. And the deeper Julian follows the signs, the clearer it becomes: something ancient is waking up. Something that wants him.

What begins with ghostly urges and small-town seductions spirals into a night of supernatural passion, possession, and a life-changing encounter with the woman who will one day become his boss at the S.E.X.D. division of Homeland Security.

Julian is a steamy paranormal prequel to the *Spectral Seduction* series. For fans of *The X-Files*, *Sookie Stackhouse*, and sex magic gone wrong.

Get it free at spectralseduction.com!

About the Authors

Devora Gray writes erotic thrillers where lust tangles with danger, and nothing is as it seems. A former sex coach and sessionist, she brings an insider's understanding of desire, power, and taboo to every page. Devora lives in Las Vegas, NV, with her partner and Wheaten terrier, H.R. Pup-n-stuff. When not dreaming up kinky situations, she's cold-plunging with Len or weight lifting with her daughter. Find her at devoragray.com

Len M. Ruth writes gothic horror, edge-of-your-seat thrillers, and steamy paranormal romances where shadows seduce and secrets kill. A lifelong horror fan, he blends eerie suspense with heat in every story. Len lives in Las Vegas with his partner, Emory, and Cooper, the cocker-blocker spaniel. When not conjuring ghosts and bad decisions, he's hiking desert trails or plotting his next haunting. Find him at lenmruth.com/